A PROUD WOMAN

A Tabitha & Wolf Mystery

Sarah F. Noel

The characters and events portrayed in this book are fictitious. Any similarity to real persons, living or dead, is coincidental and not intended by the author.

ISBN: 9798390807828

Cover design by: HelloBriie Creative
Printed in the United States of America

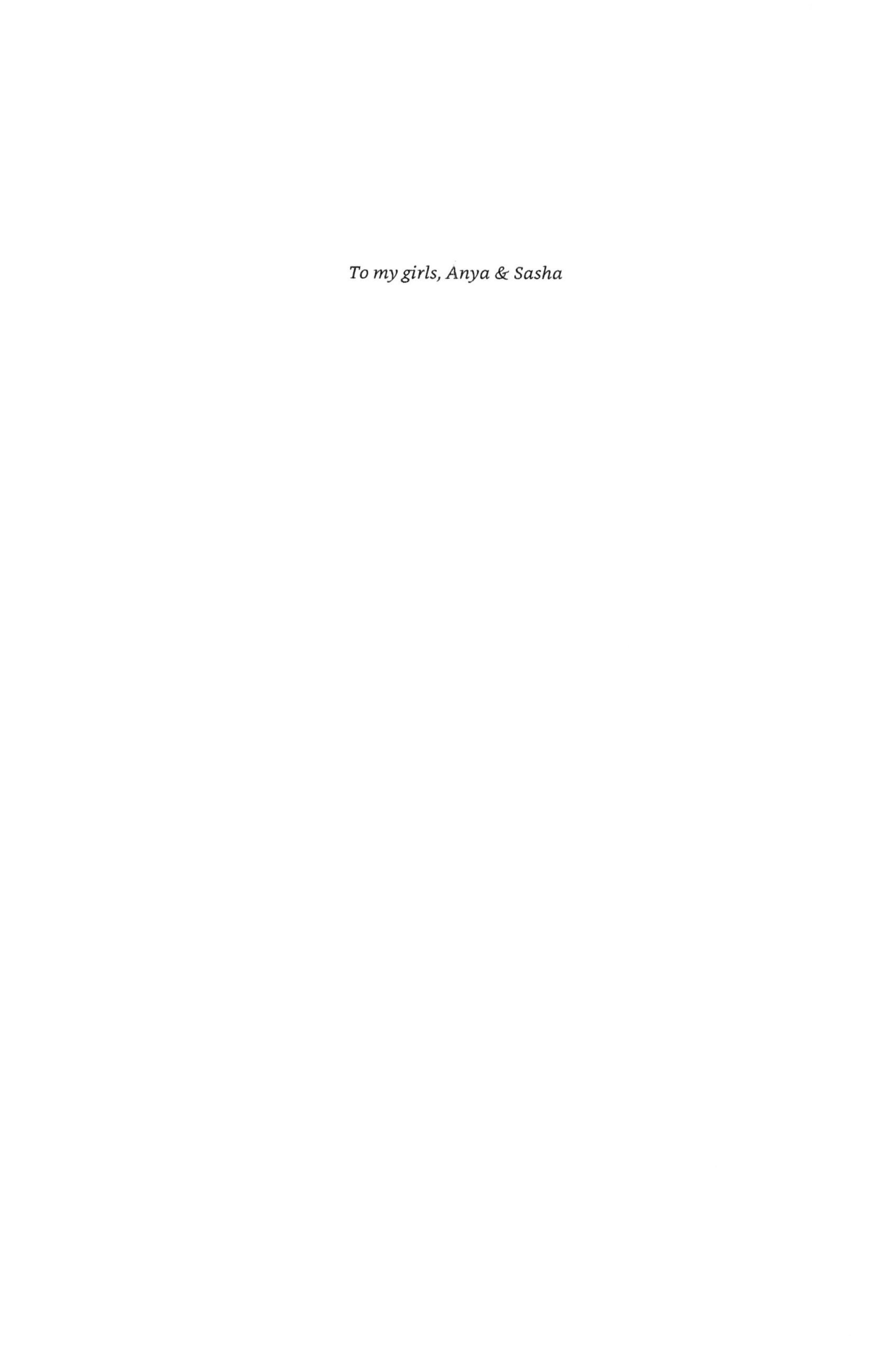

To my girls, Anya & Sasha

CONTENTS

FOREWORD

This book is written using British English spelling. e.g. dishonour instead of dishonor, realise instead of realize.

British spelling aside, while every effort has been made to proofread this thoroughly, typos do creep in. If you find any, I'd greatly appreciate a quick email to report them at sarahfnoelauthor@gmail.com

PROLOGUE

London 1897

The candlestick came down on the duke's skull repeatedly, long past the point where death was in question. The victim had been sitting in his favourite leather armchair, sipping his favourite brandy, and nibbling some superb ginger biscuits while browsing his favourite pornographic images. Eventually, he'd started to feel drowsy, and his limbs felt heavy. He'd sensed someone in the room with him but couldn't turn his head to see. The first blow wasn't nearly enough to kill him, but it did knock him unconscious. The last words he ever heard before the second, lethal blow were, "No more!"

CHAPTER 1

Tabitha had been standing in front of the mirror for a full five minutes, transfixed by her own image. To the undiscerning eye, not much had changed, only that she had moved from full to half-mourning. Her rich chestnut hair coiffured as conservatively but stylishly as usual. Her maid Ginny would allow nothing less. Her jewellery was minimal, tasteful, and clearly extremely expensive. Her now-deceased husband had deeply cared that she was always a visual representation of his power and influence. But what did seem different were her eyes. Over the two years of her hellish marriage, she had become used to seeing dead, emotionless eyes staring back at her, eyes that spoke to a crushed soul. But today, for the first time since the night of her marriage to Jonathan Chesterton, the Earl of Pembroke, those eyes had some life in them.

Jonathan's death should have ended her suffering, but it didn't. The police investigation and the attendant sensationalist publicity consumed the six months following the death. And, of course, there was the faux horror by the upper echelons of society who were secretly lapping up every bit of gossip and enjoying the spectacle of the disgrace of one of the formerly untouchable families. In the end, Tabitha was still untouchable enough, and the death had been ruled death by misadventure. After all, when the police inspector had examined Jonathan's body lying at the bottom of the marble staircase, the unnatural angle of his neck making clear that his neck was broken, the smell of whiskey emanating off him was undeniable.

Since the ruling, she had barely left the house. Of course,

society had generally shunned her, and that was more than fine with Tabitha. She had always found high society's etiquette and unspoken rules suffocating. Long before her coming out at 18, her mother had bemoaned how Tabitha could possibly be a product of her womb and upbringing.

But even though Tabitha had strained against her mother's and society's expectations for her, she ultimately complied. Because what else could a young girl do? But now, she didn't need to shun society; it had shunned her. Even her mother could barely bring herself to visit when she was still in London before leaving for the family country seat a month before. And so Tabitha had been left alone in the palatial Mayfair home that Jonathan's great-grandfather had built to impress society with his wealth and might. Alone except for the large staff. Tabitha sensed that despite most of the staff having worked for Jonathan and his family long before Tabitha had married him, they didn't miss their master and had a fondness and profound sympathy for their new mistress.

And so today, for the first time, her eyes reflected a woman returning to life. Tabitha had known for a while that she was a wealthy woman. With the dowry she had brought to the marriage and the not-inconsiderable monies she'd inherited from Jonathan's many business ventures, minus the entailed property, she would never have to worry about money. As a widow, her rights were somewhat more expansive than those of single women, even if they were still limited compared to men. With her father recently deceased, Jonathan's solicitor had explained that, assuming she wanted to, he could help establish Tabitha as the head of her household, leaving her total control over her wealth. She had always thought that Jonathan's man of business was honest, straightforward, and loyal. His willingness to manage her business and lack of condescension during their conversation had quickly confirmed her instincts.

Today, as she shrugged off her full mourning, almost certainly much earlier than most in society would consider appropriate, she looked at the face of a woman who was finally as free and independent as a woman in 1897 could be. She wasn't sure what she was going to do with this freedom. She was neither welcome back into high society nor desired a return. She certainly didn't want it enough to endure the obsequiousness and self-flagellation her mother had suggested would be necessary to ensure her entry back into the best drawing rooms in London. So she took one last look at this new woman in the mirror and took a deep breath before preparing to make her way downstairs. Because she would need every ounce of her new feelings of fortitude to deal with her caller that morning, the Dowager Countess of Pembroke, her mother-in-law.

Tabitha had seen very little of Jonathan's mother since his death. The few times she had seen her, including the funeral, the older Lady Pembroke had made it very clear that, despite the final ruling, she believed that Tabitha was responsible for her son's death, either directly or indirectly.

"M'lady." When she got no reply, Ginny tried again, "M'lady! I know what you're doing, and you need to stop it."

Tabitha turned around, yet again wondering why she not only put up with such an impertinent maid but almost encouraged it.

"What do you think I'm doing?"

"You're telling yourself your story like it's one of those gothic horror novels you like so much. I know what your wool-gathering looks like at this point."

"Ginny, I have no idea what you mean," Tabitha sniffed. Though, of course, she knew precisely what Ginny meant. She did tend to indulge in internal monologues where she sounded not unlike a Bronte heroine. But to be fair, recently, her life had been melodramatic enough in truth and didn't need any embellishment. "I'm merely preparing myself to face the dowager countess and wondering what she wants with me."

Ginny's features softened, and her voice became gentler, "Yer know what she wants with you. She wants to blame you, to shame you. What has she ever wanted from you, lass?" Rather than being shocked at her maid's use of such a familiar term, the affection, the tone, and the words relayed brought tears to her eyes, which she refused to shed as she quickly put herself under strict control again.

Ginny was the only servant who had come with her on her marriage to Jonathan. Only a few years older than Tabitha herself, Ginny had been with Tabitha's family since she started as a tweeny. She was intelligent, honest, and hard-working and quickly moved up in the household hierarchy. When Tabitha had turned 15 and had been deemed ready to move from a governess to her own lady's maid, Ginny had been given a chance to raise herself to a higher household servant.

In truth, Tabitha's mother, the Dowager Marchioness of Cambridgeshire, Lady Jameson, would typically have insisted that any daughter of hers have a more seasoned lady's maid. But Tabitha was her fourth and most challenging daughter, and at the time, Lady Jameson was busy planning her eldest daughter's wedding and her third's coming out. Tabitha had expressed a preference for Ginny, who had risen to be the senior housemaid. Her mother had no energy or patience to fight over it with her recalcitrant offspring.

Tabitha had no idea why her mother-in-law was now calling on her; the note sent around the day before had been brief, even terse. But she did not doubt that this wasn't a social call and wouldn't be a pleasant conversation. She made her way to the grand drawing room, tastefully decorated in soft shades of green. The large windows faced out towards the street and took full advantage of the morning sun.

Tabitha considered where she should sit. Under normal circumstances, she would have claimed the more comfortable settee. But it was a little low, and she had no desire to cede the higher position to her guest, thereby making it even easier for her to look down her nose at Tabitha. And so, Tabitha claimed a sturdy, straight-backed, if a rather uncomfortable, chair for herself and sat patiently. The dowager was nothing if not punctual. And as the clock chimed on the given hour, Tabitha heard a knock at the door, and her butler, Talbot, announced her visitor. Tabitha took a deep breath, stood up, straightened her spine, raised her chin, and prepared for battle.

CHAPTER 2

The dowager swept into the room. She was barely 5 feet tall and yet had a powerful presence, and her steel grey eyes were as hard and cold as granite. Her one concession to age, the beautiful, engraved ebony cane that Tabitha had often felt was as much a potential weapon as an aid for walking. The dowager countess would have made a brilliant general if she had been born a man. As it was, perhaps navigating high society as she did was a more impressive feat than moving troops around a battlefield.

On glancing around the room and seeing the chair that Tabitha had chosen for herself, the older Lady Pembroke immediately understood her erstwhile daughter-in-law's battle tactic and secretly admired her for it. Perhaps the girl had more gumption than she'd given her credit.

Though she would never admit it to a soul, the dowager countess had known that her only son wasn't an easy man. If she wasn't admitting it to anyone, he was a brute. Just as his father had been. But she had lived with her husband's drinking, whoring, and on occasion, his beatings. Eventually, after many failed efforts, she had done her duty and bourne him a healthy son and heir. After two daughters followed, she'd decided that providing the earldom with a spare was more than she could stomach, and the door of her boudoir had been locked against her husband. Luckily, while she preferred London society, he was much happier at the family estate, drinking heavily, hunting and riding. In fact, while indulging in all these pastimes simultaneously, he fell off his horse and broke his neck. A more satisfying and just conclusion his wife couldn't imagine.

Julia Chesterton, Lady Pembroke, had harboured no illusions that her son was any better a man or husband than his father. She realised he had a cruel streak when he was only a child. She had seen his selfishness, brutality, and, most damning to his mother, his weakness. But his mother had hoped to be able to temper these traits, particularly after his father's death, when she prayed that the gravitas of his new role as earl would mature her son. But she eventually silently acknowledged that what her progeny was lacking wasn't maturity. No, what the young earl lacked was far more worrisome; he had no heart. No soul. He was a narcissistic egomaniac. A man who enjoyed brutality for its own sake. He was a man who lacked the capacity for compassion. Sympathy for the new widow greeting her overcame her for one weak moment. But where did weakness ever get her?

"So, Tabitha, I see you've thrown off mourning for my son after a scandalously short period. I know you don't care what society says, but I had hoped you might show a little more respect for your late husband's memory, if only for my sake." As she spoke, she sat on the lower settee, which, given her lack of height, forced her to raise her head at an uncomfortable angle to be able to glare directly into Tabitha's eyes even as her hostess took her seat.

Despite her high spirits as a girl, her marriage had quickly subdued Tabitha, cowing her into a shadow of her former self. The blame for most of this lay squarely at her deceased husband's feet. But, her mother-in-law's acerbic comments, which seemed laden with disapproval at Tabitha's every word and action, had not helped the young woman find her footing as a new countess.

Tabitha reflected on what, if anything, she owed the dowager countess. As pointed out to her many times during her marriage and after her husband's death, Tabitha had failed to bear him an heir. But that meant that any real family ties or obligations Tabitha might owe this cold, hard woman in front of her were gone. She remembered the woman she had looked at in the mirror, took a deep breath, and replied, “Your son didn’t deserve even the six months of mourning I gave him. And I believe that you know that as well as I do. So, let’s not go through the charade of pretending otherwise; cut to the heart of why you’re here. What can I do for you, Lady Pembroke?”

While Jonathan was alive, Tabitha referred to his mother as Mama. She chose to do so no longer. There had never been affection or even respect between them, and she wished to emphasise that now there was no longer even a familial connection.

“So, the chit has a backbone, after all!” thought the older woman. “Perhaps, given time, she would have been able to control my son.” Though no sooner did that thought enter her head than she realised that standing up to her son would likely have only brought his wife more bruises. That had certainly been her own experience, after all.

“I see we are to be direct, so let me be as blunt as you have been. Jonathan died without a direct heir because you could not produce a son. His cousin is the next in line to the earldom. Nothing has been heard of or from this young man for many years. His parents are deceased, and he seemed to have vanished after their deaths. The estate endeavoured either to find him or find definitive proof of his death. He has now been found, and we are to expect him any day now.

"As I’m sure you’re aware, this house is part of the entailment of the estate. You can live in the Dower House at the country estate. Of course, I am also provided with residence there. But I despise the country and can promise you that you’ll be able to live there unencumbered by my company. That is all I came to tell you.”

Tabitha did stop to wonder why the estate lawyers had not seen fit to tell her this news directly. But she reflected that they were probably as terrified of the dowager as everyone else. She didn’t immediately answer. In truth, she was unsure what to say or how she felt about this news.

Of course, she knew that an heir would be found somewhere

at some point. Tabitha had no real connection to this house. If anything, it had been the scene of most of the misery and pain she had felt in her 22 years. But it was also her home. And if she felt no connection to the building, she had grown to appreciate the care the staff had always shown her. One thing she knew, she would not move to the Dower House and be a stale and dried-up widow before her time.

The obvious answer was to move back to her family home and live with her mother and her unmarried brother Timothy. She inwardly shuddered at the thought. Timothy was a charming if somewhat rakish young man. He was too busy running with his fast crowd, drinking, and gambling, and she didn't want to think of what else. He would have welcomed her home happily. But the prospect of living with her mother again made Tabitha's innards twist.

And so, she made the only decision she could make and said, "I will begin to pack my effects and instruct my man of business to begin looking for a new house. When the new earl presents himself, I will discuss the timing of my departure. Is that all?"

She was filled with a thrilling sense of freedom even as she said these words. She had the means to set up her own establishment. And as a widow, such a thing would not even bring society's censure down on her. Well, not for the most part. While a widow, she was also a young woman. The expectation would be that she would move back to her family until, after an acceptable period of time, she then became the wife and property of another man.

The conversation had been brief and uncomfortable. Tabitha's blatant dismissal of the older dowager was a surprise to both. For an awkwardly long period, they sat there facing off, each unwilling to give in and be the one to speak first. Finally, the dowager, Lady Pembroke, pushed herself up with the help of her cane and stood resting on it just a little.

She looked at this woman who, in so many ways, reminded her of her younger self. So much so that Lady Pembroke, the elder pondered for a moment why she could not extend even a tiny olive branch of, if not friendship, at least civility to the younger woman. She considered that not one of her two married daughters had even a fraction of the grit that this young woman was now, surprisingly, demonstrating. And so she allowed her face to relax and soften just a smidgeon. But it was enough for her daughter-in-law to look visibly shocked at the hitherto unseen expression on the older woman's face.

"I do know how it feels, you know, my dear. Jonathan's father was as bad as he was, maybe even worse. I suffered as you suffered. And when he died, I felt the same relief that you feel. You think I judge you and despise you. But I don't." And with those astounding words, the dowager made her way to the door and left the room.

Tabitha had risen when her guest rose. But now she sat down in amazement. The visit had been so brief that there hadn't even been time for Mary to bring in the tea things. The maid was now at the door apologising and asking if her mistress would like tea anyway. Tabitha honestly felt like she would like something a bit stronger. But drinking alcohol at midday reminded her too much of Jonathan. And so she said that a cup of tea and a slice of seed cake was just what she needed.

What had she just heard? Had she misheard? Had her nasty battle axe of a mother-in-law, the woman who never failed to point out her failings as a wife and who had vocally blamed her for Jonathan's death, just commiserated with her? Indeed, wonders would never cease. Tabitha couldn't wait to tell Ginny about the unexpected turn this visit had taken.

CHAPTER 3

Tabitha was a practical woman. Before the dowager's visit, she knew it could take years to track down the heir to the earldom, so she hadn't given much thought to her future plans. But now that the new earl had been found and was on his way to London, she promptly made an appointment with her man of business. Tabitha instructed him to find her a suitable house in an appropriate neighbourhood to purchase or for a long lease.

Houses hadn't yet been snapped up for the season, and Tabitha was told that suitable accommodation could be found promptly. She recognised that time was of the essence and expressed her strong preference for furnished accommodation. She could always redecorate at her leisure.

The staff was another matter. Tabitha felt guilty about leaving the new earl without help. But she also believed that the staff should be free to choose whether they followed her. She broached the subject with Ginny as she dressed one morning a few days after the dowager's visit. As much as Ginny was an upper servant, her good nature and willingness to lend a hand wherever needed meant that she was well-liked by the whole household staff, and Tabitha knew that she would have a good sense of the general mood below stairs.

"Ginny, how do you believe the staff feels about my imminent move and a new master taking over the house?"

"M'lady, are you asking who you believe would choose to follow you?" Ginny asked.

"Well, I suppose that is what I'm asking. I neither want the staff here to feel unwanted in my new household nor do I want to put undue pressure on any loyalty they feel to the Chesterton family."

At this statement, Ginny snorted. "That's not something you have to worry about. The last Chesterton anyone felt affection for and loyalty to was your lord's grandfather, the old earl. By all accounts, he was a generous and kind master. But since he passed away, the staff here have stayed put because they're well paid. Nothing more. I believe that they'd follow you, man and boy. And woman."

Tabitha was warmed by these words, even if she worried they were expressed through the rose-tinted hues of Ginny's feelings for her. Musing on Ginny's words, Tabitha descended the stairs intending to eat her usual toast, boiled egg, and tea in the breakfast room. She was met at the bottom of the stairs by Talbot. The ordinarily calm man seemed unusually discombobulated.

"If I might be so bold as to talk to you, milady. There's um, well, er, I'm not sure how to put it."

"Talbot, please tell me what has put you so out of sorts." The butler tried to compose himself and continued, "There is a gentleman here."

"A gentleman before breakfast? That really isn't the done thing. However, I'm assuming he has some sort of business to discuss. Is he waiting for me in the drawing room?"

Again, her butler looked far from his usual inscrutable, unperturbed self. "He is waiting for you in his lordship's study."

At this, Tabitha, who had been heading to the drawing room, stopped, turned, and gave her butler a narrow-eyed, suspicious look. As with many men of his acquaintance, Jonathan's study was his sanctuary. The only room in the house where the housekeeper, Mrs Jenkins, did not have free rein to clean and tidy as she saw fit.

Since Jonathan's death, the dark oak-panelled room that smelled of a combination of Jonathan's cheroots and a certain mustiness had been untouched. Tabitha had ventured in once to allow her man of business to gather up whatever bills and other relevant papers he could find before she ran out, chased by its overpowering male, dominating presence. Why would a gentleman visitor want to be in the study, and more to the point, why would Talbot allow it?

"Talbot? I feel there is more to this situation than you are saying. You know I prefer plain-speaking. Who is in the study, and why did you allow him entrance?"

"He told me he is the new Earl of Pembroke and has papers from the lawyers to support that claim. I put him in his lordship's study because, well, because he is now his lordship and asked to see it."

Tabitha realised that her butler was at the far extreme of situations he felt comfortable handling with aplomb and questioned him no longer. Instead, she made for her husband's study, full of righteous anger at the lack of decorum the new heir had displayed.

She opened the door and saw a man sitting in Jonathan's sturdy leather chair with his feet on the desk. Feet that were not clad in the soft, smooth buckskin of a gentleman's boots but instead, boots that looked like they had been with their owner for many years and through many a grimy puddle or worse. And her eyes followed the boots up through clothing that looked no newer or cleaner than the footwear. Her review of her guest ended with the face of the new earl.

Tabitha's first thought was that he was clearly related to Jonathan. Jonathan had been a handsome man when she first met him. Tall with broad shoulders and dark curly hair. He had green eyes that had so bewitched her during their courtship but which she came to realise could blaze with cruelty.

The man in front of her shared many of the same physical traits. Except his eyes were blue instead of green. They had the shape, if not the colour, of cats' eyes. They were heavily lashed and sat in a face with sharp planes and high cheekbones. But there was no doubt that he was Jonathan's cousin. His dirtier, less well dressed, but if she had to be honest, far more handsome cousin. Unlike Jonathan's dark curls, which had always been well trimmed and oiled, his heir's hair was too long and far too unkempt. And it was unclear if he was growing a beard or hadn't bothered to shave in many days, such was the dark stubble along his strong jaw.

He seemed to be reading papers that had sat on Jonathan's desk. Tabitha was sure that her man of business had taken away all her important legal and financial documents. But even so, she was immediately irate that this stranger had started going through Jonathan's papers. But, instead of launching into the tirade that was her first impulse, she took a deep and steadying breath. Tabitha reflected that she was now a guest in this house and that the man before her was its master.

Hearing the door open, the new Earl of Pembroke looked up and cocked an eyebrow. "Madam?"

"I am Lady Pembroke." She added after a brief pause, "My lord."

If possible, the eyebrow seemed to raise even higher. "So, you're the lady of the manor?"

"I was the 'lady of the manor', as you put it.' Now, I am the widowed countess, and you are the new lord of the manor. If you are married, your wife is now its lady, and then I will be the dowager countess.

The new lord chuckled. "I have no lady wife and don't plan to have one anytime soon. So as far as I see it, you're still the lady of the manor."

"I assure you, sir, I have no desire to outstay my welcome. I'm in the process of finding a new house and hope to be no more of a bother for you as soon as possible."

"You're leaving? Why? I don't know anything about running a great house like this. And I definitely don't know anything about being an earl. Would you do me the favour of staying on for a while and helping me?"

Tabitha wasn't sure what to make of this statement. Indeed, she wasn't sure what he meant, if anything, really by it. It had never occurred to her that she had any option other than moving out.

Under normal circumstances, an unmarried woman living in the same house as an unmarried man would be scandalous. Yet she was a widow, which allowed her a certain latitude. And technically, they were family, however distant and through marriage. And then there was the fact that she didn't care whether society was scandalised. In fact, Tabitha rather liked the idea that she might scandalise the drawing rooms of London. It wouldn't be the first time she had been the subject of gossip.

Tabitha looked at the handsome but scruffy man in front of her. She envisioned what would happen if she did poach all or even most of his staff. She imagined the likely mismanagement of the household if she didn't stay and realised she couldn't be responsible for such turmoil. But more than that, despite his resemblance to Jonathan, the new earl had a kindness to his face that Jonathan had never had. This man had laughing eyes and a mouth that seemed permanently ready to smile. The only smiles she ever remembered Jonathan giving were cruel, sadistic smiles when he was able to inflict pain and suffering.

For all his scruffiness and informality, this man already seemed more worthy of the earldom and certainly more worthy of her help. "If you're sure, then I'm happy to stay for a while and help you with your household and your entry into society. Though I must warn you, I'm hardly the darling of polite society these days."

"Excellent! I believe we'll rub along very well together," he said. "Given that we're going to be cohabiting, perhaps I should know your name. Or should I keep calling you Lady Pembroke?" A mischievous twinkle in his eye suggested that he wouldn't call her that even if she demanded it. Especially if she demanded it.

"You may call me Tabitha," she offered.

"Nice to meet you, Tabitha. My friends call me Wolf."

"Wolf? Is that your name?" Tabitha asked incredulously. She couldn't imagine regularly addressing the new Earl of Pembroke as Wolf.

"Well, my full name is Jeremy Wolfson Chesterton. Wolfson

was my mother's family name. But no one has called me Jeremy since I was in short trousers. And I won't answer to it if you do."

"Well, I can't imagine London high society referring to you as Jeremy, but they also won't call you Wolf. As with every nobleman, your peers will refer to you as Pembroke. And so that is what I shall call you." Tabitha said this with such finality that even Wolf realised this wasn't an argument he could win, at least for now.

The moment was suddenly awkward. This was now technically the new earl's house, but it felt like he was a guest, an interloper even. Did she leave him alone in the study? What was the correct protocol for this situation? Was there a protocol? Collecting herself and reverting to the comfort of being a practical woman, Tabitha said, "Then let me show you the house, introduce you to the staff and have your valet move you into Jonathan's old rooms. Assuming that those are the rooms you wish to take on. They are the rooms that the Earl of Pembroke has always inhabited."

The new earl chuckled, "My valet? There's no valet and not a lot to move in. I have a man who works for me in various capacities. Although I don't think he's ever brushed my coat or tied my cravat." No sooner had he said those words than there was a soft knock on the door.

"Enter!" The new Lord Pembroke, Wolf, to his friends (and enemies), and Tabitha, Lady Pembroke, both said simultaneously.

Tabitha was still standing with her back to the door, and she turned as the door opened and visibly started. Standing in the door frame, well actually filling the door frame, was the largest, hairiest man she had ever seen. At least she assumed he was a man. She might have believed it more willingly if someone had told her he was a mythical beast. He was so tall that he might need to bend his head to get through the door frame, with shoulders so broad and muscled that, if his head could get through the door, it was still doubtful whether his body could.

It was hard to believe that the gentle knock on the door

had come courtesy of the enormous hands that this beast of a man possessed. The backs of those hands were covered in thick dark hair, clearly covering his entire body. Tabitha couldn't help noticing it creeping out of the neck of his shirt to meet a full beard that reached up his cheeks to almost right under his eyes.

"Ah, Bear. Good timing. We were just talking about you."

"Bear?" Tabitha couldn't help exclaiming. "Wolf and Bear? You are jesting, are you not?"

Wolf chuckled, "Yes, we often get that reaction. But honestly, our names are just a coincidence. As I told you, mine is short for Wolfson and perhaps attributable to my bad behaviour as a young lad. And Bear, well, I assume it's obvious how he got that name. That our names go so well together and perhaps perfectly represent who we are and what we do as a pair is just a bonus."

It suddenly occurred to Tabitha to wonder where Bear had come from and what kind of consternation his appearance had caused amongst her household staff. As if reading her mind, Wolf said, "I told Bear to go and introduce himself to your housekeeper. I believe that your fine man, Talbot isn't it, took him down himself so that Bear's appearance didn't cause too much screaming and fainting amongst your female staff. And maybe even your male staff," he added.

Tabitha could only imagine what her always-in-control housekeeper would have made of this new mountain of a man entering her domain. And it did occur to her to talk to the cook about increasing the weekly food order. She could only imagine how much a man this size might consume daily.

Looking again at those huge, meaty paws that looked far more appropriate for wringing the life out of a man than dressing a member of the nobility, Tabitha noted, "I can see why there's some question as to his appropriateness to be a valet and tie a cravat with those hands."

Wolf laughed, and joining his laughter was what Tabitha assumed was laughter coming from Bear, but honestly sounded more like growling. Only his eyes, filled with amusement, assured her he wasn't angry and about to rip her head off. She was sure it was better to have Bear as a friend than an enemy.

CHAPTER 4

As Tabitha led the way downstairs to the kitchen, the central hub for the household staff, she reflected on what Wolf had said, "What we do as a pair." What exactly did they do that the names Wolf and Bear were so appropriate? She didn't know much about Jonathan's uncle's family. She remembered some allusions to Jonathan's uncle being the family's black sheep and having been spurned by his illustrious relatives. But from everything she'd heard, Jonathan's grandfather had been cut from a different cloth than his son and grandson and didn't seem like someone who would abandon a son lightly.

Given that Bear had already introduced himself, in some way or another, to some portion of the household staff, Tabitha wasn't overly worried about bringing him back into the kitchen without warning. Nevertheless, the moment she saw the new young housemaid Emily's face, she knew that not everyone was forewarned about the latest household staff member. Tabitha cleared her throat and said, "Emily, would you mind gathering the staff as quickly as possible? I would like to talk to everyone."

Preparations for lunch were well underway, so the entire kitchen staff was already present. Mrs Jenkins, the housekeeper, had a sixth sense of what her mistress needed and quickly appeared from her office outside the kitchen. From the widening of her eyes, Tabitha assumed that she had not previously been introduced to Bear either. Even though it was a large staff, it didn't take Emily long to round everyone else up. News travelled quickly through a household, and there was already a lot of curiosity about the man in the study.

"Thank you for gathering so quickly, everyone." Tabitha noticed that even the gardener and groom had somehow been alerted and were standing just by the back door so as not to dirty the kitchen with their boots. "I will make this brief. I would like to introduce you to the new Earl of Pembroke and, therefore, the new master of this house. The gentleman with him is his," Tabitha paused momentarily and then decided to keep things as simple as possible, "his valet, mister…mister Bear. I have agreed to stay on for the time being to help his lordship and ensure that the household transition is as smooth as possible.

"Mrs Jenkins, please air out his lordship's bedroom, show Mr Bear where everything is, and help him acclimate to the house's rhythms. For now, there will be no alteration to the household or the meal schedule. Once his lordship has been with us for a while, it will be up to him to decide what changes he would like made.

"Your lordship, you have many names to learn but to begin with, I'd like to introduce you to your formidable butler Mr Talbot, wonderful housekeeper Mrs Jenkins, and our very talented cook, Mrs Smith. I'm sure the rest of the staff will become known to you over time."

Tabitha turned to Wolf and asked, "Lord Pembroke, would you like to address your staff?" She noted that Wolf seemed less cocky and at ease with this request.

"Err, certainly. I assume that is the thing to do." And then he paused, clearly at a total loss for what to say. Tabitha decided to take pity on him and suggested, "Perhaps for the time being, it's sufficient to introduce yourself and your man and express your appreciation for the staff's consideration as you accustom yourself to your new role."

Wolf looked at her with gratitude and said, "Yes, of course. Exactly that. I'm sure I'll find everything excellent and won't be inclined to change anything. As you will soon discover, I was not raised to be an earl, so please excuse me in advance if you find anything I do, say, wear or eat unbefitting of my new rank. And as for my man," and he gestured at the mountain of a human standing slightly behind him, "I assure you that Bear, sorry, Mr Bear, may look threatening but is truly the kindest, gentlest, most trustworthy, and loyal man I know. He is also not used to a grand household, so I ask you to extend your patience to him. Thank you." And with that, Wolf turned and left the kitchen, and after a brief shared look with Mrs Jenkins, Tabitha followed him.

Just outside the kitchen, Wolf stopped and turned to Tabitha, "I have no wish to usurp any space of yours, but I'm assuming that the study was the domain of the previous earl, and so is an appropriate lair for me?"

"My lord, the entire house is at your disposal to use however you see fit. But yes, the study was always my husband's sanctuary, hence the conspicuous lack of dusting. My husband barely tolerated the housemaids there. If you want to get on Mrs Jenkins' good side, you'll allow her staff to tidy and dust regularly. The only reason I haven't done it in the six months since Jonathan's death is that I had no wish to open that door and be reminded of him."

Wolf's face immediately took on a look of sympathy, and Tabitha realised that he had misunderstood her reluctance to enter the study for grief. This man hadn't known his cousin, and she felt no reason to perpetuate the myth of a grieving widow and said, "I didn't want to be reminded of him because he was a cruel and violent man. I am glad he's dead and suspect the entire household feels similarly. Whether or not they take to you as a master, it won't be because you pale next to him in any way.

"My husband made enemies everywhere he went; only his rank and great wealth gave him the circle of acquaintances he had. It seems that the only person who grieves for him is his mother, and after talking with her yesterday, I'm unconvinced that she does it as anything more than a performative act."

Not sure why she was taking this virtual stranger into her confidence, Tabitha nevertheless gave Wolf a summary of her conversation with the dowager the few days prior. The earl was a good listener; she felt he gave her his full attention and saw compassion, not pity filling his eyes. She was glad it wasn't pity.

Tabitha knew full well that the treatment she had experienced at her husband's hands was not so exceptional. Indeed, from what Ginny told her, women of the lower classes almost came to expect violence at the hands of drunk husbands. At least she hadn't dealt with beatings compounded with poverty and disease. Tabitha had learned a lot from Ginny. As a younger woman, she had known, in a vague and unconsidered way, that she lived a pampered life of luxury. But growing up in a mansion in Mayfair, she had rarely had to look upon the poverty and squalor that was the inevitable lot of so many of her fellow citizens.

An avid reader of the works of Mr Charles Dickens, Tabitha had an intellectual understanding of what it meant to be poor, dirty, homeless, and hungry. She had cried tears at the plight of poor Oliver Twist. But she had never had cause to understand the reality emotionally. The stories Ginny told her of the poverty that service had enabled her to escape were eye-opening. Ginny's mother had taken so many beatings at the hand of the man Ginny called father that she had lost multiple pregnancies. And so, Tabitha had grown to learn that her unpleasant marriage was only unusual because she could hide her bruises with silk and jewels.

CHAPTER 5

The next few days went by, notable only for their normalcy. Wolf and Bear were undemanding, easygoing members of the household. The earl was happy to leave every household decision to Tabitha and was a genial master to his new servants.

Once everyone got over the shock of Bear, he did turn out to be a gentle giant. He stayed out of everyone's way for the most part, often spending most of the day out of the house - Tabitha had no idea where he went. When he was at home, from what she could tell and Ginny reported, he made himself useful in all the ways a very tall, very strong man can. The kitchen staff had taken a particular liking to him, and Mrs Smith, not usually an easy woman, made his favourite ginger biscuits daily. The scullery maid, Nancy, initially in total awe of the new addition to the household, had somehow progressed to being a particular favourite of the putative valet.

Where and how exactly Bear spent most days was a question that Tabitha did consider but didn't feel it was her business to enquire. As for his lord and master, he spent most of his first few days holed up in his study with some combination of his man of business, his estate steward, and his solicitor. Wolf took his breakfast and lunch in his study. But he joined Tabitha for dinner every evening. Perhaps because no other men were present, Wolf insisted on removing to the drawing room with Tabitha for coffee rather than staying behind for port and cigars.

Honestly, Tabitha hadn't been sure how extensive her tutelage to the new earl would have to be. After their first dinner together, she was relieved to find that his table manners and understanding of basic etiquette were perfectly acceptable. He knew which fork to use for which course and didn't seem ill at ease during the meal. Tabitha reflected, he was the grandson of an earl, after all. But she also had no idea what his upbringing had been.

Wolf's speech was that of a gentleman. His hair was still longer than was fashionable, and she did wish that he could be persuaded to shave daily. But Tabitha had to admit that, once kitted out in new clothes and boots befitting his new status, Wolf cut quite a dashing and noble figure. Although he was not much past 36 when he died, Jonathan's body was already starting to turn to fat and had he lived, his jowls would have been pronounced by the time he was 40. By comparison, his cousin's form was muscular and powerful. His jawline was strong and well-defined. Even though they had been made hastily, Wolf's new clothes suited him better than any more patiently tailored outfits had ever fitted Jonathan.

Their dinner conversations began with some formality and stiffness, particularly on Tabitha's part. Still, Wolf proved to be an easy conversationalist, and their dialogue quickly became more casual and pleasant. The new earl was reticent when it came to talking about himself and his past. And Tabitha had no wish to relive more of her life over the last few years. So instead, she educated him on the social circle into which he now found himself thrust. Initially, she merely shared names, ranks, marriages, and offspring. But she soon found herself revealing the various peccadillos or the ones most gossiped about.

As an outcast from high society herself for the last six months, Tabitha was not current on the most salacious news. But Ginny was friends with a couple of neighbourhood ladies' maids, and when they met on their half day off, Ginny typically returned with the kind of information that servants always seemed to be the first to know. Tabitha had never thought of herself as a gossip. Still, as the days and their conversation progressed, she found herself full of a new outrage that these degenerate, immoral people condemned her. And this outrage spurred her on to share more of the tattle with her dinner companion.

Wolf, for his part, found the conversation amusing. He had never thought well of the nobility that had spurned his parents. And hearing about their dark secrets felt harmless and, in fact, useful. If Wolf had learned anything in his many years at his chosen profession, it was that secrets could be powerful currency.

The new Lord Pembroke didn't quite know what to make of his housemate. Tabitha was undeniably beautiful, with hair threaded with reds and gold in the right light. Thick dark lashes framed her large, intelligent eyes. Tabitha was quite tall for a woman and wore her height well, with a stately poise. Her figure was a little slimmer than was the fashion at the moment, but the overall effect was comely.

Wolf judged her cold and distant at their initial meeting, just like the noble grandmother and aunts he had rarely visited. But over a few days, as their dinner conversation became less formal and stilted, he started to see that what he'd taken as coldness had been a layer of self-protection that he imagined she had assumed since her marriage.

There was no doubt that he was grateful for her remaining to run the household. He neither knew nor wished to learn how to manage a household, let alone one as large as the one of which he now found himself the head. Wolf had grown up in a household with minimal staff. Still, he and Bear had shifted for themselves for so long that having people to wait on his every need felt incredibly uncomfortable. He quickly picked up a trick that at least worked some of the time; by saying, "My man will take care of that," he persuaded whichever servant was hovering around him to leave him alone. And, of course, Bear rarely took care of whatever it was.

Wolf hadn't spent significant time with a lady in a long time. He spent time with women, but none deserved the moniker 'lady.' It took him a day or two to control his automatic urge to swear constantly. He'd tried to remember the table manners his father had insisted he practice. His childhood had been such a strange world where the shadow of nobility was always there. But his day-to-day reality was a family always scrambling to keep the illusion of better things alive.

Once it became clear to his grandfather that Jonathan would not have any younger brothers, the old earl took just enough interest in his other grandson to ensure that he at least had the education of a gentleman, "just in case." And so, Wolf had dutifully attended Eton and then Oxford. He had been invited to his grandfather's estate once a year for inspection until his grandfather's death when Wolf was 14.

Wolf's father had always held out the hope that he would eventually be able to make peace with his own father. He tried his best to ensure that Wolf and his sisters could return to aristocratic circles if a rapprochement ever happened. It didn't. But Wolf was raised as a gentleman between his grandfather's hedge of his bets and his father's naive optimism. While Wolf had tried his best to distance himself from this for many years, he now felt gratitude.

So, at least ten days passed peacefully, even pleasantly. The entire household had walked on eggshells when the previous earl had been alive. Even if it wasn't on their own behalf, they were terrified of doing something that would provoke his anger against the countess. They suffered the strain of hearing him scream and more at the countess. The impotence of wanting to intervene but knowing that no good would come from it for any of them. Since his death, that tension had dissipated to be replaced by the malaise of a house in mourning. Even one in mourning for someone no one actually mourned.

But as soon as her ladyship put on her lavender half-mourning and the new earl appeared, it was as if the house felt lighter, airier. Like a slowly growing mould, what had lingered for two generations in that house had been wiped clean. While it was true that the earl was a little unconventional, enough of the servants had either lived through the reigns of terror of the previous two earls or had seen enough with the younger to believe the tales told of his father. Their new master was a gentleman, which was sufficient as far as they were concerned.

But on the eleventh day, the peace was shattered.

CHAPTER 6

Tabitha had woken up from a lovely dream. Her beloved father had still been alive, and she had wandered in a field of cornflowers with him as a little boy and girl ran ahead of them. The children kept picking flowers and returning to the adults, crying, "Mama, Grandpapa, here are more for the crowns." After a while, they'd come to a green meadow at the end of the field. They'd all sat down on a blanket that had magically appeared. Tabitha had shown the children how to weave crowns out of the flowers; between them, they made one for each of them, including her father.

She had lain half out of sleep as long as possible, trying to keep hold of that dream. She knew those children; she'd dreamt of them before. They were the two children she was supposed to have, snatched from her womb too early. She had dreamt of them many times. The little girl with the red-gold ringlets and freckles was called Maryann, and the stocky little boy with the large brown eyes and cowlick was called Peter.

But as much as she tried to keep hold of the dream and the children in it, she finally woke up entirely, and the dream was just a vague memory lingering on the edge of her consciousness. She might have imagined that such dreams, of people long gone and children she never got to hold, would make her sad. But instead, she relished this time she could spend with them all and always woke from these dreams happy.

As usual, Wolf had taken his breakfast in his study, and so she dined alone. But it wasn't the solitary dining that she'd been forced into in the six months after Jonathan's death. Then, she sat alone, abandoned by friends and family. A social pariah considered deserving of her loneliness. Now, she was just a woman taking coffee and toast while the other household members went about their business. Tabitha wasn't entirely sure why it felt so different, except that she knew that Wolf was just down the hallway and that if she had wanted to interrupt him to chat, she would have been most welcome.

After breakfast, she went through the menus for the week, and some household accounts with Mrs Jenkins. Over the last few days, Tabitha decided that her half-mourning wouldn't last long. In fact, she wasn't sure why she'd bothered with it at all. You can't be more cast out and disapproved of by society than she already was. And so, she'd decided to visit her modiste and order a new wardrobe.

Jonathan had always expected her to dress as conservatively as possible, which was ironic if even half of what she'd heard of his mistress was true. While Tabitha did not wish to be immodest in her dress, she would like to be less austere and to wear the colours and fabrics she'd loved before her marriage.

That morning she was sitting in her drawing room at the beautifully carved mahogany desk she used to keep up with her, albeit modest, correspondence. She had just finished re-reading the letter from her cousin Polly who was married with a brood of children and lived in Devon. Tabitha had always enjoyed Polly's high spirits and direct manner. She had been one of the few people that Tabitha had felt able to confide in during the two awful years of her marriage and was one of the only people to immediately side with Tabitha and defend her in the aftermath of Jonathan's death.

Tabitha was just about to pick up her pen and tell Polly about the house's new inhabitants when the door opened, and the dowager countess swept in. She hadn't even stopped to remove her outer garments, and Talbot hovered in her wake, ready to catch whatever she might divest herself of as she stampeded towards the younger woman, waving her stick before her.

"What is this, I hear? You are living here unaccompanied with a single man and a creature who, by all accounts, can barely be called a man?"

"Good day to you, Lady Pembroke. Why don't you let Talbot take your coat and gloves and take a seat? Talbot, please have Mary bring some tea and some of those orange scones that the countess so likes."

"I have no interest in tea and cake and polite chit chat with you." The dowager snarled. However, she did allow Talbot to help her off with her coat and help her to the settee. "Now I demand to know what is going on and why I had to hear about it from Lady Davenport, of all people." Lady Davenport was Tabitha's next-door neighbour and notoriously nosy. It was no surprise that she had been curious about her new neighbours and even less surprising that she immediately began spreading malicious stories about them.

Tabitha arranged her face into perfectly innocent curiosity, "Lady Pembroke, Mama," she said, trying to appease the furious elder, "if you are talking about the new earl, then yes, as you yourself informed me, he has been found. And again, you were the one to tell me to expect him any day. As is often the case, you were correct, and within days, he arrived to establish himself here, as is his right. His valet, a Mr Bear, accompanied him."

"Mr Bear! What kind of name is that? And as for the rest, where do I start? Why did my late son's heir not see fit to pay his addresses to me? And more to the point, why are you living here with him? Don't you realise how that looks and what society will say? If they're not saying it already?"

So now they were at the heart of the problem. It was a bifurcated problem; on the one hand, Wolf had not immediately rushed to bow low before the dowager countess. On the other hand, what would people say? As to the latter, Tabitha cared not one whit. To the former, she admitted to herself that was probably an oversight on her part. But to be honest, Wolf had a lot to acclimate to over the past ten days, and she had been reluctant to throw him into the lion's den before he'd had a chance to settle into his earldom.

Tabitha had, of course, realised that an introduction to the dowager was inevitable. She had hoped to be able to ease Wolf into it. But she should have known that word would get out and that the dowager would take umbrage at the imagined lack of unctuous deference. She considered how to soothe the dowager's perception of slight. For herself, Tabitha didn't care. But this is the world that Wolf would have to move in now, and it was unfair to have him begin on the wrong footing with the dowager merely because of Tabitha's turbulent relationship with the matriarch.

"Mama, forgive me. The fault is all mine. I have been guiding the new Lord Pembroke in the ways of London society and what will be expected of him." At this, the dowager made a sound that was part sniff, part snort, and was clearly meant to imply that Tabitha was the last person to help someone else navigate society. Tabitha ignored it and continued, "As you can imagine, this has taken up much of our time, and the rest has been spent with Jonathan's solicitor and his man of business. The earl has made no social calls yet." This much was at least true. "And, of course, the first he planned to make was to pay his respects to you."

This speech hardly mollified the irate dowager countess, who had been working herself into a lather since she had heard the news, and certainly wasn't going to let it all go to waste that easily. However, to the experienced eye, which Tabitha counted herself, there was an obvious softening of the features, and the eyes no longer shot darts. Tabitha continued, "I believe the earl is currently alone in his study. Do you wish me to summon him?"

Tabitha knew what a dilemma this presented. The dowager was clearly extremely curious about the new heir. But she wished to meet him on her terms and in her own home where she could lay out the battlefield to her advantage.

Instead of answering, the dowager pivoted. "Regardless of his lack of manners in failing to call on me, the most scandalous part of the gossip circulating throughout society is that you are living here, unchaperoned with him."

This was a more difficult charge to answer. If only because the same concern had briefly entered Tabitha's mind. She, of course, could not admit any concerns to her mother-in-law. The only defence was a full-throated one. "Mama, I am a widow, not some ingenue. Moreover, the earl is not a stranger; he is a cousin, albeit a more distant one. There can be nothing scandalous about living with a male relative."

She could see that the dowager was weighing the logic of these arguments. Living with a brother or father was perfectly acceptable. Perhaps even a close cousin. But it was unclear what the protocol was for a man no one knew anything of until two weeks ago and who was still a mystery to everyone who mattered and was a cousin-in-law to boot.

Tabitha could see the dowager thinking this all through and trying to come up with an ironclad reason why Tabitha was bringing shame on the family name again. Seizing the opportunity, Tabitha rushed to move her piece to chess mate and continued, "The earl has never headed up a household as large and as grand as Chesterton House. He asked me if I would stay on, at least temporarily, to ensure the smooth running of the household." And now she went in for the kill, "I know that this house and the conduct of all within it reflect on you. You ran this household for years with efficiency, dignity, and decorum. I felt I owed it to you to ensure that none of the standards you set and that I've tried my best to adhere to are lowered."

A glint in the dowager countess' eye told Tabitha that she'd won the match and that the older woman knew and admired her game strategy. Unwilling to concede the battle, even if she'd lost the skirmish, the dowager rose to her full five feet and said with all the arrogance and grandiosity a countess could summon, "He will present himself for tea tomorrow, and you will accompany him." She approached the door, seemed to think of something else, and turned back. "Oh and have him bring this Mr Bear with him. I must inspect any servant at Chesterton House who is causing gossip just by his very being." And with that, she left.

The whirlwind that had been the dowager's visit had not allowed Tabitha the chance to move from her spot at her desk.

She continued to sit there for many minutes after her guest had left, her unfinished letter now ignored. What was foremost in her mind was what to say to Wolf. So far, he had shown himself to be willing to be educated in the ways of the beau monde. But it was one thing to learn about the foibles of the aristocracy as an academic exercise over dinner. It was quite another to be paraded into her mother-in-law's drawing room and almost certainly judged lacking.

However, Tabitha reflected, she could only put it off for so long. And as she had just witnessed, the longer she waited, the worse it would be for Wolf and her. Now, the issue at hand was how to present this to Wolf. Strictly speaking, he owed the dowager countess nothing. She was the nominal matriarch of the family, but he didn't seem like someone who stood on ceremony for those kinds of niceties of society. She reflected on the best tack to take as she walked to the study and knocked gently on the door.

She entered to see Wolf sitting in the same position she had first found him, feet up on the desk. Though now decidedly less scruffy, it was clear that he had no interest in dressing formally in his own home with no company present. He wore no jacket or cravat and had rolled-up shirt sleeves. Tabitha could only imagine what the dowager would make of such a lack of sartorial standards. While not a fop, Jonathan had always been turned out to formal perfection, no matter the situation. On the other hand, she couldn't help but admire the muscular forearms on display. Tabitha appreciated the likely greater comfort of such an outfit. It made her wish she could throw off her corsets and heavy skirts and instead walk around her home in such comfort.

"Tabitha, what a nice surprise. What do you need from me?"

"Am I disturbing you, Wolf?" she inquired. Tabitha had long ago given into the inevitable and started calling him by his chosen name.

"Yes, but that doesn't mean it's an unpleasant disturbance. I will admit that examining the ledgers of the estate is not the sort of work I enjoy."

"Isn't that why you have Mr Roberts, your steward? Jonathan wasn't a negligent landowner, as far as I know. But I believe he was happy to leave the day-to-day management and finances to Mr Roberts, who has been with the estate since Jonathan's grandfather's day."

"Indeed, Mr Roberts is a highly competent manager and has been very patient as I learn about the estate. But I have a duty to understand the necessary decisions more fully. Perhaps this all came more naturally to your husband because he had been born and raised to the position." Tabitha highly doubted this. "Anyway, as I said, the interruption is hardly unwelcome."

"Well," she started haltingly, "you may change your mind when you hear what I have to say."

"Then you better come in, sit down, take a glass of sherry, and tell me what's bothering you."

Tabitha gladly took the seat and the sherry and began, "I wouldn't say that this is bothering me as much as I suspect it will bother you."

"Now, Tabitha, you're starting to worry me with such a dramatic prologue."

Tabitha laughed. "I'm sorry, Wolf, I am making this into a bit of a drama. It's just that the dowager countess, Jonathan's mother just visited. Maybe visit is too polite a way to put it. She stormed in and rang a peal over me because you have not waited on her yet."

Wolf looked genuinely confused, "Why ring a peal over you? If there is a fault, and I'm not entirely sure why there is any, surely it is only a fault of mine."

Tabitha hesitated for a few moments, unsure how much candour was appropriate. Finally, she realised that Wolf deserved and would appreciate utter candour. "The dowager countess, Lady Pembroke, has been greatly disappointed by the earldom no longer being in the direct line of succession. She blames my childlessness for this situation. To retain her importance, she must be seen to have your respect, even your deference. Anything else will seem like the cut direct, at least in the eyes of society. You may not care what society thinks of you, but they are certainly watching and making judgments. And Lady Pembroke definitely cares about such judgments. She believes you owe her deference in virtue of her rank, age, and status as the mother of the late earl."

When Tabitha finished, she saw a wide grin appear on Wolf's face. She couldn't imagine what there was in her statement to make him smile. She was about to ask when he said, "Now I understand fully. I have dealt with enough gang captains to understand the desire to have others kiss the ring."

Tabitha was shocked. She wasn't sure what shocked her more, hearing that the new Earl of Pembroke had personal and frequent interactions with the gangs in London or having the upper echelons of society compared to such a gang.

Wolf continued, "I understand that gangs, however outwardly vicious and disruptive, nevertheless exist with their own internal codes of honour and etiquette."

At this, Tabitha had to interrupt, "Surely, sir, you're not comparing a brutal street gang's notions of honour to that held by polite society?"

Wolf laughed, a pleasant-sounding baritone of a grumble. "'Polite society?' Is that how it sees itself? Consider this, in polite society, a man is honour-bound to treat an unmarried young woman with nothing but the greatest gentleness, civility, and respect. But once that young woman is his wife, now considered his property, he is no longer honour-bound to continue this behaviour and can beat her until he breaks her bones. Society will not consider him any less honourable for this behaviour. How is this notion of honour any better than a street thug?"

As he said this, Tabitha felt herself go cold. She was sure all the blood must have drained from her face. While she had alluded to Jonathan as less than an ideal husband, she had never mentioned her treatment at his hands. She suspected that one of the staff had told Bear, who had then told his master.

In reality, Wolf knew none of these particulars of Tabitha's wretched marriage. Still, the look on her face told him everything he needed to know. He felt awful at having caused her such anguish, even if inadvertently, and so quickly changed the subject. "But we have digressed. I will, of course, be happy to rectify my lapse in etiquette as soon as possible, if only for your sake."

Tabitha was happy with the quick reversion to the original topic and exclaimed, "Wonderful! She is expecting me to escort you to tea tomorrow afternoon. You will need to shave and, in every way, meet her expectations of how the Earl of Pembroke should look, sound, and act. Oh, and one more thing," she added, "we're to bring Bear."

The response to this was as sudden and surprising as she'd expected. "What the devil does she mean by demanding that? Or even desiring such a thing? Since when are my associates her business?"

Tabitha smiled sympathetically, "Of course, she has no business making this or any demand of you. You owe her and me," she added, "nothing. The fact of the matter is Bear is conspicuous in the neighbourhood, and people's tongues have been wagging. That a man who looks as he does is the valet to the new earl, a personage who is the topic of much speculation and gossip can only add to the interest. Such talk has winged its way to the dowager's very receptive ears.

"I'm sure part of her peeve is that she has no first-hand account to brandish. She walks into evening parties, and everyone is all atwitter about the new heir and turns to her, expecting her to be a fount of information. Yet, she must admit, to her shame, to know not much more than everyone else. This situation must be excruciating for her ladyship.

"She means to rectify this situation, and, as such, she needs to meet Bear and be able to testify personally to his proportions and generally terrifying countenance. Nothing less will right the ship of her pre-eminence in the gossip mill."

For a moment, Tabitha thought that Wolf might be justifiably outraged by the idea of displaying his friend and putative servant as some sort of carnival sideshow merely to give tongues some new information on which to wag. But she was relieved to hear him chuckle again.

"I'm sure it will amuse Bear that the cream of society is this interested in him. Should he shave and put on his best coat, or will the rumour mill be better served if he looks as much like a wild beast as possible?"

"I believe that, while we may indulge her curiosity up to a point, we do not need to indulge the most outrageous impulses of a bunch of bored, spoiled aristocrats. Mr Bear should also shave and wear his best coat and cravat and in every way present as, while a large specimen of a man, nonetheless a model of rectitude. "

CHAPTER 7

Thus, it was that at the appropriate visiting hour, the three of them set off in the earl's carriage to take tea with the dowager countess. When Wolf and Bear had presented themselves for inspection before leaving, Tabitha had marvelled at how well-suited Wolf was to society's expectations of a noble. Except for the length of his hair, which she had given up trying to remedy.

His looks could rival any Corinthian; tall and broad-shouldered, he had a physique that showed off his new, fashionable attire to great advantage. He had a chiselled jaw, high cheekbones, and those penetrating eyes. She reflected that it was merely a matter of birth order that had made Jonathan's father the earl rather than this man's, and so perhaps it should not be a surprise that he so looked the part.

Even Bear had cleaned up remarkably well. His sheer bulk was indisputable. But with a proper jacket and cravat, his overall hairiness was somewhat disguised. And shaved, he looked younger and less terrifying than usual. Bear's eyes had a gentleness she hadn't seen when they first met. But she wasn't sure whether she hadn't noticed or it merely reflected what she now knew about his gentle and kind demeanour.

"Gentlemen, you both look debonair and every inch the part of the Earl of Pembroke and his valet. However, the dowager will not be impressed by looks alone. We need to run through some items of etiquette and just general prudence.

"To begin with, you are Lord Pembroke or Pembroke. You are not to request or even suggest that she call you Wolf. And likewise, you are Mr Bear. Wolf, there will be no throwaway comments about gangs or whatever the two of you used to get up to. It will never occur to her that someone who has now inherited the earldom ever had to earn his living, assuming that is what you were doing. And we do not need to disabuse her of her assumptions.

"The dowager is rather fonder of speaking than listening and this is to our advantage. She will ask you very little about yourself and instead spend as much of our visit gossiping about her acquaintances and lecturing you on what you ought to be doing. Just nod and murmur polite agreement with whatever she's saying. No matter how pompous or absurd.

"Bear, I'm assuming you will make your way below stairs. I would like to believe that my staff is not constantly gossiping about me. But perhaps I am deluding myself. However, I can assure you that the dowager's household is a positive viper's nest of intrigue and gossip, taking its lead from the woman herself. I advise you to take heed of as little as possible and to say even less."

Both men looked down at their feet and nodded their heads. Tabitha felt like her governess as she warned Tabitha and her siblings how to behave as they were trotted into the drawing room to say polite good evenings to their parent's guests before being shuffled out again.

She clapped her hands, "Good, then I believe we're ready to go."

Jonathan had set his mother up in a lovely house that, if somewhat less palatial than his own, nevertheless allowed her to entertain with no shame. On his marriage to Tabitha, he had suggested to the dowager that she did not need to leave the home she shared with him. But she insisted that a woman must be allowed to take charge of her household without her mother-in-law looking over her shoulders. Privately, Tabitha wondered whether she wasn't just looking for any opportunity to leave a son who was far too much like his father.

The diminutive dowager seemed to compensate for her vertical challenges by hiring the tallest butler Tabitha had ever seen. Even so, he wasn't as tall as Bear. And unlike the massively muscled valet, Manning was rail thin. As inscrutable as any seasoned butler, Manning's face gave away none of his surprise when Bear followed Wolf and Tabitha into the house's lobby. With her coat removed, Tabitha explained that Mr Bear was the earl's valet and asked if the butler could show him below stairs.

"Excuse me, your ladyship, but the countess, Lady Pembroke," Tabitha noticed that in Manning's eyes, the dowager had never been relegated out of her pinnacle role, "specifically requested that the earl's valet accompany you into the drawing room."

Wolf quirked an eyebrow at her in question, and she gave a slight shrug of her shoulders in reply. Tabitha had no idea what the dowager was up to now.

Tabitha hadn't been in the dowager's home for quite some time, and she had forgotten the oddity of the drawing room. Its petite owner had set the room up very much for her own convenience. It was as if, in selecting furniture, she had overlooked that one of the primary functions of a drawing room was to receive guests. Many of whom were likely to be significantly taller and larger than their hostess. Instead, she seemed to have gone out of her way to find the smallest adult furniture possible. Looking at the room from the doorway, Tabitha wondered if the furniture had originally been made for a nursery.

One of the results of the placement of such furnishings was that most visitors were usually supremely uncomfortable in their chairs, and visits rarely lasted long. Perhaps, Tabitha reflected, that was the point. Certainly, one of the dowager's aims was to place every guest at an immediate disadvantage as she sat comfortably in a chair that was the perfect size for her frame.

The dowager indicated that they all, including Bear, should be seated. Wolf looked uncomfortable and unbalanced on a gilded chair into which he could barely squeeze. Poor Bear looked around him, clearly wondering which chair he wouldn't break and finally chose a chaise longue just slightly behind where

Tabitha and Wolf had taken seats. Even with the extra width this seating afforded him, seeing this enormous man perched on the delicate, tiny furniture was one of the most absurd sights Tabitha had ever seen. Trying her best not to giggle, she took a moment to smooth her skirt and compose herself before looking up at her hostess.

"Lady Pembroke, I'd like to introduce you to Jeremy Chesterton, Earl of Pembroke, and his man, Mr Bear." Bear stood and executed a neat bow at this introduction.

"Countess," he said, sitting back down, "please allow me to apologise for my inexcusable tardiness in waiting on you. The other Lady Pembroke bears no blame; she mentioned several times that introducing myself to you must be one of my top priorities."

Well, that was laying it on a bit thick, Tabitha thought to herself. By the smirk on the dowager's face, she agreed. But she accepted the lie with a gracious nod of her head and answered, "Your apology is accepted. I am sure you have much to do and learn as you take on an earldom you were not prepared or educated for as a distant cousin."

If Wolf got the subtle dig, he was diplomatic enough not to acknowledge it in any way. Instead, he continued, "As you know better than anyone, I had not expected an honour as immense as this one. With her time, knowledge, and patience, Lady Pembroke has been generous beyond measure. But, of course, no one's guidance could be more valuable and more welcome than your own."

The dowager repaid this patently disingenuous flattery with an equally disingenuous simper and replied, "Why Tabitha dear, you never mentioned what a charming flirt the new earl is." It was all Tabitha could do not to roll her eyes. However, she couldn't blame Wolf. He was only doing what she had told him to do. In fact, he seemed to be exceeding her expectations of his ability to charm when necessary.

"You know your lordship," the dowager continued.

He interrupted her, "Please call me Jeremy if it isn't too great a breach of protocol."

At this, the dowager giggled. Yes, thought Tabitha, 'giggle' was the only word for the sound that the dowager was making. Tabitha just had an awful thought. She prayed it wasn't the case. But was it possible that the dowager wasn't playacting but was flirting with the much younger man? She had expected a melodramatic, self-righteous dowager. And then, when the conversation turned, she had assumed that she was witnessing a particularly brilliantly fiendish shot over the bow, a dire warning delivered with the affectation of an ingenue. But now, she wasn't quite sure what she was witnessing.

"Well, usually, I'm quite the stickler for observing the customs of good society. But, when a handsome and charming young man pleads with me to use his given name, it would seem churlish to deny his heart's desire," the dowager continued.

Tabitha did roll her eyes now. She didn't remember anyone pleading and claiming their heart's desire. She stole a glance at Wolf, who was somehow not breaking character and assumed the air of a young lover granted a kiss from his love.

"Jeremy, you do look awfully uncomfortable in that chair. You're far too well-built a young man for such a spindly chair. See that chair in the corner? Bring it and place it by me. You'll be much more comfortable, and we can speak more intimately. "

Wolf rose, got the chair, and put it at the dowager's elbow. He sat down, and they proceeded to put their heads together and talk like old friends, or perhaps more like lovers, Tabitha thought wryly.

After a few minutes of this, Tabitha decided that she could stomach no more and cleared her throat and said, "Mama, you had requested that we introduce you to Lord Pembroke's man, Mr Bear."

The dowager looked momentarily confused, as if she'd forgotten that Bear was even in the room at her request. "Ah, yes, but of course. Dear Jeremy, please introduce us."

Wolf jerked his head to indicate to Bear to get up and come over. The man was enormous next to anyone, but looming over the tiny, seated dowager, even Tabitha felt momentarily alarmed. But the dowager seemed anything but perturbed. Wolf introduced her to Bear, and she laughed and said, "Well, I can see what all the commotion in your neighbourhood was about now. I'm sure that the sight of Mr Bear had every young maid quaking and every mother in fear that her household was coming under attack. What a hoot!

"I think, Mr Bear, I may need to borrow you occasionally to hang around my home and put the fear of God into some of my neighbours. I can think of a few in particular who I wouldn't mind terrifying." She began to chuckle as if there was nothing more amusing than being able to scare her neighbours at will.

After this introduction, Bear was excused and allowed to go to the kitchen. Manning brought in tea and cake, and it was only after another 30 minutes when Tabitha felt that an acceptable length of time had passed for their escape, that she rose and began to make their apologies.

"I'm so sorry to drag Lord Pembroke away. But I believe he has his man of business coming shortly."

"Pish posh. Your man of business waits on you rather than the other way around. However, I expect Lady Willis soon, and I like you too much, Jeremy, to subject you to that harpy. But you must promise me that you'll come and visit again soon. In fact, I'm having a little supper party on Thursday that you must attend. It will allow me to introduce you to all the best people." She paused, looking a little embarrassed. "I'm sure you understand, Tabitha dear, why I can't extend the invitation to you. And you're only just out of full mourning. People would be appalled."

Tabitha knew why she wasn't receiving an invitation, which stung a little. But she also had no desire to spend an evening making polite conversation with a roomful of people who were judging her and gossiping about her behind their hands. She certainly had no wish to contaminate Wolf's likely triumphant entry into society with her presence. With a little inclination of her head, Tabitha acknowledged the dowager's point.

CHAPTER 8

Although Tabitha insisted that Bear was welcome to share the carriage with them, she could understand why he chose to sit with their driver, Madison; his height alone would have made the carriage an uncomfortable ride.

Their privacy assured for the ride home, Tabitha felt little compunction in speaking her mind, "That was quite the performance!"

Wolf assumed a look of total innocence and replied, "Lady Pembroke, whatever do you mean?"

"I mean, I realise that I was the person who suggested that you get on the dowager's good side. However, I don't believe I included outrageous flirting with a woman old enough to be your grandmother as one of the suggestions."

Infuriatingly, Wolf continued to maintain his look of angelic naivety, "Flirting? Is that what you say I was doing? I cannot answer for the dowager countess' behaviour towards me. Still, I can assure you that I responded to her with the deference you had specifically ordered me to display."

Tabitha wasn't sure which part of this statement to attack first, "Ordered? Is that how you remember the conversation? Please excuse me if I overstepped. I intended to prepare you adequately for your meeting with a wily old battleaxe who was predisposed to disapprove and has the power to make your entry into society difficult."

"And indeed, you prepared me, and I assume you won't argue, that I met the challenge of that 'battleaxe' head-on and neutralised the threat."

Tabitha had no reply to this. Wolf had indeed won the dowager over to an extent she had never anticipated. Perhaps that sat at the heart of her irritation; for so long, she had tried to please her mother-in-law. Even before her marriage to Jonathan, Tabitha had sensed that his mother didn't wholeheartedly approve of his choice. It was unclear where this disapproval stemmed from; Tabitha came from a noble and wealthy family. She was a young, innocent debutante, untainted by any prior liaisons or even gossip of some.

After her marriage, Tabitha had always assumed that the dowager's primary problem was her inability to bring any baby, let alone a male one, to term. And then, with Jonathan's death and Tabitha's short time as the chief murder suspect, the relationship had degenerated even further. The dowager had always made it quite clear that no matter that there was no charge in the end, she firmly believed Tabitha wasn't innocent.

Wolf was happy to take advantage of Tabitha's pause in attack to move the conversation away from his behaviour and asked, "You did not seem surprised not to be invited to the supper party. Why is your exclusion such an accepted fact?"

Tabitha realised that she needed to address the reason for her status as a social pariah at some point, so she answered, "I'm not sure if you were told, but Jonathan died falling down the stairs while drunk. He and I had been fighting in the hallway just before it happened, and I was sporting what became a black eye. An overly enthusiastic young police inspector raised the possibility that I had pushed my husband down the stairs in anger. While they could never make the accusation stick legally, it nevertheless stuck socially. I believe that the dowager was at least in part responsible for both spreading and endorsing the story. I do not doubt that my early move into half-mourning confirmed what those wagging tongues suspected."

"You don't seem very upset at this. Indeed, you must have suspected that anything less than a long, visibly anguished period of mourning would spur on such salacious rumours. And yet, you came out of full mourning anyway."

Tabitha shrugged. Wolf was only vocalising what she had been internally debating for the last few weeks; why feed grist to the mill by not maintaining the illusion of the grieving widow? "I decided that I didn't care. Those people's opinions are unimportant to me.

"The callow, foppish pups draining their estates dry with their whoring and gambling. The demure debutantes stabbing each other in the back for the chance to win one of those pups. The fine upstanding members of society those pups matured into crushing those debutantes into submission once they attained their maidenhoods. And finally, perhaps the worst of all; the bitter, mean-spirited matrons into whom those debutantes harden. Finding joy in the weaknesses and foibles of their so-called friends.

"No, I don't care what they think of me. And realising that has been liberating. At least now, the pretence is over. I no longer am invited to parties I never wanted to attend anyway. They were going to whisper lies and half-truths about me anyway. At least now, I don't have to catch them doing so in loud whispers in my company."

This information was more than Tabitha had revealed about herself and her marriage to Wolf or perhaps anyone. The emotional effort seemed to drain her, and when done, her raised hand indicated he didn't need to reply. She turned her head and looked out the window for the rest of the trip home.

When the carriage pulled up outside Chesterton House and Wolf helped her out, Tabitha continued holding his hand, looked into his eyes, and said, "Do not make my battles your own. Go to the party."

Then she let go of his hand and swept into the house. Wolf watched Tabitha go for a few moments and reflected on what a fine and proud woman she was.

CHAPTER 9

The evening of their visit to the dowager had been awkward. Tabitha felt she had revealed too much, and dinner was a quiet and strained affair. Wolf feared that the confidences shared in the carriage may have permanently undone the ease of conversation they had fallen into since his arrival. It was so uncomfortable that he found himself grateful that the following evening was the dowager's soiree. It meant he could give Tabitha some space for another day in the hope that some time would undo some of the forced formality that seemed to have sprung up between them.

Tabitha was embarrassed. Embarrassed that she had let down her guard and spoken so freely and candidly. Ginny had long been a confidante. But even sharing a warmer relationship than existed between most women and their maids, certain things could not be shared with a servant. Even a servant as intelligent, loyal, and brave as Ginny.

When she thought of demure debutantes whose only aim was to secure a fine husband, she felt ashamed that she had been one of those girls only a few years ago. And when she spoke so bitterly of the dowager and her ilk, she was only too aware that, if Jonathan hadn't died when he did, she too might have aged into another such ugly creature. Tabitha was worried that her dismissal of high society sounded like sour grapes. And she felt the most shame over her admission that she had been under scrutiny for her husband's death.

Tabitha was as relieved as Wolf himself that he was otherwise engaged for the night at the dowager's. She ate alone and then retired to the library to curl up with a book in front of the fire.

When Talbot knocked and entered, she had just settled down with a glass of sherry and her favourite Charles Dickens novel, Bleak House.

"Milady, I apologise for the interruption, but there is a scruffy young visitor at the backdoor. He's asking for his lordship or Mr Bear. The earl has already departed for the evening, and Mr Bear seems to be out. The young man is quite insistent that he has a message for his lordship and became quite agitated when I tried to send him away."

Tabitha put down her book, stood up, and smoothed her dress. She was very curious about what a young street lad wanted with Wolf and Bear. "I'll come down with you, Talbot, and talk to this young man."

She followed Talbot downstairs to the kitchen. It seemed that the young boy, who didn't look much older than eight or nine, had somehow persuaded cook to let him past the back door, and he was now sitting at the kitchen table with a glass of milk and one of cook's delicious raisin scones. As she entered, he looked up, and Tabitha couldn't help but smile at his milk moustache.

Cook slapped him on the back of his head and said, "Mind your manners and stand up when your betters enter a room."

The lad put down his scone and hastily got to his feet. Tabitha waved him back down and sat opposite him. She took a scone from the plate in the middle of the table and smiled at the young boy. "Now, let's start with your name."

"Rat it is, miss." He replied with an accent that made it clear that he had grown up in the roughest, poorest part of London.

Talbot quickly interjected, "This is the Countess of Pembroke, Lady Pembroke. You should refer to her by milady or your ladyship. Certainly not 'miss'."

Tabitha quickly took over from her prickly butler, "Now, Master Rat, is that your real name?"

The boy shook his head, "Nah, but it's what I've been called since I started working with Wolf and Bear. See? Wolf, Bear, Rat. Wolf is the brains of the group. Bear is the muscle. And me, Rat, I'm the one who can 'ide in holes, shimmy up buildings, and run along roofs. I'm the one who gets the goods wot they need and stuff. My real name is Matthew, Matt. See? Rat. Matt." He smiled with great pride at the rhyme of his nickname.

Tabitha wasn't sure whether to be amused or alarmed at what the 'goods' and 'stuff' might be that Wolf had a child procuring for him by running across roofs. "So then, Master Rat, how can we help you this evening? I hear that you asked for his lordship and Mr Bear. As I believe you've been told, neither of them is here at present. However, I'm happy to pass on a message."

Rat narrowed his eyes as he assessed the situation. Tabitha continued, "I realise you don't know me, but I'm a new friend of his lordship's, and I promise you I'm very trustworthy and reliable. If you give me your message, I promise to deliver it to the earl as soon as he comes home. "

Rat's face showed confusion. "I don't want no lord or earl, m'lady. I'm looking for Wolf and Bear. Bear showed me your 'ouse before they left if I needed them."

Tabitha could see that there were some basic facts that needed clearing up. "So, Mr Wolf is now the Earl of Pembroke. We refer to him as his lordship or milord. This is now his house."

"So, wot? Wolf, his lordship like, is now 'ammered for life to you, miss? I mean, m'lady?"

Tabitha guessed that he meant marriage and answered, "No, his lordship and I are not married." At this, Rat raised his eyebrows and then winked at her.

Grasping which way his thoughts had headed, she immediately corrected him, "Nor are we engaged in another kind of, well, any kind of romantic entanglement. My husband was the previous earl, and he died recently. Mr Wolf, his lordship, has inherited the title and has asked me to stay here for some time to help him with his household."

Comprehension seemed to have dawned on Rat, and he said, "Right then, so you're keeping 'ouse for Wolf?"

Tabitha decided that this conversation had been side tracked long enough and said, "Something like that. So, as you can see, I'm someone that his lordship trusts, and so can you. What is your message?"

"Well, tell Wolf that Bruiser 'as been round asking for him. Says he has a big job needs doing and that he needs it done sharp and maybe there's plenty of brass for the taking. Wolf is to meet Bruiser at 10 tomorrow, at the Cock, for some morning scran and ale."

Tabitha tried to make sense of this message, relaying it back to the boy to ensure she had understood correctly, "So a Mr Bruiser wants his lordship to meet him at the Cock? A pub called the Cock. Tomorrow morning for breakfast?"

"Yeah, that's what I said, ain't it?" Rat replied.

"Yes, I was just making sure that I had it correctly so I could accurately deliver the message."

"M'lady, maybe I should just wait 'ere and give it to m'lord Wolf himself. Bruiser said there's another 'a'penny in it for me if I bring a reply tonight."

"Master Rat, it is possible that his lordship will be back late tonight. You should be in bed long before that. Your mother will be worried."

Rat laughed, "I sleeps when I need to. Don't be worrying about me. The best pickings are at night, so I'm used to it. And me ma and pa have been gone since Melly was a little chavvy of three or so."

Tabitha realised on an intellectual level that poor orphaned children scrabbled on the dirty streets for what they could find. But it was quite another thing to confront the reality of that in one's own kitchen. She then thought about the last thing that Rat had said and asked, "Who is Melly?"

"Me sister. We call her Melly, but 'er real name is Melody. She's older now. Not sure 'ow much, maybe a year or so."

Horrified at the thought of a four-year-old girl alone in the dark, Tabitha said, "Where is Melody now? She's not alone, is she?"

Rat looked offended, "Nah, what do you take me for? She's out back 'ere. I told her to 'ide and not make a sound."

"She's waiting outside my back door for you while we speak?"

Tabitha rose and hurried to the back door. She opened it and called out, "Melody? Melly? You can come out. It's safe. Rat is with me."

There was no response. Tabitha tried again, "Melly, we have milk and scones. You should come in before Rat eats them all." There was rustling in the bushes at this, and a tiny figure emerged. As the child walked into the light cast from the kitchen, Tabitha caught her breath. With her red-gold ringlets dancing around her face and freckles sprayed all over her nose, this child was the Maryann of her dreams come to life.

Tabitha felt tears spring to her eyes and threaten to spill over. She took hold of herself and bent to the child's level, "Melly, my name is Tabitha. But my very good friends call me Tabby. Would you like to come in with me and have something to eat?" The child nodded and took Tabitha's outstretched hand. They walked back into the kitchen, and Tabitha lifted her and put her on the chair next to Rat. The little girl still hadn't said a word. She just stared at Tabitha with large blue eyes that seemed full of wonder, if a little scared.

Rat patted his sister's hand, "It's okay Melly, these are friends of Wolf and Bear. This is m'lady. Want a scone?"

"I've asked Melody to call me Tabby if that's ok with you, Master Rat?"

"Like a Tabby cat?"

"Yes, just like that, I suppose. So, you're Rat, and I'm Tabby cat." At this, Melody started to giggle. A childish giggle of such innocence that Tabitha was scared she'd well up again. "Then, I think I should call you m'lady Tabby Cat!" Rat announced.

"Milady Tabby Cat? I think I like the sound of that." Tabitha could sense Talbot's disapproval emanating from him behind her back. "Talbot, I believe Mrs Smith and I have things under control. Please send his lordship down as soon as he returns home."

As shocked as Tabitha had been at the thought of a boy Rat's age living on the streets, the idea of this angelic little girl, who looked like she had walked right out of Tabitha's dreams, doing so, helped her make her mind up. Her housekeeper, Mrs Jenkins, had entered the kitchen during the conversation with Rat, and Tabitha now instructed her, "Please make up a fire in the nursery; we will be having guests tonight."

Then she addressed the children, "Rat, as I've told you, his lordship might be home late tonight. You can both stay here and speak with him tomorrow morning. But I will ensure that Talbot or I give him your message tonight. And I will give you the ha'penny to compensate you for the one you will lose from Mr Bruiser."

Rat seemed very unsure what to make of the invitation. Tabitha thought about how the offer of food lured his sister in and decided to try the same tactic, "Mrs Smith here makes the best breakfast; eggs, bacon, sausages, toast, kidneys."

Tabitha could also see Rat salivating and knew she'd won the round. She saw Mrs Jenkins eyeing the dirty children with horror as she contemplated them sleeping in her sheets. But Tabitha could sense that the threat of a bath would send these children back to London's dark, dangerous streets. So, she considered a compromise.

"Rat and Melly, why don't you finish your scones and milk and then go with Mrs Jenkins. You can wash your hands and face," even this made Rat visibly baulk, "and she will find you clean clothes to sleep in. And in the morning, you can tell me more about yourselves over breakfast."

They finished their milk, and, making clear with her expression that it was against her better judgement, Mrs Jenkins led them upstairs. She had assured Tabitha that Jonathan's childhood clothes were packed away somewhere, and she was sure she could find something for them to sleep in.

Tabitha returned to the library, determined to stay awake and talk to Wolf when he got home. She asked Talbot to inform Bryans, the footman, who would stay up once the butler had retired, to ensure that Wolf came to find her.

Tabitha had intended to stay awake and read while she waited for Wolf's return, but she found her eyes growing heavy, and the next thing she knew, Wolf was gently touching her shoulder and calling her name. Looking at the clock, she realised it was past midnight, and she'd been asleep for some time.

"Tabitha," Wolf said. "Bryans said you needed to talk to me. What is so important that you've slept in an armchair so that you could say it tonight?" He looked genuinely concerned. She indicated that he should pull up another chair near her.

"You had a couple of little visitors tonight. Two children."

Wolf looked thoroughly confused. "Children? I don't know any children. What were their names, and what did they want?"

"Matt, known as Rat, and his little sister Melody, known as Melly." Comprehension finally dawned on Wolf's features.

"Oh, Rat, why didn't you say? I suppose he is a child, technically."

"Technically?" Tabitha exclaimed. "He can't be more than 8 or 9. How is that only technically a child? And what kind of dealings do you have with a boy his age? In fact, what kind of dealings do you have at all?" Because this was the real question hanging out there. What profession had Wolf pursued before rising to the earldom? "What kind of profession involves street urchin messenger boys and clandestine meetings with men called Bruiser?"

There it was. The question Tabitha had been burning to ask for days now. She had grown to like and even started to trust Wolf and Bear. Tabitha feared discovering some nefarious activities that might make her reassess that judgement.

Wolf, for his part, had hoped that he could postpone this conversation or even avoid it entirely. He wasn't ashamed of how he earned his keep before his surprise inheritance. But he also realised he had operated in a world of shadows and deceit. This was totally unlike the world that Tabitha knew. He sighed and began, "Bear and I were thief-takers, for want of a better phrase?"

"Thief-takers? Does such a profession still exist? Like Jonathan Wild?"

Wolf sighed again at the mention of the most notorious thief-taker. "Well, as someone who was more thief than a taker, Wild gave the profession a bad name. Though, to be fair, he was hardly the only one. And yes, even with the establishment of the Metropolitan Police earlier in the century, private individuals still need to supplement the official investigations."

Whatever Tabitha thought she was going to hear, it wasn't this. She had led such a secluded life, first in her parent's home and then in the gilded cage of her marriage. Tabitha knew about poverty and violent crime only in the abstract. She read Dickens' books and had occasionally glanced at Jonathan's newspapers. So, she had a vague sense that the brutality she experienced at her husband's hand was just a genteel version of the brutality that so many others dealt with daily.

Of course, when Jonathan had died, she had briefly been exposed to the police force and had even experienced what it was like to be considered a criminal. But, even then, she was aware, at least on some level, that she was being handled with kid gloves because of her rank and wealth and that a poor woman suspected of killing her husband would have received very different treatment. "So, what exactly did you and Bear do as thief-takers?"

"For the most part, we were paid by victims of crimes, usually robberies, to find and return their property. Sometimes, to track the perpetrators of other crimes. Even murder."

Tabitha wondered, "Why isn't that left to the police?"

"Sometimes it is," Wolf answered. "But sometimes, the police don't have the resources, patience, or inclination. Sometimes, they want to make a quick arrest and are less concerned about finding the truth. Often, once a suspect is in their custody, they care even less about retrieving the stolen goods. Bear and I fill a void in these cases."

Tabitha was fascinated, "And how did you and Bear come to such a profession?"

"Ah," Wolf replied, "Therein lies a story. And perhaps a story too dramatic and certainly too long for this late at night."

Tabitha acknowledged that she longed for her bed, but there was one part of this story she needed to know. "And Rat and his sister? How did they come to be part of your enterprise?"

"Well, firstly, I've never met his sister. Bear and I stumbled across Rat about a year ago when he made an inept attempt to pick my pocket. I got hold of the lad by the scruff of the neck and threatened to turn him in to the nearest constable. He started to whine and begged me not to. He told me that his parents had died in quick succession, his mother barely a week before. He was paying a neighbourhood woman to shelter and feed him and his little sister, and he had no money to pay her for the week.

"The story was so melodramatic, and he was so pitiful that I believed him. I told him he was a terrible pickpocket and that the next person who caught him likely wouldn't be as kind and generous as I was. I said I would pay him to run messages for me and the like. And that's all there is to the story. The boy proved himself to be intelligent and diligent. That one attempt at thievery aside, he's honest and is good at picking up information for me on the streets.

"As far as I know, he and his sister have continued to pay the neighbour for food and shelter. And that's it. I guess you could call him an employee. Well, an ex-employee. When I moved here the other week, I had Bear show him where to find me, just in case but told him that I would not need his services regularly. By this point, he'd proven himself useful enough that I was sure he'd find similar work elsewhere."

"You were sure? But you didn't know?" Tabitha challenged, trying very hard to keep her face and tone as neutral as possible. "You had taken responsibility for two young children and abandoned them when it was no longer convenient for you."

Wolf looked shocked at her characterisation of his actions, "Abandoned is a rather harsh word. I hardly took responsibility for them; I gave the boy some work when I had it. And my change of circumstances has made it unlikely that I'll need his particular talents, for now."

"And what of this Mr Bruiser? What does he want, and will you go to meet him?"

"Well, despite what his name implies, Bruiser is actually a

detective inspector. I wouldn't say he's honest, but he's not a total crook. He has a very fluid sense of morality. It is not generally known in my old stomping ground that I've ascended to my new noble heights. I had no wish to make myself such an easy mark. Only Rat knew where to find me. And when to find me. If Bruiser wishes to talk to me, I will meet him. He knows enough about me that I have no desire to have him seek me out here and make any trouble for any of us."

This entire conversation left Tabitha with more questions than it answered. What kind of trouble could this Bruiser make? What did he know about Wolf? What exactly did 'fluid sense of morality' connote? But she was exhausted and wanted breakfast with the children the following day. She quickly explained to Wolf that the children were sleeping in the nursery. His surprise at this announcement was evident, but he said nothing. She then told him they should all have breakfast together and discuss the next steps. He wasn't sure what next steps there were to discuss, but he could see how exhausted Tabitha was and decided to postpone that conversation.

CHAPTER 10

Tabitha would have loved to sleep longer the following morning, but she wanted to talk with Wolf and the children before he left for his appointment with Bruiser. She dragged herself down to the breakfast table to find the children tucking into what turned out to be their second helpings of food. Both children were malnourished and undersized, but there was nothing wrong with their appetites. Wolf sat with them, sipping coffee and nibbling on some toast.

Everyone looked up when she entered, and she attempted to sound more awake and cheerier than she felt, "Good morning, everyone. Did we all sleep well?" The children's mouths were full of what looked suspiciously like iced buns, not a typical breakfast staple in the house. Instead of answering, they nodded as she took her place next to Melody.

Tabitha decided she might as well dive into the matter at hand. Turning to Rat, she asked, "I'd like to learn more about you and Melody and how you've been living since your parents died."

Rat looked at the last of the iced bun on his plate and decided that continuing to eat it while talking was probably frowned upon in this house. Instead, he replied, "Our ma and pa died a few months apart, just before Christmas about a year ago. Pa worked down the wharves, and ma sewed clothes for people. I'd been bringing in some money making meself useful around the neighbourhood, but it was never very much chink. Not enough to pay the rent. With 'em gone, the landlord kicked us out, and Mrs Miller, wot was friendly like with our ma, offered to take us in.

"Mrs Miller has a lot of nippers of 'er own and said that we could stay with 'er for a shilling a week, and she'd watch Melly during the day while I worked. She has older girls who look after the nippers during the day cause Mrs Miller sells flowers at Covent Garden. I didn't sleep there much, but knowing Melly was okay was good.

Tabitha was reluctant to ask where Rat slept and what 'making meself useful around the neighbourhood' meant. Rat continued, "Then I met Wolf here, I mean his lordship Wolf, and we became partners." Wolf raised his eyebrows at this characterisation of the nature of their relationship but let it slide. "About a week or so ago, Mr Miller came home from sea and wasn't happy to find more nippers than he'd left two years ago. Even with my shilling being paid regular like, he threw us out."

"We had nowhere to go. Nippers like us end up in an orphanage or, worse, the work'ouse. There was a chance that Melly and I could get separated. A family might even adopt her, and I'd never see 'er again. I couldn't let that 'appen. I'd been doing some errands for old One-eye that runs the Cock. He said that we could sleep in his cellar at night if we were gone during the day. So that's what we've been doing. Cause of that, I've 'ad to take Melody out on my errands, like last night. But at least we're together."

During the last part of this speech, Melody solemnly nodded while gazing adoringly at her older brother. Tabitha realised she still hadn't heard the child speak and wondered if she could. She was just considering how to ask this question gently when the little girl suddenly said, "Matty looks after Melly. Us 'gainst the world." Rat nodded his vehement agreement with this statement.

Tabitha felt tears spring to her eyes. Taking control of herself, she took a sip of the coffee Talbot had poured for her and said, "I think you're a very enterprising young man and a wonderful brother for looking after Melody so well. I'm sure your parents would be very proud of you. But you must realise that this isn't the best answer for Melody. I'd like to make a proposal.

"I'd like to suggest that you come to live and work here. You can live in the carriage house with our coachman, help him with the horses and help our gardener out as well. You can also run errands for Mrs Jenkins and his lordship, should he need them. You'll be paid a wage and fed and housed. Melody will continue to live in the house, in the nursery, be well cared for, and even learn her letters. And you can eat supper with her every night and see her whenever you wish."

At this, Wolf's eyebrows raised so high that they almost disappeared into his hair. Seeing his surprise, it occurred to Tabitha that this was his house, not her's and that offering to take in orphaned ragamuffin children was probably something she should have asked his approval for before making the suggestion. Considering this, she said, "Talbot, could you please take the children back to the nursery and ask Mary to stay with them? I believe there are some old toys up there that they can play with while I talk with his lordship."

With the children out of the way, Tabitha waited for Wolf to say something. When he didn't, she began, "I realise that I spoke very much out of turn, your lordship, when I made that offer. This is your house, not mine any longer. There is no reason that you would want to bring two young children into it. If you can give me a week or so, I can revert to my original plan and take a house for myself and the children."

Finally, Wolf spoke. His voice was gentle as he asked, "You know London is full of orphaned children, don't you? Are you going to save them all? It can't be news to you that poverty, disease, and hardship are the lot of most people in this city. "

Despite the gentleness of his tone, Tabitha was irritated by the seeming condescension of the question. Perhaps her actual irritation was that he was right, of course. What did it say about her that she had no problem overlooking all the other Rats and Melodys when the realities of their lives didn't intrude on her own? Why had it been so easy to ignore the problems that she knew, at least intellectually, lay beyond the mansions of Mayfair and Belgravia? And so she answered him rather more shrewishly than she wished, "Of course, I know I cannot save everyone. But

I can save these two. And so I will. As I said, we will not trespass on your hospitality any longer than necessary."

"Don't be absurd, Tabitha. Of course, you will continue living here. But I do want you to understand the ramifications of what you're suggesting. Rat is a street kid. As I said, I believe he's honest, notwithstanding the pickpocketing attempt. He's used to fending for himself and, in many ways, is old beyond his years. I have no idea whether he's suited for service, even in a carriage house. What if he's not? What if he wants to go back to his old life?"

"Then he's free to do so. This is an offer of a job and a roof over his head, not indentured servitude," Tabitha countered."

"And what of Melody if he does leave? Your offer's stated point was to ensure that they're not separated. So, will you be okay with him taking his sister if he leaves? No matter how attached to her you may have become?"

Tabitha wasn't sure how to answer because Wolf had hit at the tender underbelly of her offer; the chance to have the little girl she had dreamed of living in the nursery. The chance to raise her and fill Tabitha's life with that childish giggling. What would she do if, in a month, a year, or more, Rat wanted to leave and take Melody with him? Would she be able to let the child go back to life on the streets? This was a question that Tabitha couldn't honestly answer, so she said the only thing that came to mind, "Then I will just have to make sure that Rat is happy here and doesn't want to leave."

Wolf sighed heavily, "I want to go on record as saying that I think this plan is fraught with possible issues and heartbreak. But, if this is what you want, and if Rat and Melody agree, then I will go along with it, and you are all welcome to continue to live here for as long as you want to. And now, I have an appointment to attend to." And with that, he rose and left the room, leaving Tabitha to muse on what she had just undertaken.

Mrs Jenkins went up to the attics and found various gently used, appropriately sized children's clothes and shoes. She also found some toys, including a rag doll and a range of outfits for her to wear. Tabitha was very aware that Rat hadn't accepted her offer yet, but she decided to proceed as if he had.

Mrs Jenkins had insisted that he have a bath. Clearly, a bath was a rarity for Rat, and he had approached the tub as if it were a terrifying beast about to ravage him. Melody was far more open to the experience, and once she was in the warm water, she began to have fun splashing around.

With both children clean, hair washed, and nails scrubbed, Mrs Jenkins had got them into their new clothes and shoes. Tabitha had let her highly competent housekeeper take the lead but had stayed in the nursery to help where she could. When the children had removed their old clothes and shoes, Mrs Jenkins shook her head and said to Tabitha, "I'm not sure these can be considered shoes at this point. The poor boy had to cut the toes to allow for their growing feet. And I'm not sure these soles would keep much muck and water out. I'm throwing all of these out. " Tabitha concurred with this decision.

Freshly bathed and in clean clothes, tightly clutching her new doll, Melody seemed a little less shy. The nursery had a little table and chairs, just the right size for a little girl. Melody went and sat on it and started putting her doll into a new dress. Tabitha went over, and gestured to the second small chair and asked, "Melly, can I help you with your doll?"

The child nodded solemnly, and Tabitha perched on the tiny chair. "What do you think her name is?" Tabitha asked.

"Gemmy," Melody answered without hesitation. "was my friend before mean Mr Miller made us leave."

"Well, Melly. Gemmy is a lovely name, and she's a very lucky doll that you came along to look after her. I bet that Gemmy was missing having a mommy." Melody nodded again and finished dressing her doll. Rat dressed and then approached the table and watched his sister play. He stood there for a few minutes deep in thought, then he looked Tabitha in the eye, held out his hand and said, "I'll take your offer, m'lady. It's the best thing for Melly, so I'll do it. Thank you."

Tabitha shook his hand and said, "I'm delighted to hear that.

I promise Melly will be well looked after, and you can see her whenever you want. I'll ensure you can eat with her in the nursery every evening. I'll have Madison, our driver and groom, show you where you're to sleep and what you're to do. And Old Fred, our gardener, will also find chores for you."

Tabitha paused, a thought suddenly striking her, and she asked, "Is it a problem for you that you will live and work as a servant for us while your sister lives in the house?"

Rat laughed and shook his head, "Nah, m'lady Tabby Cat, it's the right way to do it. Melly is a young'un and can learn her lessons and 'ow to be a lady. I'm too rough. Learning and regular baths and the like aren't for me. I'm too old to start doing all that."

Tabitha suddenly felt very sad and sorry for the world-weary little boy. Was he right? Was he, even at his tender age, too old to change? "Well, let me be clear, regular hygiene is still required, even for servants." And then she thought of perhaps a middle ground, "Rat, I'd like to teach you your letters when Melly learns hers. Even as a servant, it's a great advantage to be able to read. Would that be okay?"

Rat thought for a moment, then nodded his assent. Tabitha acknowledged this and added, "And as for your name, wouldn't you prefer if the servants, indeed all of us, called you Matthew or even Matt? Instead of Rat."

The answer was swift and sure, "Nah, I'm Rat. If Wolf and Bear are good enough names for them, then Rat is good enough for me."

Tabitha paused, then decided to pick her battles, "Then Rat, why doesn't Mrs Jenkins take you to the kitchen and start introducing you and explaining your situation to the rest of the staff." She considered her next words carefully, "Rat, your situation and Melly's are a bit unusual for the household staff, his lordship, and me. I shall leave it to Mrs Jenkins to explain the situation to the rest of the staff. It may take everyone a little time to get used to your presence. The staff here are kind, and they're honest. But there may also be some petty resentments that arise.

If anyone is anything other than welcoming and understanding to you or Melly, please let Mrs Jenkins know immediately. " Rat nodded yes.

Tabitha and Mrs Jenkins agreed that Mary would continue to look after Melly for now. Mrs Jenkins had told her that Mary was the eldest of twelve children and knew how to look after a little girl. She'd also said that Mary had a younger sister ready to enter service and suggested that Mary become the new nursery maid, that Nancy be promoted to second chambermaid, Jane, from second chambermaid to first, and that the sister, Ellen, join the household as the new scullery maid. Tabitha indicated that she fully believed in Mrs Jenkins' ability to manage the staff and would agree to whatever she thought best.

CHAPTER 11

On leaving Tabitha in the breakfast room, Wolf collected Bear and headed to their appointment. The Cock public house was in the infamously criminal and violent Whitechapel area of London. A densely populated, poverty-stricken area of London. It was home to a large population of immigrants who lived in overcrowded, rundown tenements.

Whitechapel was known for its high rates of crime and vice, including prostitution, theft, and violent assaults. The streets were often dirty and poorly lit, making them dangerous for residents and visitors alike. Thrust into infamy almost ten years before with the unsolved Ripper murders, Whitechapel remained a rough and dangerous place, with a reputation for lawlessness and violence despite the authorities' best efforts.

Bear had immediately agreed that taking the carriage was asking for trouble. Wolf would prefer that as few people know of his recent good fortune as possible. When they had left their lodgings near St. Paul's, they had put the word about that they were leaving London for the time being.

Stepping out of his palatial Mayfair residence, Wolf looked up and down the street for a hackney cab. It was a chilly day and he was in a hurry to get to Whitechapel as quickly as possible. He finally spotted an empty cab and hailed it over. The driver, a gruff-looking man with a thick moustache, leaned out of the cab.

"Where to?" he asked in a less than friendly tone.

Wolf told him their destination, and his expression immediately turned sour.

"I ain't going there," he said firmly. "It's too dangerous, even with that giant of a man you've got there. Find yourselves another cab."

Wolf offered him double his usual fare and then triple until the man's greed finally overcame his fear.

The ride from the open, clean, opulent streets of Mayfair to the gritty, rundown streets of Whitechapel was a stark reminder for Wolf of the extreme wealth divide existing in London and on which he suddenly found himself on the other side.

The Cock was a notorious public house located in the heart of Whitechapel. Swinging by the door was a large, hand-painted sign featuring a rooster, which creaked in the wind. Inside, the pub was dimly lit and smelled of stale beer and tobacco smoke. The patrons were a rough crowd, mostly dockworkers and factory labourers, who spent their evenings drinking and gambling away their wages. But it also was popular with certain criminal elements in Whitechapel.

The publican was a gruff and burly man named Bill, known to many as Old One-eye because of the empty eye socket, now sewn up. He was known to have a short temper and a penchant for throwing out unruly customers or anyone who irritated him. Despite its rough reputation, The Cock was a popular spot among the working-class men of Whitechapel, who found solace in its cheap drinks and rowdy atmosphere.

Before ascending to the earldom, Wolf had used the Cock as an informal office. Years before, Wolf had done the publican a favour, which Old One-eye had always remembered. People knew they'd find Wolf and Bear there, or Bill would take messages for them. The Cock was always an excellent place to keep an ear out for news of the criminal activity swirling around London more thickly than the densest smog.

Before leaving the house, Wolf and Bear had changed out of their new clothes and into their old ones. Even so, after only a few weeks, their reappearance was notable, "Sent you packing back to London with your tail between your legs, did they?" and similar jokes filled the smoky air. Old One-eye saw Wolf and nodded towards a dark corner where Inspector Trotter, commonly known as Bruiser, sat eating a meat pie and drinking ale.

Bruiser had grown up in Whitechapel alongside the thieves he was now supposed to arrest. Good with his fists as a youth, he'd earned his nickname from the many street fights he'd won. Now as part of the Metropolitan Police force, he patroled the dimly lit alleys and dark corners of Whitechapel, always on the lookout for trouble, Bruiser was feared by the criminals and respected by the locals.

But, Wolf also knew that Bruiser wasn't above supplementing his income on occasion working on the other side of the law. Bruiser had always walked a fine line between the law and the criminal underworld. Although he had officially joined the Metropolitan Police force, he couldn't deny his roots in the streets of Whitechapel. So, when he was approached by the local gang leaders to "assist" in their extortions, Bruiser couldn't say no.

Bruiser would use his badge and authority to intimidate other criminals, making it clear that they would have to pay up if they wanted to operate in Whitechapel. And, in return, he would receive a cut of the profits. Of course, this did sometimes mean turning a blind eye to the activities of his gang bosses.

Given the dual nature of Bruiser's professional life, Wolf was curious about which side of the criminal fence the "job" he had for him lay on. Bruiser and Wolf had always been cautious around each other but also shared a mutual professional respect. Wolf knew that the inspector wasn't always straight, but he also realised that the man had his own sense of honour; he would never hurt the innocent. The men he victimised deserved what came their way.

Wolf had known the man to be compassionate and generous to the Whitechapel locals, particularly the children. He suspected the inspector had persuaded Old One-eye to let Rat and Melody shelter in his cellar.

Walking up to the older man, Wolf lifted his chin in greeting and in turn, Bruiser indicated that he sit down. Bear had gone to get them some ale and a pie each. Just because it was mid-morning didn't mean drinking wasn't acceptable, even expected in Whitechapel.

"I got your message. What's so important that you must send the lad to search for me?" Wolf asked.

The inspector swallowed his mouthful of pie, took another swig of his ale, and replied, "He must have found you easily. I thought you were out of town."

"If you thought that, why did you send him to find me?"

Bruiser chuckled, "Do you think I ever bought that story? You were just a little too careful to whisper it in the ears of all the best Whitechapel gossips. Clearly, you wanted the news spread about. A man slinking out of town usually does so with more subtlety."

Wolf nodded in acknowledgement at the man's astute observations. "Let's just say I've left Whitechapel, and that's all anyone around here needs to know."

"Then why come and meet me?" Bruiser asked.

"Because I may want to leave this life behind, but I'm not so naive as to think that to do so is easy. You work for powerful men on both sides of the aisle. A request from you is not one that an intelligent man turns down." Bruiser nodded his own acknowledgement. A policeman couldn't walk both sides of the law without high-level protection from his higher-ups. There were well-placed men in the Metropolitan Police force who recognised the value of Bruiser's criminal connections.

"So, what do you need? What is this big job that Rat was talking about?"

"It's one of Mickey D's boys. He thinks he's been set up for murder."

"And, of course, he's innocent and was nowhere near the crime scene," Wolf said sarcastically.

"Look, you know Mickey and his boys. They're thugs, they're thieves, and they've done their fair share of roughing up. But they're not murderers. It seems they got word about some diamonds just begging to be lifted, to hear Mickey tell it. It seemed an easy enough job, and he sent one of his nephews, not more than a kid.

"The lad cracked the safe and took the diamonds and left. The next morning, the newspapers reported that a body was found bludgeoned to death after a burglary gone wrong. There was a bloody candlestick near the body.

"My colleagues at Scotland Yard consider it an open and shut case. They're obviously investigating some of the known gangs of thieves in London, and Mickey has no doubt they'll be sniffing around his group before long."

"And who was the dead man?" Wolf asked.

"The Duke of Somerset," Bruiser answered, clearly always intending to end his story with that dramatic flourish.

Wolf remembered seeing a headline in the morning paper but hadn't had time to read the whole piece. "Why exactly does Mickey D think I can prove his nephew's innocence? Assuming he is innocent, which seems unlikely given the tale you've just told."

Bruiser chuckled again, "Why, my lordship? Because these toffs are your people now, aren't they?"

Wolf groaned. He had always known that news of his new situation would carry to Whitechapel eventually. But he'd hoped that it would take more than two weeks.

"Word carries fast," he commented. "How did Mickey D find out so quickly?"

"Mickey may be a Whitechapel lad, but his network is all over London. Did you really think that you could slip away and inherit an earldom, and no one here would be the wiser?"

"If Mickey knows all this, he must realise I've hung up my thief-taker hat for good. I no longer need the income and don't want the notoriety."

Bruiser gave him a long stare. Then he said, "It's not my business what's between you and Mickey D. But he gave me to understand that you know it's in your interest to help him."

"If he knew about my recent good fortune, then I'm assuming

he has some idea where to find me. So why all the subterfuge? Why have you delivered the message with help from young Rat?"

"Again," the inspector continued, "I'm not privy to the inner workings of Mickey's organisation, but I believe he's worried he has a rat of his own. Potentially. He thought it would be more discreet if you and I had a little chat."

Wolf hadn't hated his life as a thief-taker. He'd been good at it, and it had been a regular income. But it wasn't the life his father had wanted for him or the life he'd been born to lead. He may not have been born the heir to an earldom, but he was an earl's grandson, which meant something to him. He didn't care about the title itself or even the money. Never worrying again about having enough food to eat was nice. But the power that the title brought with it meant something to him. Not political power. He didn't care about that, though he realised he was now a member of the House of Lords. But the power to make a difference in people's lives. That meant something.

He'd been learning from his steward, Mr Roberts, how many tenants he had on his various properties. The crops they grew and the animals they raised. And more to the point, the needs they had. It hadn't taken many reviews of Jonathan's papers to realise that he was a miserly landlord. That was something that Wolf had already directed Jones to start rectifying. He told him to mend roofs and fences. And that was just for starters. It turned out that the steward was enterprising and had many ideas for ways that the lands of the earldom could be more productive, both for the tenants and the earl.

When he was finally tracked down and told that he had inherited the earldom, Wolf was initially unsure how he felt about it. But as he reflected on his newfound status and wealth, he realised this was an opportunity to do something with his life. And to help make other people's lives better. Yes, life as a thief-catcher often meant assisting people in a roundabout way. He helped people retrieve their stolen property and often helped ensure the acquittal of innocent people accused of crimes. But it was a messy kind of helping. There were jobs he couldn't take; whenever he even suspected Mickey D's gang's involvement, he had to turn the work down. And sometimes, the clients who paid him seemed worse than those he was supposed to be catching.

Wolf wasn't sure what his new societal position meant for Mickey's hold over him. But he wasn't sure he was quite established enough in aristocratic circles to risk finding out. So, he told Bruiser he would take the work. "But if Mickey thinks he has a mole, how am I supposed to communicate with him?"

Bruiser answered, "Use the boy as a go-between when necessary. But first, Mickey will come to you tonight. Give me your exact address and expect him at 11."

Wolf was unsure how he felt about having a thug like Mickey D show up at Chesterton House. But he didn't seem to have a choice, so he nodded his assent. He then got up, indicated to Bear that they were leaving, and said farewell to Bruiser.

There wouldn't be any hackney cabs hanging around Whitechapel, so they began to walk back towards Mayfair. On the way, Wolf filled Bear in on the job that they had to undertake.

"I'm sorry, Wolf. I know this is my fault. If it wasn't for me..."

Wolf interrupted him, "It's not your fault. Men like Mickey D thrive because they excel at finding people's weak spots and exploiting them. He knows your weak spot and that you're mine." They walked the rest of the way back to Mayfair, mostly in companionable silences. It was more than an hour's walk, but Wolf was glad of the time to clear his head and think about what might happen when his two worlds inevitably collided.

CHAPTER 12

When they arrived back at Chesterton House, Wolf and Bear changed into more suitable clothes. Descending the staircase on his way to his study, Wolf found Tabitha waiting for him at the bottom. She had her arms crossed and a very determined look on her face. Wolf had pondered how much to tell Tabitha and when during the walk home. One look at her face, and it was clear he would probably have to tell her something, and now. If nothing else, she needed to be prepared for Mickey D turning up at the house.

Raising a hand to forestall her inevitable questions, he said, "In my study. Not out here."

Tabitha followed him into his study, and he shut the door behind her. She sat in one of the armchairs, and he sat opposite her. "Do you want to ask me questions?" he asked.

"I'm not sure where to start," she admitted. "You told me that you and Bear were thief-takers previously. I assumed that career was behind you."

"As did we," he replied. With that, Wolf told her the entirety of his conversation with Bruiser. He decided that, at this point, he had no choice. The worst that she could do was to choose to leave the house. He acknowledged to himself that, if that happened, he would miss her. Wolf would miss her company and her help navigating society. And he would definitely miss her management of the household. But he'd get by.

Tabitha didn't say anything while he spoke. Her countenance remanded remarkably unreadable, and Wolf honestly had no clue what she would say when he finished.

"So, just to be sure that I understood all that," Tabitha said at the end of his story, "this Mickey D has a hold over you and has used that, in the past, to manipulate you to turn down certain cases that involve his gang. He is now trying to force you to help prove that one of his gang members is innocent of the murder of the Duke of Somerset?"

"That's the long and short of it," Wolf acknowledged.

"And while you won't tell me the hold he has over you, it is something about Bear. Correct?"

"Yes, that is correct. I do feel that, given more time and friends in society, this hold he has will have less power over us. But, at this point, I have no choice but to do his bidding and take this job."

Tabitha continued, "And this Mickey D will be coming here tonight to tell you more about the case?"

"Yes. I'm truly sorry for that part. But it seems the most discreet way for the Earl of Pembroke to meet with a known gangster at short notice. Mickey is a pro. He'll slip in around the back, and no one will be the wiser."

Tabitha stood up and looked down at Wolf in his chair. "I'm going to the nursery now to see how Melly is adjusting to her new home. We can talk more over dinner about how we will manage Mickey D."

Wolf stood up and exclaimed, "There will be no 'we' managing this situation. Mickey D is a thug and inappropriate for a countess to be around."

"Indeed!" Tabitha replied, "But, without my help, how do you expect to gain entry to the Duke of Somerset's home? You may be an earl, but the house is mourning their slain patriarch. You will not gain admittance."

"And you will? Aren't you a social outcast?"

"I have known the family for many years. The new duke, the murdered man's son Anthony, was a childhood friend of mine. I read about the duke's death this morning and was already planning to pay a visit to the family. It is appropriate that I pay my respects to the family. I will bring you with me."

Wolf deferred to her greater knowledge of the social niceties of such things but countered, "Even if it makes sense for you to visit the duke's family with me, I still see no reason for you to meet Mickey D tonight. The two conversations are unrelated."

"Unrelated!" Tabitha exclaimed. "How am I to help you question the duke's family delicately if I haven't heard first-hand from Mickey why he believes his man is innocent?"

Wolf could see that he would not win this argument. He'd been so busy trying to figure out how to get out of helping Mickey D that Wolf hadn't considered what he would need to do if he took the job. His typical clientele, as a thief-taker, rarely ran to the aristocracy. Generally, they were not the people who could not get the police's attention and resources. The profile of his typical client was solidly middle-class, lawyers, doctors, and even clergy on occasion. Given this, he didn't have much experience questioning the upper classes. He had assumed that his recent elevation to their ranks would help, but beyond that, he wasn't sure how to begin. He silently acknowledged that Tabitha's help could be essential.

"I need to go and talk with Rat. How's the lad doing so far?" Wolf asked.

"I believe he's settling in. I did check in with Talbot and Mrs Jenkins. Both reported back that the boy is a fast learner and eager to please. Of course, it's early days. I worry that he's so used to caring for himself and Melody that he will find it challenging to be given orders and expected to work as a part of a larger group. But we'll see."

"And the girl?"

"Children are so adaptable. It's as if she's spent her entire life in that nursery with Mary. We've found more toys in the attic, and Bryans even found a doll's house that he brought down and cleaned up for her. She seems to have already won the hearts of everyone on the staff. She has Talbot wound around her little finger. I even caught him up there, sitting on one of those little chairs having a tea party with Melly and her doll this morning! I never thought I'd live to see the day!"

Wolf laughed. But a somewhat wry laugh. He hadn't had

much exposure to children beyond his dealings with Rat. So wasn't sure how a little girl Melly's age usually acted. But he did know that she and her brother had lived a hard life, particularly since their parents had died. He was sure that Melly had internalised how to ingratiate herself and fit in with whichever group she was a part of. He acknowledged that it was sad when a four-year-old had to have those kinds of life skills. But he'd seen enough of life's hardships in London's most poverty and crime-stricken areas, not to be surprised.

Tabitha continued, "I'm going up there now. Would you like to join me?"

The suggestion caught Wolf by surprise. He continued to be very sceptical of the wisdom of the children living at Chesterton House. He could already see that Tabitha and the rest of the household had become very attached. This was unlikely to end well for anyone. He saw no reason to add his own potential attachment to the little girl into the mix. Not that he was particularly worried about becoming attached to Melody or anyone. He had his emotions under tight control. But then he would have thought the same was true of Tabitha until this little girl came along.

But he saw no graceful way of refusing the invitation, so they both went to the nursery. Opening the door quietly, it looked like Mary had more experience as a nursemaid than less than 24 hours. She and Melody were sitting at the little table playing some game involving clapping their hands together while singing a nursery rhyme. Wolf vaguely remembered his sisters playing a similar game when they were young.

On catching sight of Tabitha and Wolf standing in the doorway, Mary leaped up and curtsied, and Melody ran over and hugged Tabitha's legs, squealing, "Come and play, Tabby Cat."

Wolf raised an eyebrow, "Tabby Cat?"

Tabitha ignored the sarcastic question and bent down to return the child's embrace.

"Have you been having fun with Mary?" The child nodded happily. "And have you been good for Mary?" Melody nodded a little more solemnly. Tabitha glanced at Mary.

"She's been a little angel, m'lady. I was thinking we'd go for a walk out in the square in a bit if that's ok with you and his lordship."

Unprepared to give an opinion on raising the child, Wolf immediately indicated this, and all decisions were Lady Pembroke's to make. Tabitha, in turn, approved the outing as long as appropriate outerwear was to be found in the attic.

Tabitha had spent the morning scouring the library for appropriate books for a young child. She had sent Talbot up earlier with The Water Babies, The Adventures of Pinocchio, and The Happy Prince and Other Tales. She suggested to Wolf that he choose one and read to Melody until it was time for her walk. He stared at her with disbelief. It was one thing to accept this child up in the nursery; it was another to be asked to play the role of genial uncle. And, of course, Wolf realised this was precisely Tabitha's scheme; she wanted him to bond with the little girl. He protested, but when a little hand slipped into his and began to pull him over to the large armchair by the fire, he felt impotent to do anything other than follow.

The new Earl of Pembroke sat in the comfy chair, and the child had climbed onto his lap without being invited. He gave Tabitha a hard stare, but she smirked back at him with a knowing look confirming his worst suspicions about her motives in suggesting he read. Mary brought over The Water-Babies, and before he knew it, Melly snuggled in his lap, and he was reading the book to her.

Tabitha, for her part, felt no shame or guilt about the situation. She was very aware the children stayed in the house at the earl's pleasure. While she would move if she had to, she had no desire to. And so, it was vital that Melody conquer the heart of the last holdout in the household. She found Wolf's discomfort mildly amusing. Tabitha sensed this was a man who would have no qualms staring down the barrel of a gun but had no idea how to manage an adorable little girl.

As for Melody, Tabitha wasn't sure whether it was fair to

attribute conscious manipulation to a young child, but there was no doubt that the girl's command of the situation and the earl was one that the dowager herself would have commended.

Wolf had no idea of the expectation for how long he would sit and read, but there was a wide gap between Melody's sense of the length of a story time and his own. He had planned to read for 5-10 minutes and then escape to his study. But after the first chapter and the second, she had pleaded for more, and he found himself bizarrely unable to say no. Finally, after at least 30 minutes, Tabitha took pity on him, and at the end of the chapter, she came over, lifted Melody off his lap and said gently but firmly to the child, "That's enough for now, Melly. You have your walk with Mary now, and the earl has some important things to do."

Melody looked down at the earl, still sitting in the armchair with the book on his lap and asked, "Wolfie, will you come back and read some more?" Wolfie? At this, Tabitha couldn't help but chuckle. "This is the earl, my love. You must call him your lordship." Wolf had put up with all the formality that Tabitha had insisted on so far for the rest of the household, but this was beyond the pale. He refused to be so addressed by a young child and said so.

"Wolfie is just fine with me!" He stood up, put the book aside, and told the little girl, "If you are a good girl for Mary, perhaps I will come by tomorrow or the next day, and we can read some more. Would that be okay?"

He didn't know what had come over him making such an offer. But the look of glee on the child's face was almost worth knowing that Tabitha had achieved her aims. The smug smile he noticed she directed at Mary confirmed this suspicion. He finally managed to escape to his study, and Melody and Mary went for their walk.

CHAPTER 13

Wolf braced himself for more questions over dinner, and Tabitha didn't disappoint him. He'd explained that while his grandfather had paid for his education, no additional money had been set aside for him. His grandfather had died when Wolf was 14, and Jonathan's father had ascended to the earldom. He had made it quite clear to Wolf's father that he had no intention of doing anything more for their family than he was legally obliged to do by the terms of his father's will. And so, Wolf was turned out into the world, a highly educated man with no practical skills.

He had considered joining the army but realised he wasn't born to take orders. The clergy was out of the question - Tabitha didn't ask why. The only other career suitable for a man of his birth and education was the law, and Wolf's father strongly encouraged him to enter the legal profession. They fought, and his father banished him from the house, much as his own father had banished him on his marriage to Wolf's mother.

Wolf acknowledged that his father's intention was likely not to banish him but rather to bend him to his will. However, that didn't happen, and Wolf ended up in London with not much more than the clothes on his back and a few trinkets he hoped he could sell.

"Did you ever go back to see your father before he died?" Tabitha asked.

"No," Wolf acknowledged. "We were both stubborn. I was determined not to return until I had made something of myself, and he may have wanted to reconcile but likely had no idea where to find me. No one did. It's why it took the solicitors so long to track me down after Jonathan died."

Tabitha wanted to ask more and know how he had met Bear and become a thief-taker, but she sensed that Wolf could only open up and share so much. She understood that. She had shared more with him about her marriage to Jonathan than she had intended and more than she felt comfortable sharing. But there was still so much he didn't know and perhaps would never know. If anyone understood the need to be very protective of how much of oneself to share and to whom, it was Tabitha.

Instead, she asked, "How was your evening at the dowager's? With all the commotion with Rat and Melody and then Mickey D, we never had a chance to discuss it."

Wolf laughed, "It was much as you had anticipated. The dowager barely let me out of her sight and was thrilled to be the person introducing the infamous and hitherto mysterious new earl into society. The conversation was bland, the food and wine at least copious, and I couldn't wait to make a polite exit as soon as possible."

Tabitha couldn't help but be secretly pleased that Wolf hadn't been drawn in by an aristocratic circle that spurned her. She wasn't even sure why she was so happy about it, except that Wolf had provided her with pleasant company when everyone else had made their disapproval of her very clear. While she genuinely wanted to help him enter society smoothly, a part of her selfishly didn't want him to glide into it so easily that he no longer needed her help and company.

After dinner, they retired to the parlour. More comfortable than the drawing room used to receive visitors, it had long been Tabitha's sanctuary. In place of the drawing room's more formal and stiff furniture, the parlour had comfortable armchairs and sofas dotted around the room. The colour scheme was in calming pastel shades and floral patterns. Taking his customary armchair, Wolf drank brandy, but Tabitha wanted to stay awake and to be sharp for their guest's arrival, so she drank coffee. Wolf seemed perfectly at ease and read a book. Tabitha tried to read but couldn't concentrate. She sat at the piano in the corner of the room, trying to soothe her nerves with some Chopin. But this didn't help either.

Finally, sensing that Tabitha was on edge about their meeting later that evening, Wolf suggested that she have a sherry or port, just enough to relax a little. She realised the wisdom of his suggestion and accepted a sherry. Finally, just as Tabitha managed to relax enough to enjoy her book, there was a sound at the door. She had never asked about the etiquette of receiving a known gang member in one's home, thought clearly the parlour was acceptable. Naively, she had assumed Mickey D would come to the front door and be announced by Talbot just as any other guest would be. Instead, he suddenly appeared in the room with the butler seemingly none the wiser.

Tabitha started at his entry. She wasn't sure what she'd expected a gang leader to look like, but Mickey D didn't fit the bill. He was a man of middling years with thick hair that would soon be more white than grey. He had bright blue eyes that seemed to twinkle with mischief. There were no noticeable scars, no eyepatch, no visible trophies of a hard life given over to crime and violence. Mickey D most resembled her roguish but charming uncle Jack, always a favourite when she was a child.

Wolf looked up when he entered, seemingly unsurprised that their guest had somehow circumvented the staff and managed to track them down in the house. "I'd say 'nice to see you', Mickey. But I won't insult your intelligence."

Mickey D chuckled and replied, "Now, there's no reason to take that attitude with me. We were always friends, weren't we?"

"Friends? Is that what we were? Friends don't normally hold each other for ransom with blackmail."

"I'm not sure what kind of friends you have then. Most of mine do things like that regularly." Mickey D walked into the room and, without invitation, sat on a chair opposite Tabitha. "But there's no matter; I'm here anyway. So, why don't you start by introducing me to your charming companion."

Wolf sighed and answered, "This is Lady Pembroke."

Mickey D looked confused and asked, "You're leg shackled

already?"

"No, she is not my wife. She was the wife of the late Lord Pembroke, my cousin Jonathan." At this, Tabitha inclined her head.

Mickey D looked around the room. Tabitha had the feeling that it was more of a professional assessment. Mickey D continued, "You've suddenly come up in the world, Wolf. You were very close-lipped about being the heir to all this."

There was a tightness around Wolf's eyes, and his tone was as cold as ice when he replied, "Not that you, or any of the scum you have around you, are owed any explanation, but this was all a surprise to me as well." As he said this, Wolf gestured around at the room's grandeur. "I have no desire to prolong this conversation any more than necessary. Tell us what you need to, and then you can be on your way."

Mickey D pointed to Wolf's brandy and asked, "Isn't it customary to offer a guest a tipple?"

"You're not a guest. Do you want to tell me your story or not?"

The other man sighed, but realising the futility of pushing harder, he launched into his tale. "So, as you well know, we don't usually go for the big flashy jobs. Too much focus from the coppers on those. But word got round to me about a job that seemed too good to pass up. A diamond necklace was being taken out of the vault at the bank for a few nights only. I had an inside connection who could give us the scoop about when to slip in."

He paused, and Wolf clarified some issues, "When you say word got around to you, what do you mean?"

"I mean that when I can, I try to have helpful young people placed in service around London. You never know when having someone sympathetic inside will become useful."

Wolf asked, "And I assume that by 'sympathetic', you mean someone you are blackmailing to do your dirty work?"

Mickey D chuckled, "I know that you don't much like me, Wolf, and that you see our arrangement as coercion, but believe it or not, there are plenty that are happy to help me and the boys and to see that their family gets taken care of in turn. I keep my word and am loyal to them that's loyal to me. And the people in Whitechapel know that.

"When their nippers are sick, who is helping them? Not the likes of her," he nodded towards Tabitha, "that's for sure. When the menfolk are injured and can't work, who makes sure the family doesn't starve? Mickey D, that's who." He thumped on his chest as he pronounced this.

Wolf knew well enough that most of this wasn't idle boasting and nodded to acknowledge so. As gangs went, Mickey D's, if not quite Robin Hood robbing the rich to give to the poor, certainly tried to help the people of Whitechapel. Even if that help usually came with some kind of strings. Accepting food, money, or medicine from Mickey D was to make an implicit deal with the devil; one day, he would come knocking for some kind of payback, and you better not be found wanting when he did. On the other hand, he at least offered help, usually the only help the impoverished of Whitechapel could expect.

Mickey D continued, "So when there's an opportunity for one of them to enter service, they don't forget who was there for them and their family. They're happy to be able to pay me back in some minor way. I don't ask them to steal for me, just for information when it comes up."

Tabitha wasn't sure what to make of this conversation. As far as she knew, her parents and then her husband had engaged in charitable activities of some sort. She knew that her father had been known as a good and generous landowner with a well-deserved reputation for caring for his tenant farmers and their families when hard times struck.

Jonathan did not have such a reputation, but she remembered that he had once accepted an invitation to a benefit gala that the Duchess of Swanley had thrown. The duchess, an acknowledged eccentric, had claimed that The Salvation Army was a worthy philanthropic endeavour and that she had decided to champion them personally. The gala had been quite extravagant but included some activities to raise monies. Of course, on reflection, Jonathan's interest in going and contributing was likely more related to his desire to curry favour with the Duke of Swanley, a man with significant influence in the government.

She felt she was a good person, but Mickey's D casual accusation made her feel defensive, and then she was almost immediately guilty. She suddenly felt much as she had when Wolf had asked why she was so concerned about Melody and her brother when surely, she knew about London's childhood poverty before meeting them.

Tabitha shook her head to dispel these uncomfortable thoughts and said, "Gentlemen, I don't believe this squabbling is getting us anywhere. Mr D continue with your story."

Mickey D interrupted her, "I'm no mister. Plain Mickey or Mickey D is fine by me."

"As you wish. Mickey, you have come to ask Lord Pembroke to help you. Why don't you explain the nature of this help and why you're in need."

Mickey D sat back in his chair, steepled his fingers together and said, "Indeed, that's the tale to be told. But I do believe I need to wet my whistle a little to be telling it." Wolf huffed loudly but did get up and poured the other man a brandy. After an appreciative sip, the man continued. "As I said, young people of my acquaintance do find their way into service occasionally, and when they do, they keep their ears open for me.

"One such lad, who is a boot boy at a grand old house not far from here, sent word back through his mam that this diamond necklace, so valuable that it was kept in the bank, was being brought to the house for just a few nights before one of those toff shindigs I guess you'll be dillydallying at yourself now.

"The boy gave the layout of the house. The safe was in the duke's study. The family kept to a regular schedule. And the night before we planned to do the job, the boy sent word back that the butler was away, so the house was even less well guarded than usual. I've a nephew, Seamus is his name. Good lad. Eager to prove himself. This seemed like the perfect job for him to lead. We had a lot of upfront info. We planned it well. The risks seemed low.

"That night, Seamus watched the house until he saw the light go off in the study. Seamus enters through the window and makes quick work of the safe. He's a smart lad, and safe cracking is something he's picked up on fast. Took the necklace and left through the window. The whole thing probably took about 15 minutes.

"The following day, the newspapers are full of the murder of a duke and the theft of a diamond necklace. Seems the duke had been napping in a chair when Seamus was working on the safe and never woke up. A servant had come into the study to make up the fire in the morning and found the duke with his head bashed in and a bloody candelabra next to him. The police have said that the murderer was a thief disturbed by the duke in the middle of the thieving."

Tabitha interrupted the story, "The duke was killed still sitting in his armchair? Why would a man, even one sleeping in his chair, be awoken by an intruder but not immediately stand up?"

"Aye, that's the first question. According to the papers, the police believe he had been pushed back into the chair during the attack. But that makes no sense to me. And anyway, it didn't happen. Seamus tells me it didn't happen, and I believe him."

Wolf asked, "So you're saying the duke was already dead when Seamus broke in?"

"I'm not saying anything except that Seamus didn't kill him."

Wolf asked the next obvious question, "Do the police have reason to suspect that your gang is involved?"

"Not yet. But the murder of a duke isn't a crime they'll let go of. I want to prove his innocence before they get around to thinking of me and the gang. And they'll think of us before long, don't you worry."

Tabitha pondered the story they'd been told, "And why did the light go off in the room if the duke was in there reading? That doesn't make any sense. Was he reading by candlelight or by gaslight? How do you hit someone over the head with a lit candelabra? There are definitely elements of this that don't make immediate sense."

CHAPTER 14

After unceremoniously kicking Mickey D out, Tabitha and Wolf retired to bed without discussing the gangster's request. But Tabitha found Wolf waiting at the breakfast table the following morning, ready to discuss the night before. She poured herself a coffee, took a slice of toast from the buffet, and sat opposite him. She wasn't sure if he was waiting for her to comment or had already decided what to do, so she waited a few minutes, sipping her coffee and chewing her toast.

When it was clear that he was waiting for her to begin, she said, "Do you believe him? Do you believe his man is innocent of murder?"

Wolf gave her a wry smile and answered, "Those are two very different questions. Do I believe that Mickey believes the story he told us? Yes, I do. There is a sort of honour amongst thieves, or at least among some. In his own way, Mickey D is an honourable man." He saw Tabitha about to jump in and continued, with the caveat, "Yes, he's a thief. And something more than just a thief; he runs a gang. He's not above some intimidation and, as I know too well, some blackmail. But in his way, he's honest. Probably far more honest than many of the nobility you know. He's honest about who he is and how he makes money. He doesn't put on a veneer of gentility while being a thug underneath it." He lifted his eyebrows at Tabitha as he made that statement, and she knew he was thinking of Jonathan.

Wolf's next statement confirmed that she'd correctly read his thoughts, "From what I can see from his books, Jonathan was as much a thief as Mickey, maybe more so. He stole food out of the mouths of his tenants and business away from competitors whenever he could, using whatever means available, legal or not. At least Mickey owns his thievery and has some genuine concern for the people of Whitechapel, even if there is a self-serving element.

"So, when he says his man didn't do it, I believe he believes that. Whether or not the lad did kill the duke, it's easy to see how it might have happened. Seamus believed the study would be empty. He didn't see the duke when he first entered because the man was sleeping. Partway through the robbery, the duke wakes up. Seamus impulsively hits the other man over the head with the nearest thing to hand, a candelabra. Then he panics and denies that he did anything but the robbery. I'm sure that to the detective police inspector in charge, it's an open-and-shut case. And I'm not sure I disagree."

Tabitha nodded in agreement, "My father explained the concept of Occam's Razor to me when I was a child."

Wolf replied, "Yes, the most straightforward answer is usually correct. Don't muddy the water with overly complex models. Without any reason to think otherwise, the most obvious answer is that Seamus murdered the duke during a burglary.

"However, Mickey D demands that I investigate, so I must. At the very least, providing concrete proof that only Seamus could have committed the crime will hopefully appease Mickey D. Even if he's not happy."

"And will he be assuaged with such proof? He seems like a man who usually gets what he wants," Tabitha asked him with concern writ plainly on her face.

Wolf considered her question for a few moments while he sipped his coffee. "My experience of Mickey D is that he's an intelligent and rational man. From what I've heard, he has a surprising interest in science for someone who doesn't seem to have had any education. I think that, when presented with facts, he will believe them. Regardless of what he would like to think to the contrary."

Tabitha wiped her mouth with her napkin, drained her coffee

cup, and replied, "Then we best get to finding those facts. My suggestion is that we divide and conquer. On reflection, I don't believe there's any real benefit to you visiting the grieving family with me. Instead, I will take my maid Ginny with me." Wolf raised his eyebrows in question, and she continued, "Most of the accurate and interesting gossip I've heard over the years had come via Ginny through the servants' network. People ignore servants and are shockingly candid in what they'll say and do in front of them."

"Isn't it unusual to turn up for tea with your maid in tow?"

"Somewhat, but I believe that Ginny has a friend in that household, the dowager duchess' maid, so it won't be particularly noteworthy if I let her tag along for my visit. She can then go down to the servants' quarters and see what she can learn.

"Meanwhile, I will pay my respects to the duchess and the dowager, and hopefully, the new duke, Anthony, will be at home. I'm assuming the family has no reason to believe anything but the murder during a robbery story, but it will be interesting to hear their take on it."

Wolf leaned slightly towards her, a concerned look on his face suddenly, "Just remember, Tabitha, you cannot indicate that you know anything other than the information in the newspaper reports. Nothing we've heard from Mickey can be spoken of or even alluded to. Apart from anything else, if Mickey even suspects that the police are focused on Seamus because we've let something slip, we will both find ourselves in great danger. This is not a game."

Tabitha's first instinct was to take offence and assure him that she was more than up to the task of such a covert operation, but in truth, what he said wasn't something she had considered fully. And so, she said, "You are right to warn me, Wolf, and I will remind Ginny. She's a smart girl, but neither of us has ever been involved in something like this before, and we will take our lead from you."

Wolf sighed in relief and sat back in his chair. Then,

remembering Tabitha still hadn't told him what his part would be, he enquired where he would be going if not with her. Tabitha smiled slyly, "Why, you will be paying a call on my mother-in-law." Wolf's eyebrows shot up again, and Tabitha chuckled. "There is no more enthusiastic collector of gossip than the dowager. If the Duke of Somerset had any skeletons in his closet that society whispered about, she would know what they were.

"As we have seen, while she has no love for me, you are quite the new pet. The duke's death will likely be the topic of conversation in every drawing room in London today. If you stop in for tea, I'd be shocked if it doesn't come up. And once it does, some gentle prodding to find out what she knew of the deceased should be the easiest of things for someone with your charm." Wolf sighed the sigh of a man who knows he's been hoisted by his own petard.

As Tabitha had predicted, the dowager was delighted to see the handsome new earl and eager to gossip about the deceased duke. Wolf tried to tease information out of the older woman as subtly as possible.

"Oh, my dear Jeremy, I know that one is not supposed to speak ill of the dead, but the late Duke of Somerset was an awful man." Wolf leaned in to encourage her confidence but said nothing, aware that someone who delighted in gossip as much as the dowager would rush to fill the silence. "You may think I speak in hyperbole, but you would be wrong."

The dowager dropped her voice slightly and confided, "It will probably have come to your notice by now that my son was not the best of husbands or men. So, I will share that neither was his father." She must have seen something cross Wolf's face because she continued, "I suspect you then wonder why I don't extend more sympathy to my daughter-in-law. Let me answer that plainly, Tabitha's crime is a lack of stoicism.

"When one finds oneself in a marriage such as Tabitha's or mine, it is important to keep one's dignity, find a lady's maid who is good with cosmetics to conceal bruises and accept that such is a wife's lot. Instead, my daughter-in-law goaded her husband, fought back, and now he is dead."

"Your ladyship, surely you don't blame Tabitha for your son's death? I understand he had drunk too much and fell down the stairs."

"Yes, I'm sure that is your understanding. However, it is not mine. I will say no more about the matter except this; it was Tabitha's duty to stand by her husband's side no matter what. To obey and honour him and to accept some brutality occasionally."

Wolf didn't know how to answer this, so he didn't reply. Instead, the dowager continued, "I believe the lot of men is to be brutal creatures, and the lot of women is to suffer their excesses with as much grace and dignity as one can muster.

"Men do not all have the same vices; some drink, some gamble, and many whore. Often, they do all three to excess."

"You believe all men are this depraved, Lady Pembroke?"

She smiled at his question. "In my experience, all that truly separates a thug from a gentleman is a well-tied cravat. And perhaps, due to private boxing lessons, a gentleman's aim is surer when he strikes a blow. I realise that this makes me sound quite the radical. To suggest that a duke is no better a man than a labourer reminds one, to quote the great Mr Wilde, of the worst excesses of the French Revolution."

Wolf felt that the conversation was getting off-track and so gently prodded her away from philosophising and back to the dead duke. "Yes, well, my point was, my son was a brutal, cruel man, and yet even he was appalled by the Duke of Somerset's behaviour."

"What behaviour?" Wolf asked, trying to curb his impatience.

"Some years before Jonathan married, while I still lived at Chesterton House, I was approaching his study, and the door was ajar. He was inside talking to his man of business and steering him away from some investment involving the duke. At first, I wasn't sure what I was hearing, but it became apparent; the duke has a taste for youthful flesh."

The dowager raised her hand, expecting Wolf to protest, "No!

I also believed he meant lush young debutantes. But instead, it became clear Jonathan meant children. Young girls before the first blush of womanhood. Something so shocking that it seemed depraved even to my son."

The dowager didn't have any more details to add to this accusation. The overheard conversation had not divulged any more information, and it was hardly something about which she could ask her son. But over the years, some rumours had reached her ears, confirming what she had overheard.

The conversation then moved on to other society tattle, and after an acceptable amount of time and tea, Wolf made his excuses and returned home.

Wolf's afternoon visit had taken quite a bit longer than Tabitha's, and when he arrived home, he found her drinking tea in the parlour and reading a book. They quickly each told their respective findings. Tabitha's were far less dramatic than Wolf's. The story told by the grieving family was much the same as related in the newspapers; a burglary gone wrong.

"I did note that the duke's widow, Cassandra, seemed more dry-eyed than one might expect. But I suspect that he was not a pleasant man to be married to and, rather like me, she cannot summon any genuine sorrow over his death." Wolf had to agree that was likely the case based on the intelligence he had received from the dowager.

Tabitha continued, "Ginny did get a few titbits out of the servants; the burglary happened when the butler was away for the night. The household considers it unfortunate timing; we know Mickey D had a spy in the house, so the reduced staff made him even more inclined to steal the necklace. There were also some murmurings about the upper footman taking advantage of his temporary status filling in for the butler. That he was drunk that night on the butler's brandy. So, there's no doubt it was a good night for Mickey's gang to enter the house.

"Also, while no one came out and spoke against their employer directly, Ginny got the sense that the duke won't be missed and that there was a lot of sympathy towards the women of the family."

Wolf had seated himself in his now customary armchair and sat back in contemplation. After a few minutes, he spoke, "We have two events: a burglary and a murder. The simplest explanation is that they are connected, which is certainly the explanation the police are following. Mickey D would have us believe they are entirely unconnected and rather an unlucky coincidence for his lad Seamus. We have doubts about the veracity of Seamus' story, but let's assume that he's telling the truth. Let's assume the duke died before Seamus entered that study and broke into the safe.

"I believe the only way for us to proceed is to make this assumption, for now. We must ignore the burglary and focus on who else might have wanted the duke dead and why. Only once we have exhausted those lines of enquiry, assuming we find nothing, will we have to fall back to the simple conclusion that Seamus killed the duke during the robbery. "

As he spoke, Wolf watched Tabitha closely. She had insinuated herself into this investigation against his better judgement. Still, now that she was involved, he greatly appreciated her as a sounding board for ideas. She had a sharp mind, and while she had led a sheltered life, she was surprisingly hard to shock and had taken the coarser aspects of the case in her stride. Bear was an incredibly loyal and trustworthy partner, but his ability to make intellectual contributions to Wolf's work was minimal.

While much of Wolf's thief-taking had involved physical danger, he felt this case's solution lay in drawing rooms rather than in back alleys. Because of this, he was inclined to allow Tabitha to continue to help if she wanted to. Having decided this, he said, "I believe it is time for a war council."

"A war council?" Tabitha asked, raising her eyebrows slightly at the rather dramatic terminology.

"There are various lines of enquiry to investigate at this point, and I believe that we will need more capacity and capabilities than you and I have together."

Tabitha did note Wolf's inclusion of her in the ongoing

investigations. She had wondered if he would put up more resistance to her continued participation beyond her afternoon visit to the duke's household. If he did, Tabitha had already decided to insist that he continue to include her in this case, though she couldn't say exactly why she was so determined or how she would have managed to persuade him. She knew it felt good to use her brain for something other than approving the menus for the week. Mrs Jenkins and Mr Talbot ran a tight ship at Chesterton House, and there was not much for Tabitha to contribute towards the household management except a light hand at the tiller and bestowing her blessing on the decisions made by her housekeeper, butler, and cook.

Of course, in the normal run of things, a smooth-running household was necessary for an aristocratic lady with a busy social life and a gaggle of children. Tabitha had neither and had spent much of her time since Jonathan's death feeling quite bored. She had always been an avid reader but could spend only so many hours a day reading a book. She had never been as interested in shopping as some of her friends, and there was nothing fun about shopping for clothes during a mourning period. And anyway, her need for new clothes and accessories had been minimal with no social life.

But now, suddenly, she had a child in the nursery for her to fuss over and a man in the household who was interested in her thoughts and seemed to respect her mind. Even before Mickey D had forced Wolf to take on the case, Tabitha had relished their evenings together discussing everything from art to politics to history. But this case had given her something she had lacked for a long time: purpose. And Tabitha was damned if she would give up her role in it without a fight. So that it seemed she didn't need to argue for her continued role was surprising and gratifying.

"So, who will be in this war council?" she asked.

"The two of us, obviously, and Bear. If you approve of her inclusion, your maid could continue to be of great help. And Rat, of course."

Tabitha sat up straighter at the mention of the young boy.

"Why Rat? From what I hear from Mrs Jenkins, he's just starting to settle down nicely and learn the ropes. He's working well in the stables and garden and proving himself a very adept errand boy. Why should we interrupt his new routine?"

"Because, as you said, he's a very adept errand boy. We'll need to communicate with Bruiser and Mickey D. Do you imagine it would be more appropriate for me to keep hoofing it back off to Whitechapel? And anyway, wasn't part of our agreement about Rat and Melody staying here that he continues to run errands for me?"

"Yes, but that was before I knew the full extent of those errands. At the time, I envisioned him running to collect new boots for you or sending messages to you at your club. Not acting as a go-between with a violent gang."

"Be that as it may, Rat has always kept his eyes and ears open and may have heard something pertaining to this case. We need to include him." Tabitha could see she would not win this argument and inclined her head to acknowledge his opinion.

CHAPTER 15

Tabitha and Wolf had agreed to gather their new war council just before dinner. Tabitha had wanted to spend the rest of the afternoon in the nursery with Melly. Wolf had retired to his study to write to his solicitor and man of business to instruct them to investigate the duke's finances and business.

Ginny had been very excited when Tabitha asked if she wished to help further with the case. She had very much enjoyed her afternoon of domestic espionage. They gathered in the parlour, and Wolf insisted that everyone, even Rat, be seated comfortably. Rat had been cleaned up by Mrs Jenkins, much against his will, and now looked quite respectable, though even younger than when Tabitha first met him.

Ginny was excited but uncomfortable sitting in the earl and countess's presence. Bear seemed as uncomfortable as he always was when trying to fit his enormous frame into delicate furniture.

Wolf quickly laid out the facts of the investigation as they knew them. He omitted nothing. Tabitha saw Ginny's eyes widen in shock at the dowager's accusations against the duke, but she said nothing. When Wolf had finished, Rat cleared his throat nervously, and Wolf indicated that he should speak up.

"Yer lordship, Wolf sir, I'd heard some rumours like. That Mr Miller who threw us out when 'e came back from sea, well, 'e's not a nice 'un. Drinks and bashes his lady around. Seems he wasn't just back from sea for a bit but 'ad lost his place on the ship. Their oldest girl's in service and sends 'ome 'er money. But the next girl Janey, she was maybe nine at the time, she was right pretty. Maybe the prettiest girl I've ever seen. So, about a few days after 'e was 'ome, I heard this story that Old Abbess 'utchins 'ad come to talk to 'im about Janey, and then the girl 'ad disappeared, and Mr Miller was suddenly throwing a lot of brass around.

"People said that Mr Miller must have been paid for Janey to go into service, but why would Old Abbess 'utchins be paying 'im for that? Yer knows 'er trade, yer lordship Wolf."

Wolf nodded and enlightened Tabitha and Ginny, "Mrs Hutchins is a madam; that's what he means by an abbess. She runs a mid-end brothel in Holborn, but her roots are in Whitechapel. I know that many of her girls are from the old neighbourhood."

"What is a mid-end brothel?" Tabitha asked, genuinely curious.

Wolf was uncomfortable with this conversation but respected Tabitha too much to answer her with anything but the unvarnished truth. "I would consider a high-end brothel to be one a man of Jonathan's rank might frequent. The next level down or two is in a clean, respectable-looking house catering to solicitors, reasonably successful men of business, perhaps the odd vicar or two." Tabitha couldn't hide her shock at Wolf's last statement. He continued, "Tabitha, men are men, even ones wearing a dog collar. Perhaps, even more so, when forced by their profession to pretend rectitude they may not feel."

Tabitha acknowledged to herself how shocked she was. She knew she'd had a sheltered upbringing, but quite to what extent, she was just starting to realise. But she also knew that even a hint of discomfort from her, and Wolf would insist that she no longer help him on the case. And so, she stiffened her spine, looked him in the eye and asked, "So is the implication that this Mrs Hutchins has been recruiting very young girls for her brothel?"

Wolf considered her question and answered, "I doubt it's as simple as that. Congress with a girl under 16 was outlawed more than ten years ago. The men who frequent Mrs Hutchin's brothel are established enough in society that she couldn't afford to flaunt overly young girls in front of them. At least in her main establishment.

"Bear, go down to Whitechapel and ask around. See if Mrs Hutchins has bought up other young girls recently. Be discreet." Bear nodded in acknowledgement of his task. "Rat, you ask around about girls as well. And then go and tell Mickey D what you told me. Tell him to go and talk to Mrs Hutchins. Say we believe it may be relevant to the case. Tell him, from me, be insistent but not too forceful."

"Do you not think it better if we go and see Mrs Hutchins?" Tabitha asked.

Wolf ignored her inclusion of herself in that proposed expedition and replied, "Mrs Hutchins is a tough old bird. She will respond much better to the threat that a visit from Mickey D and his boys implies. Rat, make arrangements with Mickey to rendezvous and find out what he can uncover."

The young boy nodded with a seriousness of purpose that broke Tabitha's heart. This shouldn't be the kind of thing a boy his age should be involved with. But she knew she had lost that argument, at least for now. She consoled herself with the knowledge that he was well-fed, had a safe and warm bed, and no longer had to worry about his sister's safety and health. Rat's life may not be all she wished for him, but it was better than when she had met him only a few short days before.

"How can Ginny and I help?" Tabitha asked.

"Ginny, your friend is the Dowager Duchess of Somerset's maid, right?" Ginny nodded her head. "Good. Is tomorrow your afternoon off?" Ginny nodded again. "And would it be her's too?"

Ginny finally found her voice and answered, "Yes, m'lord. Me and Annie often meet up and take a walk in the park or even go to a teahouse for a piece of cake if we've got a bit of extra money."

"Excellent. Can you arrange to meet up with this Annie tomorrow and do just that? I will happily pay for you to take tea wherever you would like. I want to know more about what that household is really like. Could this attack come from a disgruntled servant? What visitors might the duke have received? Anything you can find out without revealing our investigation. Do you feel comfortable doing this, Ginny?"

"Oh yes, m'lord. I'm happy to help you in any way I can." Wolf couldn't help but notice the eagerness in the young woman's voice and hoped that he wouldn't regret drawing her into what was quickly becoming a sordid case.

"So now Ginny, Bear, and Rat all have tasks. How can I help?" Tabitha reiterated.

"You can help educate me," Wolf answered. I want to understand the day-to-day life of a duke better. Where might he go? Who might he see?"

Tabitha fought down a desire to pout and tell him that everyone else had some skulduggery to undertake while relegating her to glorified schoolmistress. Instead, she answered, "Then, if we're finished here, let's you and I go in to dinner, and we can begin your education immediately.

Wolf adjourned the meeting, and Tabitha and Wolf moved to the dining room. Over Dover sole, quail, and finally a delightful trifle, Tabitha told Wolf all she knew of how a man of the duke's status might spend his days. Tabitha based most of her information on what Jonathan had done. But she suspected that the life of a debauched duke was not so different from that of an equally unpleasant earl.

Some of what Tabitha described was how Wolf was now filling his days, time with his steward and his man of business. Jonathan had been quite intrigued by the technological advances that were taking place in industry and attended meetings at the Royal Society and periodic meetings with inventors. Tabitha believed he'd invested in some inventions, and Wolf confirmed this. As far as he could tell, Jonathan had a good eye for such things, and his investments had returned good profits over time.

Jonathan had no interest in politics and had not bothered to take advantage of his position in the House of Lords. As far as she knew, he'd spent a lot of time at his club, White's. Tabitha knew he'd had a mistress, but she didn't know the details. She'd got the sense that Jonathan gambled heavily. But again, didn't know where or when.

What she couldn't tell Wolf was how similar to Jonathan the duke might have been in his habits. But she could say with certainty that he was a member of White's, "As, of course, you are now."

"I am?" he asked. "How am I a member of a club?"

"Because it's a hereditary membership. As the new Earl of Pembroke, you will automatically have membership there. That is how I know the duke was a member."

"Well, in that case, perhaps White's is as good a place to start as any. Will it seem bizarre if I just turn up on my own? It's not like I know anyone. Will any of those god-awful bores I met at the dowager's be members?"

"Oh, I think it's very likely that most of them are. I suggest that you plan to dine at your club tomorrow night. Drink some claret, make conversation, and see what you find out. I suspect that the men gathering at White's are as big a bunch of gossips as any bored matrons gathered in a drawing room for tea and cakes."

Wolf chuckled at this, "There are elements of my new status that my life so far has not prepared me for; indulging in tittle-tattle with a bunch of dissolute aristocrats is definitely high on that list. But, for the sake of the investigation, I will follow your advice."

While Tabitha was grateful that he took her counsel so seriously, she realised this left her even more out of the investigation. Everyone had some little adventure to undertake, and she was stuck at home, dining alone the next night to make it worse.

The following morning, after breakfast, Tabitha asked Mrs Jenkins to send Rat to the nursery when he finished whatever task she had him working on so they could begin their reading lessons. Mrs Jenkins looked a little uncomfortable as she replied, "Apologies, m'lady, but the lad has gone out on errands that he said were on orders from his lordship." Ah yes, Rat had his messages to run to Mickey D. Wolf was meeting with his solicitor and then his man of business to see what they had uncovered about the duke's financial situation. And Ginny would be getting herself ready soon for her afternoon out doing her own espionage.

Tabitha realised she was being silly and determined to spend the rest of the morning in the nursery with Melly. She felt a little guilty about neglecting the little girl because of the investigation. Tabitha had longed for a child for so many years, and now she had the care of a delightful one, and suddenly that didn't feel like enough, and she wasn't sure why that was. However, despite these conflicted feelings, she was genuinely delighted to spend time with Melly that morning and very conscious of the obligation she had undertaken when she had brought her into the nursery.

Tabitha spent the next couple of hours having a doll's tea party and helping Melly begin to learn her lessons. Tabitha was grateful that Mary knew her letters at least and could practice daily with Melly. The little girl was a quick learner and seemed to delight in learning her letters and pleasing Tabitha when she was correct. It became clear to Tabitha that, before too long, she would need to hire an actual nanny to take care of the child if she were to receive a proper education.

But seeing how Mary and Melody had taken to each other was gratifying. In many ways, it was remarkable that they'd only been together in the nursery for a few short days; the little girl shadowed Mary as she moved about the nursery when Tabitha first arrived. She'd insisted that Mary had to be part of the tea party and had only started to be more comfortable being away from the maid when she had become absorbed in her letters.

Tabitha was thrilled to see the bond created in such a short period of time, but there was also a bittersweet feeling that went alongside that; whether it was this child or a baby of her own, it was the nature of Tabitha's class, that a mother made periodic visits to a nursery, while servants provided the bulk of the childcare and love. It was how Tabitha had been raised and how any child she might have had with Jonathan would have been. Nevertheless, she felt a pang that whatever bond she might form with Melly would never have the same quality as the relationship she would create with the woman paid to look after her.

CHAPTER 16

While Ginny was quite a few years younger than Annie, they had been friends for several years. In fact, they were distant relatives through Ginny's aunt's husband. When Ginny had first entered service for Tabitha, Annie had sought her out and helped guide Ginny in navigating the inevitable politics of the servant's hall. They now spent at least one afternoon off a month together and had formed a genuine friendship. It would not be unusual for them to take tea together, and with the fiction of Ginny's windfall courtesy of her new employer, it would be natural for her to share her good fortune with her friend.

Despite their long friendship, Ginny felt an unseen barrier during their conversation that afternoon; her friend seemed distant and cool. Thinking back to her attempts to gain information from her friend's colleagues earlier that week, Ginny wondered if Annie felt that her friend had been sticking her nose where it didn't belong. Ginny's purpose was to do more of the same, and she was unsure how to address the awkwardness head-on. Finally, after two cups of tea and some very stilted conversation, she determined to be blunt. "Annie, is everything okay? You seem distracted."

The other woman didn't answer immediately, and Ginny saw something shifting in her friend's eyes; was it fear? Uneasiness? Ginny saw it flicker, and then Annie composed herself and answered, "Well, of course, everything is not okay. With the duke's death, the whole household is turned upside down. There are all the preparations for mourning and the funeral on Friday.

And, of course, my poor mistress beside herself at her son's loss. No parent should have to bury a child." Ginny nodded in agreement, even though many parents buried a child in their world. Even in aristocratic circles, death in childhood was not uncommon. But she did get Annie's point; a woman of the dowager duchess' age did not expect to outlive a grown son.

Given that Annie had volunteered information about the family in mourning, Ginny considered how delicately to pry that door open a little more. She decided to talk about her recent experience with a similar situation, "I do understand. When his lordship died, his mother was beside herself. So much so that she held my mistress responsible; I believe she still does."

Annie looked interested in this turn in the conversation and asked, "But didn't the police also suspect Lady Pembroke initially? How did that come about, and what made them dismiss any charges?"

"Well, firstly, no charges were ever brought against her ladyship. Lord Pembroke had been drinking to excess, as he often did. There had been some words said between them on the landing outside her room, and he had struck her. As he often did. Then he stumbled and fell down the stairs to his death." Ginny heard the defiance in her voice, more vehement than she had intended. "They questioned her ladyship, and finally, the coroner's inquest returned a verdict of death by misadventure. However," and she paused here, "her ladyship, the dowager, never accepted that. M'lady was very gracious and often told me she couldn't imagine the dowager's pain when burying her only living son."

Annie nodded in acceptance of the version of events that Ginny was relaying, so the younger woman felt encouraged to carry the analogy further. "Though, I will admit that m'lady did not shed tears over her husband's death. She may not have had a hand in it, but that doesn't mean she was sorry. He was cruel and didn't even deserve her shedding crocodile tears, let alone real ones." She saw Annie nodding in agreement, but it wasn't clear whether it was in sympathy with Lady Pembroke or if the story she was hearing resonated closer to home.

After a brief pause, Ginny took a slightly different tack and commented, “By all accounts, your young lord, the new duke, is a very different kettle of fish to his father.”

This seemed to be a statement that Annie felt she could wholeheartedly agree with, “Oh yes. The young master, I mean the new duke, is a good man. Always good to the servants, a good son and grandson. Kind, generous and gentle. A very different man to his father.”

Ginny considered this statement; while it had been difficult to induce her friend to speak ill of the dead duke, in giving a glowing comparative review of the son, she had effectively told Ginny all she needed to know about the father. She felt that she was unlikely to get more information at this point, but did ask one direct question, “From what the newspapers said, the diamond necklace had only been taken out of the bank vault the day before and was due back a day later. It’s quite a coincidence that the burglary happened at such a suitable time. And with the staff being shorthanded over that time as well.”

The young woman wasn’t quite sure what she expected as a reply to such a statement. In truth, it was merely an offhand observation she might have made in talking with anyone about the incident. What she didn’t expect was the flush that made its way up her friend’s neck and the look of, what could only be called guilt, that crossed her face. Ginny pretended not to notice it, but she made a mental note to mention this to his lordship when she reported back.

As soon as Ginny returned home, she went to Wolf’s study and nervously knocked on the door. In the ordinary course of her duties, she would have little to do with the master of the house and certainly would have no reason to seek him out in his private rooms. But this was not the ordinary course of her duties, so when he called to enter, she turned the doorknob, swallowed her fears, and walked in.

As it happens, Tabitha had just sought Wolf out in his study to find out what his agents had reported.

"Ah, Ginny, great timing," Wolf said. "Take a seat", he said as he gestured towards one of the room's armchairs. Ginny had not been expecting such informality and glanced over at her mistress for an indication as to what she should do.

"His lordship said to sit Ginny, so please sit," Tabitha said kindly. "Now, do you have anything to report from your tea?"

Ginny cleared her throat and lifted her head slightly, proud that she'd had some success with her assignment, even though she felt guilty that she might be betraying her friend. Nevertheless, duty won out, and she relayed the highlights of her conversation with the other maid. When she reached the part that had made Annie uncomfortable, she paused, reflected on what had happened, and chose her words carefully: "What she seemed to react to was that there was a great coincidence in the burglary being that night."

"Well," Wolf pointed out, "we know it wasn't a coincidence. The boot boy had informed Mickey D that the jewels would be there only for a couple of days. I'm guessing he had no idea then that the butler would be gone or the upper footman drunk, so those were still lucky coincidences for the thieves."

Ginny considered his words and answered, "I do see that, m'lord. But I know that Annie is a distant relative and, like me, her people are Irish, and some live in Whitechapel. I know she's as loyal to the duchess as I am to her ladyship, but even so, that part of the conversation caused a reaction."

"No, you're right, Ginny. We need to follow up on this. I'll have Bear and Rat check in with Mickey D on what he knows about this Annie and her family. Good work." The maid blushed with pride, then got up, curtseyed and let herself out.

Wolf and Tabitha sat in companionable silence for a few minutes, each contemplating what they had heard. Finally, Tabitha broke the silence and said, "You were just about to tell me what your various agents have managed to discover."

"Yes, at first blush, there doesn't seem to be much they were able to dig up. The Somerset estate is in good shape. While the deceased duke was a gambler, it wasn't to excess. His father had made some good investments over the years, and the son was astute enough to continue to reap their benefits. There's a portfolio of property holdings, throughout London, with some interesting additions made quite recently, most notably, a townhouse in Holborn, a popular neighbourhood given all the theatres and music halls, but hardly one you would expect to draw a lot of interest from one of the richest and most powerful men in Britain.

"What was particularly interesting about the townhouse was that he didn't purchase it directly but instead had tried to hide the purchase using a company that seems to have been set up solely for this purpose. The duke went to great lengths to protect his name from any association with the company. My solicitor had to do a lot of digging and be quite persistent to unearth what he did."

"Why would the duke go to such lengths?" Tabitha asked.

"Well, in my experience, people hide things for one of two reasons: they're illegal or shameful."

"And so, the question is: what kind of activity was he hiding? Your men couldn't find out any more than that?"

"No, but I've asked them to keep digging." Wolf pulled the bell, and within moments, Talbot appeared. Wolf asked, "Has Rat or Bear returned yet?"

Talbot looked pained at having to refer to the valet and the child by these names. However, he replied, "The lad returned a few minutes ago and is having something to eat. I'm not sure about Mr Bear, but I'll check in the kitchen and ask," he paused for a moment, then forced himself to use the name "Rat to come up when he has finished his meal."

"Thank you, Talbot. That will be all."

Tabitha barely held her chuckles until the butler left the room, "Poor Talbot. It was bad enough to introduce Bear into the household, but that he now has Rat to contend with, it's almost more than we can ask of the man. Mrs Jenkins confided that they all tried to call the boy Matt, but he refused to answer to the name, so they quickly gave up. And, you know, it's all your fault."

"How is it my fault?" Wolf asked, pretending to take offence.

"Because the boy idolises you, and being called Rat marks him as one of your men. If you and Bear had less absurd names, I'm sure he wouldn't choose to be called that."

Wolf laughed at her characterisation of his name. "My name is absurd, is it?"

"You know it is. And even if it wasn't in and of itself as a nickname, partnering with someone called Bear is just ridiculous. And I suspect you relish that absurdity, so you didn't discourage Rat from using that nickname for himself." Wolf acknowledged she might have a point, but Bear knocked and entered the study before they could continue the conversation. Even this room, with its larger, more comfortable armchairs, didn't seem to have a chair in which the mountain of a man could be comfortable. But he managed the best he could.

"So, what did you find out?" Wolf launched right in.

Tabitha hadn't heard Bear speak much since he entered the household. Mostly, just the odd word or phrase. Because of this, she was very interested in his report to Wolf.

"Well," the large man began, "the story young Rat told us wasn't a one-off. There have been others. Mostly, same story; very young, very pretty girls from impoverished, desperate families. Money exchanging hands that could be life-changing for the families."

As he spoke, Tabitha reflected on how well-spoken and articulate Bear was. She wasn't sure what she'd expected, perhaps some barely human grunts. As she reflected on this, she felt ashamed of her prejudice. And determined to get to know the man better. He continued, "In all the cases, the families claimed that they believed their daughters had been taken into service. But when pressed, they acknowledged that they had no real reason to believe that and admitted they had never heard from the girls again. There were no visits home on a half-day off, no money sent home, and no letters. The girls just disappeared, and the families tried to forget they had ever existed."

Tabitha had to ask, "How did you ever get any of them to

admit to this?"

Bear laughed a deep-throated sound, "I have my sources. I ask around. People tend to be scared enough of me to answer when they realise that all I want is some answers rather than to bash their heads in. Wolf and I have been doing this for a while. We know what we're doing." Again, Tabitha reflected on how badly she had misjudged Wolf's associate. She had immediately assumed that Wolf was 100% the brains and Bear the brawn. Even their nicknames led to that easy assumption. But their relationship was more complex.

"So, girls are being taken. Young girls. We must assume that they've been sold into prostitution," Wolf said.

Tabitha had a visible reaction to this statement, "Girls that young? They're children. How can that be possible or allowable?"

Wolf sighed and answered, "Tabitha, you wanted to be involved in this, and unfortunately, this world, the world Bear and I used to be part of, is full of the unimaginably awful but possible. The illegal but the accepted."

"Well, it's not accepted by me!" she exclaimed, her eyes wide and bright, glistening as if unshed tears were gathering.

"Unfortunately, the world is full of things unacceptable to you and me," Wolf added. "Unacceptable to most decent people, at least in the abstract, but which nevertheless can happen. You and I likely even indirectly benefit from things like child labour or hazardous working conditions in factories. Do you ask how the materials for your fine dresses are made and by whom? Do you ensure that there are no underage workers and that the conditions are safe before you buy something made in a workshop?"

Tabitha started to protest, and Wolf held up a hand. "This isn't a criticism of you; it's a general statement about us all. Particularly those of us with wealth and privilege. Part of that privilege is never confronting the ugliness of the systems we implicitly uphold. Prostitution is part of that ugliness."

Tabitha could hold back no longer and said forcefully, "I don't believe there is anything I do or buy that implicitly helps to uphold prostitution, let alone child prostitution!"

Wolf spoke gently but firmly, "Again, this is not an attack on you, Tabitha, but just a statement of fact. Women go into prostitution because they have no other economic choices. These families are selling their children into prostitution for the same reasons. Why do they have no economic choices? Because of decisions made by people in our social class. We run the government, own the factories, and are the end consumers. They're the tenants, and we're the landlords. We own the land that they till. If we allow a world where we have all of this," and at this, he swept his arm before him to include the room and its contents, "and they don't have enough to eat, where does the fault with that lie ultimately?"

Tabitha didn't answer for a minute or so, but the look on her face told Wolf that he had shocked her. Then she answered quietly, "You are quite the radical."

"Am I? I would prefer to think of myself as a supporter of reform rather than revolution. I'm certainly not alone in our class in believing in the cause of reform and acknowledging that, while there has been progress, there is much more to do."

Tabitha had to admit that she had never taken much interest in politics. She knew that various reform bills had been passed into law during her lifetime and before. Her father had supported them; she knew that Jonathan had been fervently against most. If only for this reason, she'd always had a bias towards reform, but in a very general way.

Before this conversation could get any more uncomfortable for either of them, there was a timid tap at the door, and then Rat entered. He looked very young and small to Tabitha standing there, and it squeezed at her heart. "Wolf, your lordship, m'lady Tabby Cat," Rat said as a greeting.

"So, lad, what do you have to report?" Wolf answered.

"Well, the Miller girl wasn't the only one Ma 'utchins bought. There are all sorts of tales, but from what I can tell, about fifteen young girls over the last few years, maybe more. They're all around my age. None of them is more than about 10."

Tabitha put her hands over her mouth in shock but did her best not to interrupt the boy's story. He continued, "There's at least one girl at Old Abbess 'utchins' now, who's been out of Whitechapel for a couple of years, but suddenly turned up again."

Wolf was less concerned about interrupting and asked, "From whom did you hear this gossip? Are they reliable sources?"

The boy nodded, "I heard about the one girl from Jimmy, the grocer's boy. He makes deliveries to the Hutchins place. The cook has taken a fancy to him and often invites him in for a bowl of soup. One day, he's sitting at the kitchen table, and a girl comes into the kitchen looking for food like. 'E said there wasn't much to her, and she had these big old eyes staring blankly out of this pale, tiny face. But there was something about her that looked familiar like. She saw 'im looking at her, and she scarpered.

"Jimmy kept thinking about why 'e knew 'er chivvy, and then 'e realised she was the kid what lived in the room next to 'im a few years before. Big family, all cramped in that one little room. But 'e always noticed 'er because she 'ad a nice smile. Then one day, she was gone. She was probably about eight or nine back then.

"Then a couple of other people told me about families they knew where a pretty little girl wasn't around anymore one day, and nothing said of where she'd gone."

"And what did Mickey D have to say about all this?"

"'E said you should go with 'im to talk to the abbess."

"Why on earth should I do that?" Wolf asked in exasperation. "The whole point is that she will talk to him, not me."

"Mickey says 'e's not so sure that's true now you're a toff. Mickey thinks that something will come out between you and that you're better off both working 'er. 'E says 'e'll see you there at 11 tomorrow morning." Rat indicated he had nothing more to tell, and they excused him to get dinner with the other servants.

Wolf and Tabitha sat silently for a few minutes, each deep in thought about all they had heard that afternoon. Finally, Tabitha broke the silence, saying, "It seems that we are visiting Mrs Hutchins with Mickey D tomorrow."

Wolf had been sipping tea as she said this and nearly spat a mouthful across the room at this statement. He quickly apologised but added, "You surely can't be serious? Moreover, you surely can't imagine that I will allow it?"

At this, Tabitha sat up a little taller in her chair and asked, "Allow it? I'm sorry, milord, but you are neither my father nor my husband. You cannot permit me anything except the right to continue to live under this roof."

"You are wrong, madam. I have control over my activities and the power to say whether you participate in them with me. But why would you want to come? You have no idea what horrors abound in London, and there's no reason to go out of your way to learn about them."

Tabitha sighed as she said, "Wolf, you were only just chastising me for my narrow, sheltered view of the world. And you were right. I have no idea how the people live who make my life comfortable. And I have no idea about the conditions people are forced into because of a system that exists to make the life of people in my class as easy as possible. I want to fix that. I want to do better. I'm no delicate flower, and my reputation is already in tatters. I want to come with, even if it's ugly and even if it'll upset me. It should upset me, and I should face it anyway."

As she said this, Wolf watched the animation on her face. He had never admired someone more than he did Tabitha at that moment. He had to admit to himself she was right. He couldn't accuse her of leading a sheltered life one moment and then seek to continue enforcing that cloistered life the next. Nevertheless, he didn't answer her immediately. While he considered his reply, she sat with her hands folded in her lap, never breaking eye contact with him, never wavering in her determination.

Finally, he made up his mind, "You are right. It is unfair of me to make such a charge against you and then refuse to help you rectify it. However, we need to be smart about this. At the moment, no one knows that we're investigating the duke's death. We don't even know that the duke and Mrs Hutchins are connected. We have a rumour that he had a taste for very young girls. And another rumour is that the owner of a brothel is buying up very young girls. We have nothing, at the moment, to connect the two rumours or confirm any of them.

"Mrs Hutchins is a wily, tough old bird. She won't just give up information, particularly to a pair of toffs. I had hoped that Mickey D would have more luck by himself. But he seems to feel otherwise. So, the question is, what story is the most plausible for why we are asking her questions, and not just plausible, but most like to be effective?"

They sat in silence for a few minutes more. Finally, Tabitha rose and said, "Why don't we continue this conversation over dinner? Perhaps some food, and some wine, will help fuel our imaginations.

CHAPTER 17

As Tabitha and Wolf ate, they discussed credible backstories for their visit. "I'm assuming Mrs Hutchins knows you from your old life," Tabitha asked.

"Not well, but I'm sure she knows who I am. There's a good enough chance of it that it's not worth the risk of trying to pretend otherwise."

"But like most people from that life, she likely has no idea about your recent good fortune?"

"I doubt it. Mickey D is many things, but he's not a gossip. For him, information is power, so he plays his cards close to his chest. I also think it's the case if I turn up suddenly claiming to be an earl, she'll laugh me out of her house."

Tabitha considered his words, "Then perhaps we can use all this to our advantage. What motivates a woman such as Mrs Hutchins? I assume only one thing, really, money?"

"I would agree with that."

"Then, what if I'm what I seem to be, a woman of status and wealth who has hired you to find her daughter? We can construct a plausible story. What about a daughter led astray by a wastrel who promised to marry her, but cast her aside once he realised that her family would disown her? I couldn't look for her while my husband was alive because he refused to mention her name. But he died six months ago, and since then, I've paid you to try to hunt her down. With the promise of a large reward for her return."

Wolf marvelled at how quickly she had come up with such a plausible story, "Lady Pembroke," he said with mock formality, "I believe you've wasted your talents to date and that they are far better suited to a life of deception."

Tabitha laughed, "I believe you mean that as a compliment, so I'll take it as such."

"Indeed, I do mean it as such. I'm assuming that I have searched the country and received intelligence that the girl may be plying the oldest trade in a brothel in London. We wish to talk to all her girls to discover what they might know. Of course, there will be a payment just for helping you find your long-lost daughter."

"Exactly! Given this story, I believe we should advise Mickey D not to join us. I don't believe he adds anything to the story's credibility and may spook the woman."

"I agree," Wolf concurred. "I'll send Rat to him tomorrow morning to advise him of the change in our plans."

As much as she wished that Rat would not be involved in any more of this plan, she realised the futility of expressing such a sentiment. Instead, she said, "Ginny and I will devise an outfit tomorrow that screams wealth, status and power. I'm assuming you will be donning your thief-taker clothes again?"

"Indeed."

"One last thing, is there any reason to use my real name?"

"I'm sure Mrs Hutchins does not own a copy of Debrett's and so won't know a countess from a marchioness. You will look and sound the part and, most importantly, have a heavy purse. That will be all that is important to her."

"We must find a way to talk to all the girls privately."

"That will be easy enough, again, for a price. Let me do all the negotiations. The story will be that you want to feel confident in the girls' answers and are worried they will feel intimidated if she is in the room. Under normal circumstances, I can't imagine that a woman such as the one you are pretending to be would accompany a man such as me to a brothel. So, your story must speak of desperation. Your husband has died, and this daughter is your only child. Your husband has left you an extremely wealthy widow, but with no one to love, you are resorting to desperate measures to track down the only family you have left."

They agreed that this would be the story they would playact tomorrow. Wolf secretly worried whether Tabitha's acting skills would pass muster. But he also realised their plan was more likely to succeed than the original plan to have Mickey D threaten Mrs Hutchins. First, a prostitute and then a madam, threats of violence would not have been a novelty to her. Women such as Mrs Hutchins only cared about one thing: money.

The following morning, Rat was dispatched with his message and returned with a reply that agreed with the change in plans. Ginny had taken great care with Tabitha's toilette and outfit. Usually, Tabitha wore her hair quite simply, but Ginny insisted that she had to look every part of the grand dame. They wanted to cultivate a look that said great wealth and status. There should be no doubt how rich the woman who walked into that brothel was.

They chose an old dark plum-coloured, silk walking dress with a matching hat and an imposing feather plume. Ginny performed some sewing magic on the dress, and suddenly it was a little more plunging and daring than anything Tabitha would typically wear. They accessorised the dress with a somewhat old-fashioned necklace that had belonged to Tabitha's grandmother. It had large sapphires set in a heavy, ornate gold setting. She wore a matching ring to finish the outfit. Tabitha had never worn the jewellery because it had always seemed too ostentatious. It's certainly not something she would have worn outside of a ballroom. But Lady Chalmers, her fictional persona, seemed like someone who would like every opportunity to dazzle and show off her wealth as much as possible.

Tabitha had always been very conservative in her dress. But she decided that Lady Chalmers did not have such qualms. Tabitha remembered the phrase her mother had always liked to chant when moralising about another family's failings. Tabitha's mother would have spoken of the terrible disgrace that befell the Chalmers family by saying of the young fallen girl (named Lucy Chalmers by Tabitha), "Apples that bad don't fall far from the tree." At this point, her mother would have sniffed in disapproval, indicating how far below her family and their possible conduct she considered such behaviour.

Tabitha considered what kind of woman her mother would have looked up and down and judged her dress licentious enough to explain how such a woman might end up with a daughter of loose morals. And then Tabitha dressed as that woman.

Dressed and ready, she looked in the mirror and barely recognised herself. Following the lead of Queen Victoria, it had been almost unheard of for a society woman to paint her face in any way. Such artifice was the stuff of whores and actresses. However, some women had started using a little rouge, powder and even tinted lip salve. Tabitha had decided that Lady Chalmers would be one such woman. Of course, she had not owned any of those products, and Ginny had gone out early to procure the necessary items.

Looking herself over, Tabitha was sure that her mother would have been suitably appalled at Lady Chalmers and convinced that her display of bosom alone was enough to deserve the disgrace Lucy had brought upon her family. However, Tabitha looked at her character with an altogether more charitable eye. She thought that Lady Chalmers looked like the kind of woman Tabitha had often wished she could be: confident, dismissive of society's judgement, and comfortable with her beauty and body. She thought that Lady Chalmers might be someone she would enjoy calling a friend.

"You look right pretty m'lady, if I can say so." Ginny said, interrupting her thoughts. "I'd always wished to have you wear a little more colour and do up your hair, even before you went into mourning. I know that his lordship would have never allowed such a thing. But perhaps now that he's gone, once you're fully out of mourning...." Ginny left the sentence unfinished. But Tabitha nodded in acknowledgement of the sentiment.

"Let us go down and see what the new Earl of Pembroke thinks of my outfit." They had agreed that Ginny would accompany

Tabitha and Wolf to the brothel. It was more appropriate that Lady Chalmers bring her lady's maid to accompany her, and Ginny was astute and could pick up things from the girls she and Wolf might miss. They'd also agreed to bring Bear because Wolf said, "It never hurts to have someone his size with you."

Tabitha and Wolf had decided to meet for a late breakfast to go over their personas and plans, and she found him at the bottom of the stairs, having descended just before she did. He looked up as she came down, and Wolf couldn't help the look of surprise that took over his face. He had always thought Tabitha was a handsome woman. She had that lustrous, wavy chestnut hair and hazel eyes with little flecks of gold. But her clothes and hair were always so austere, even for someone in half-mourning, that he'd never really thought of any word for her but "handsome." But in her Lady Chalmers outfit, she was stunning. Yes, it was a little more gauche than he could imagine Tabitha wearing even when totally out of mourning, but the style of the newly altered dress showed off a fine figure. And the cosmetics were subtle enough to bring a healthy brightness to her face.

"You look lovely," Wolf couldn't help saying. "That colour is perfect for you, and I like your hair done that way." Tabitha blushed, not sure what to say. She had dressed modestly as a debutante, as directed by her mother. Then she had dressed conservatively because that was what Jonathan had dictated. And then she had been in mourning. It had never occurred to Tabitha that she could now dress according to her tastes. While unsure what those tastes might stretch to, she was sure they weren't as daring as Lady Chalmers. However, she wondered at that moment whether there might be a little more Lady Chalmers in her than she'd realised.

As she reached the bottom of the stairs, Wolf extended his arm to her in an unusual show of courtly manners. She had always appreciated that he treated her more as an equal than an insipid, incapable woman. However, she surprised herself at the little stab of pleasure it gave her to see the clear admiration in his eyes now and translated to his behaviour.

Over breakfast, they went over their backstories. They decided that Lady Chalmers would not be particularly sharp. There would be liberal use of a handkerchief to dab at her eyes and a simpering quality to her speech. There should be nothing about her manner to make the madam feel threatened. On the contrary, they hoped Mrs Hutchins would immediately see Lady Chalmers as a likely soft touch easily milked for money. They expected this realisation would lead to a greediness that might supersede any wariness the woman might usually exhibit to a titled lady asking about her girls.

They had agreed that Tabitha would stay in the carriage while Wolf approached the brothel and asked to speak to its madam. He would then give a quick overview of the conversation they wished to have with her and a heavy-handed indication of the size of the purse involved.

As they had hoped, Mrs Hutchins took one look at the grand carriage and immediately invited her titled visitor and entourage of servants into her parlour.

Tabitha was unsure what she expected a brothel to look like, but the entranceway and the parlour didn't look all that different from what she would expect from a solidly prosperous middle-class home. The paintings on the wall were perhaps a little more risqué, and the silks and velvet that seemed to cover every piece of soft furnishings were a little gaudier, but overall, there was nothing overtly shocking about the room.

Mrs Hutchins matched her drawing room in many ways. A full-figured woman, her dress showed perhaps a little more bosom than would be considered acceptable in polite society. Still, overall, she wore no more paint on her face than Tabitha herself did as Lady Chalmers. The madam's dress was perhaps more extravagant than a lady in Tabitha's circle would consider appropriate for the morning but not garish and was clearly of excellent quality. The woman's speech was that of someone trying very hard to be cultured while occasionally dropping an h.

Over tea and cake, Wolf quickly elaborated on the story

they had agreed on. Tabitha sat with a cup of tea in her hand, occasionally sniffing and bringing her handkerchief to her eyes at the parts of the story that might be supposed to be particularly painful to a mother. As Wolf finished the story, he made his request of Mrs Hutchins while bringing a full purse out of his pocket.

“Let me make sure I understand you sir; you wish to question all of my girls, in private?”

“That is correct,” Wolf answered. “And for this service, you will be paid handsomely.”

“How ‘andsomely?” the woman asked with avarice gleaming in her watery blue eyes.

“Name a price.” Wolf could see the mental calculations the woman was doing. How much was too much? She finally named a hefty price, but well within what Wolf had told Tabitha he expected to pay. When he immediately accepted it, he saw Mrs Hutchins's greedy recognition that perhaps she could have asked for even more.

With the negotiation complete, the madam left the room and returned with a skinny young woman, perhaps in her early twenties. Girl after girl entered the room to talk with them. Tabitha was relieved that they all seemed in good health, adequately nourished, and with no apparent signs of violence upon their bodies. Most girls looked at least 16, even though there was a world weariness about them all that broke Tabitha’s heart. But she realised that compared to herself at 16, they also had a worldliness about them compared to her extreme naivety at that age.

Tabitha reflected on Jonathan’s brief courtship of her and her parents' enthusiasm over the match. Her mother had been thrilled at snagging an earl and the subsequent rise in status for the family. Her father had been equally enthusiastic about his prospective son-in-law’s coffers and the potential to join their family business ventures. While Tabitha had felt the full force of the honour Jonathan’s attentions bestowed on her and was undoubtedly impressed by his sophisticated charms, she could now see her marriage as merely a more high-class, expensive version of the situation in which these girls found themselves.

Knowing that Jimmy, the grocer's boy, had only recognised one girl, Tabitha and Wolf quickly questioned the other girls. They had made the description of Lady Chalmer's fictional runaway daughter so memorable that a question or two would soon determine whether a girl had seen her; Lucy Chalmers had one blue eye and one brown. They had spoken to ten girls when a girl entered the room who was so young that it made Tabitha gasp. She would have been surprised to learn that the girl was any older than 11. And yet here she was, a prostitute in a brothel.

Given that the age of consent had been raised more than ten years before, from 13 to 16, Wolf was surprised that Mrs Hutchins had been willing to bring the girl out. But he had told her they were prepared to pay for each girl they spoke with. And so, again, greed won out.

Mrs Hutchins had accompanied the child into the room and seemed inclined to try to stay for the interview. But Wolf made it clear that her presence was not welcome, and she reluctantly left. Becky, because that was the girl's name, was exquisite. She had white gold ringlets and deep blue eyes. Her skin was like the finest porcelain, and she had a rosebud mouth with cherry-red lips. But just as Rat had described her, those beautiful eyes had a vacant, haunted look.

Tabitha quickly decided to drop her Lady Chalmers act and indicated to the girl that she should come and sit next to her on the sofa. She offered the girl a slice of cake, which, after an initial reluctance, was accepted and eaten hungrily. Tabitha and Wolf had already decided that she would take the lead in questioning this girl. But she waited until the child had eaten her cake, then took the plate from her and put it down.

Using a soft, kind tone, Tabitha asked, "How old are you, Becky?" The child looked up fearfully, clearly wary about this topic. "Becky, I know you can't be more than 11 or 12, so you won't get into trouble for confirming that."

In a very quiet voice, the child confirmed, "I'm 11."

"And where did you grow up, Becky?"

Again, Becky hesitated but answered, "In Whitechapel, miss."

"Thank you for telling me that, Becky. How long have you been in Mrs Hutchins' house?" Tabitha was careful to make Becky's residence in the brothel sound as benign as possible.

"I'm not sure, miss. I think I came around Christmas." Tabitha quickly calculated and realised that the child hadn't been in the brothel for more than a few months.

Tabitha felt that the child beside her had relaxed during these questions and thought she could now ask what they wanted to know. "Becky, I know this is difficult for you, and I appreciate your honesty. I hope that you can continue to answer my questions honestly." At this, she took hold of one of the little hands. Becky nodded her head in answer. "That's wonderful, Becky. Were you in another house, like this house, before you came here?"

At this question, Tabitha felt Becky's hand stiffen in hers and could sense the palpable fear emanating from the young girl. "Becky, I promise I won't let anything happen to you if you tell me the truth." At this, Becky's eyes went to the door, clearly in fear of the madam. At that moment, Tabitha made a decision. On reflection later, she realised that she didn't decide because to say that implied that she could have done otherwise. She told the girl, "Becky, when I leave here after this conversation, I will take you with me."

Wolf's head jerked up, and Tabitha heard a gasp from Ginny, who was sitting quietly in the corner the whole time. Reminded of Ginny's presence, Tabitha indicated she wanted her maid to join her and Becky on the sofa. Ginny stood up and came across the room. "Becky, this is Ginny. She works for me and will look after you when we take you home. You will stay at my house and work for me. Ginny will teach you how to be a lady's maid. Would you like that?" Becky nodded her head enthusiastically. Tabitha continued, "So you see, you have nothing to fear from Mrs Hutchins. You may tell us the truth; she cannot hurt you."

With that assurance, the story started coming out; Becky had been taken from her home when she was 8 and brought to a house with other young girls. A mean woman looked after the girls. They were locked in their rooms at night and never allowed to leave the house. Men would come to the house daily and lie with the girls. As Becky started to talk about what had happened to her, she began to cry. Tabitha squeezed her hand and assured her, "You do not need to go into details, Becky; we understand what happened to you."

Becky told them all the girls were no older than 11 or 12. Depending on how quickly they matured, they disappeared from the house around that age. No one knew what had happened to them. Then, new little girls arrived to take their place. Tabitha wanted more details but realised it wasn't the time or place. They knew enough and now had to persuade Mrs Hutchins to release the girl.

Becky had been provided with another slice of cake and was busy eating it. Tabitha indicated to Wolf that she wished to talk with him privately across the room by the window. He followed her and, keeping his voice low, asked, "What are you thinking, Tabitha? You're planning to take the girl home with you?"

Tabitha had expected this reaction and gave him a long, hard stare, "She's a child, Wolf. What would you have me do? Leave her here? Take her home to parents who knowingly sold her into prostitution? Drop her off at the workhouse on our way home?" Wolf didn't answer, so Tabitha pressed home her point, "This child is an innocent, cruelly used. I have no choice but to rescue her and take her home with us. I will repeat what I said to you when we brought Rat and Melly into the house; if this does not sit well with you, I will understand and find a residence of my own."

Wolf sighed, knowing that she had won the argument. "Of course, you are right," he conceded. "What is the story we will give to the staff?"

"I'm not sure why we owe our servants an explanation, but to make things as easy for Becky as possible, we will say that I came across her when visiting an orphanage I am considering patronising. I was immediately charmed by her sweetness and beauty and determined to bring her into our household." That is all they need to know. We will see what schooling she has received, and I will hire a well-educated nanny to help Mary with Melly and teach Rat and Becky the basics of reading, writing, and arithmetic. Now, the only question is, how we persuade Mrs Hutchins to let her leave with us."

"Leave that to me," Wolf replied. "I have the measure of the woman." And with that, he jingled the bag of coins in his pocket. Indeed, Wolf truly did have the measure of Mrs Hutchins. He nimbly combined a mild threat that he knew Becky's real age and wouldn't hesitate to report the brothel to the authorities for keeping underage prostitutes while dangling more money in front of her than she could hope to earn in a month.

Wolf had taken the woman aside and told her confidentially that the wealthy but very lonely widow was beginning to despair about finding her daughter. He claimed that this was the third brothel they'd visited this month and that no one had heard of the girl with two different colour eyes. But when she first saw Becky, the desperate mother immediately latched on to the physical resemblance between Becky and Lucy. She now felt that taking this girl home with her might make up for the inevitable loss of the other.

The truth was, Marjorie Hutchins had never been very comfortable with the arrangement to procure very young girls. She had gone along with it knowing that if she didn't, there would be another madam who would. And so she might as well take the money as put it in another's pocket. Becky was one of the earlier girls to "mature too quickly" and she had agreed to take her in because she worried what the alternative was for getting rid of girls who no longer had their childish innocence. The gentlemen who frequented her brothel did not have the same taste for overly young flesh, and she mostly had Becky doing some cleaning and mending. Being offered money to take her off her hands seemed like the answer to her prayers. And if she'd been worried about what her protector might have said about such an agreement, he was dead now, wasn't he?

As Wolf told the tale, he clinked the coins in his pocket. The rest was a quick negotiation, and before they knew it, they were back in the carriage with Becky sitting between Ginny and Tabitha.

CHAPTER 18

Tabitha had told Mrs Jenkins and Talbot the agreed-upon story about Becky, and Ginny had spirited her away to the nursery. There weren't many appropriately sized clothes in the attic, so Ginny was tasked with procuring whatever was necessary and more clothes for Melly.

After changing their clothes, Wolf back into his earl's wardrobe and Tabitha into a more appropriate day dress, they reconvened in the parlour. Tabitha had arrived with a stack of paper squares and some pens. Wolf looked at it all inquisitively, and Tabitha answered the silent question, "When I was in the schoolroom and was trying to understand a challenging problem that my governess had set me, she always suggested that I write each part of the problem out on a square of paper and then set them in front of me to look for patterns. So, that is what we're going to do."

They then spent thirty minutes writing out everything they had learned or even guessed about the duke's murder. They laid them all out in front of them on the tea table. Then, as Tabitha read them out, they began to move and group them. They also then started writing down the questions they didn't yet have answers to.

"So this is what we know: someone in the duke's house tipped off Mickey D about a diamond necklace that would only be a prime target for theft for a couple of days. Question number one, how did the boot boy find out this information? We also know that at some point on the evening of the theft, someone killed the duke with a candelabra while he sat in his study.

"As of this point, the police do not have the burglar in custody, but Mickey D worries that if they follow the trail to his gang, they will assume that the same person did the murder and burglary. Mickey believes that his gang member did not kill the duke and didn't even realise he was in the room when he opened the safe. So, my next assumption is, if Mickey's guy didn't kill the duke, he must have already been dead when the theft happened, or surely he would have gotten up and tried to stop it."

Wolf agreed with these facts and assumptions. Tabitha continued, "Therefore, question two, when was the duke killed? There was a window between the end of dinner and the time of the theft. Who could have entered his study during that time?

"Then, the second grouping: the duke himself. What do we know? We have good reason to believe that he had an unnatural taste for very young girls. We also know that over the last few years, Mrs Hutchins has been recruiting young girls for a brothel. Furthermore, we know the duke purchased a house in a neighbourhood we would not expect to interest him. Third question: did the duke own a brothel to indulge other men with his unnatural tastes?"

Tabitha hesitated after asking this question and added, "I think that we should have a categorisation of 'if then'". Wolf raised his eyebrows, questioning her comment. She elaborated, "Well, we don't know that the duke is behind the brothel; we only guess that he may be. However, if he is, we have a new question of why this might be the motive for killing him."

Wolf laughed, "My dear Lady Pembroke, it is a great shame that women cannot enter the legal profession or most professions. I would gladly hire you to advocate for me. Your logic is impeccable."

Tabitha blushed. She had always enjoyed logic puzzles, and her indulgent governess had happily tried to work them into their studies. "So, I'm going to put a mark next to any 'if then' question. What else do we have?"

"Well," Wolf answered, "there is your observation that the duke's widow didn't seem to as distraught as one might expect."

"Yes," answered Tabitha, "but as I know all too well, that may indicate nothing more than a cruel husband. However, you're correct, this is not the point at which we draw conclusions, it's the point at which we lay out what we know. And there seem to be clear indications that he was not a good husband."

"Let's not forget Ginny's observation, that the maid Annie got visibly uncomfortable when the subject arose of the perfect storm of coincidences that enabled the theft to happen so easily. So, another question is, what is Annie's relationship to Mickey D?"

They laid out all the squares and stared at them for a while. Finally, Wolf said reluctantly, I believe we have to show this to Mickey D and put some of our questions to him. I would prefer not to have him darken this door again, but it's likely the best way. I will send Rat with a note asking him to come after dinner." Tabitha was about to protest but then thought better of it. Her recent addition of yet another waif and stray to the household in the form of Becky, made Tabitha consider whether it was the best time to question Rat's duties.

They left their pieces of paper where they were and went in to dinner. Over poached halibut followed by roast quail, Tabitha outlined her plans to educate the three children she had recently taken under her wing. "I don't think that anyone is at the point of needing the educational rigour that a governess will bring. I was taught to read by my nanny, and I think that if we can find a sufficiently well-educated woman, she will suffice for now."

Wolf was hesitant to start another argument over the children with Tabitha. Still, he couldn't hold back his questions, "Melody is one thing. She's a toddler and will never remember anything other than this nursery in a few years. But we've already created an awkward situation for the entire household staff with Rat. He's a lower servant and sleeps in the carriage house, but he spends time in the nursery and is now going to be singled out to learn how to read. What about the other servants? Can the maids all read? Why are we singling him out?

"And now we're adding Becky into the household," he continued. "And yes," he held up a hand in anticipation of her objections, "I realise that what happened to Becky is appalling and that she is still a child. And no, I don't have a good alternative for what should be done with her. But the reality is the child was a prostitute for more than three years. I'm not sure she counts as an innocent at this point."

At this last statement, Tabitha put down her wine glass and gave Wolf a look that very much reminded Wolf of the look his nanny used to give him when uncovering one of his many transgressions as a boy. "The child has been abused in the most appalling of ways. No guilt or shame is attached to her; I refuse to accept otherwise.

"However," Tabitha continued, "you do make an excellent point. Rat and Becky will be part of the household staff, yet I am singling them out for an education. That is unfair to the other staff and will likely cause resentment towards the children. My solution is to offer classes to anyone in the household staff who doesn't know how to read and wishes to learn."

Wolf slapped his hand against his forehead, "That was hardly the remedy I was proposing."

"Yet, it is the obvious and fair one. So perhaps a nanny is not the answer. I need to find a tutor who is prepared to work with anyone on the staff who is willing. This will not be mandatory, but if someone wishes to improve themselves, I will insist they be given an hour off multiple times a week. I will instruct Talbot to place an advertisement for a tutor tomorrow."

Wolf sighed inwardly, aware that any outward signs of disapproval wouldn't be welcome. He had no idea where this was all going to lead. Being accused of running a radical household was the least of his concerns. But was this the end of it? Three stray children and the entire servant body learning to read and write? What other ideas might Tabitha get into her head? He was definitely a Tory as opposed to a Whig, and his new status and the wealth that came with it did not sit easily with him. Wolf had considered how he might use some of that wealth and power to improve the lives of others. But, when he had thought about it, it had been more like endowing an orphanage rather than turning his home into one.

After dinner, they returned to the parlour, picked up novels, and read. One thing Tabitha had learned during her logic lessons as a child was that there was value in stepping back from a problem for a while and focusing on other things.

They had been sitting in companionable silence for a while when the door opened, and unannounced, yet again, Mickey D ambled in.

"Wolf, your ladyship. Nice to see you again." He gestured at the brandy that Wolf had poured for Tabitha and himself, and Wolf decided not to antagonise the man at this point and stood up to pour another. The visitor took the offered brandy and settled in an armchair beside Tabitha's. He gestured to the pieces of paper on the table before them, "What do we have here?"

Tabitha answered, "These are all the pieces of information we've gathered so far. And any questions that the information has thrown up. We'd like to ask you about some of them."

"Ask away, lass."

Wolf continued, "We want to understand more about how you came to have a lad installed in the duke's home."

"As I mentioned, I'm always looking for opportunities to get some of my people embedded in the big houses. A boot boy is in a perfect position; no one talks to or pays him any heed. He can overhear conversations without anyone noticing him. It's always a great starting position for a young lad keen to impress me.

"And how did you hear of an open position in the duke's household?" Tabitha asked.

"Me niece works in the household as a lady's maid." At this, Tabitha and Wolf exchanged glances but said nothing. "She's not my greatest fan, to say the least. I've wanted to get someone in that household for a long time. My first thought was that the lass would work for me, but her mother put paid to that idea. And the girl is as loyal as the day is long to that duchess of hers, and so I've long since stopped hoping anything helpful would come out of that connection.

"However, as luck would have it, this maid happened to be back home in the neighbourhood on her afternoon off and was overheard saying they needed a boot boy. I took advantage of what she'd said and sent my lad over."

"Did the maid not realise he was one of your plants?" Wolf asked.

"Oh aye, she was very suspicious. Sent her ma over to give me a good tongue lashing and swear me off causing any trouble for her Annie." Tabitha and Wolf traded even more loaded looks at this confirmation of the maid in question. "And she made it quite clear to the lad that she would be watching him. Course, she didn't know he was one of me lads, for certain. She had her suspicions, though."

Wolf sat back in his armchair, cradling his brandy in his hands, then said, "So let me understand this - Tabitha, can you write up notes for these points, please - Annie had a strong suspicion that this new boot boy was spying on the household for you? And yet, she never pointed the finger at you after the robbery?"

"Annie's many things, but she's no snitch. However much loyalty she has to that high and mighty duchess, we're her people at the end of the day. Her ma made clear it's why Annie has never wanted my people in that house; she hasn't wanted to be in a situation caught between her lady and putting down one of her own."

"Which you had no respect for, given that you put the boy there and then committed the burglary," Tabitha pointed out.

"I had enough respect that I wouldn't use the lad to do any run-of-the-mill click on that house. But this diamond necklace was something else."

"Another question," Wolf asked. "How long after your lad was in place did he overhear about the diamonds?"

"That was the lucky part. He'd hardly been there two weeks when his ma came running to me with the news. "

"Hmm, that was lucky, wasn't it? And he sent word that the butler would be away for a night, which emboldened you further and ensured which night you would choose for the theft."

"That about sums it up."

"What does Bruiser have to say about where the police are in their investigations?" Wolf asked.

"They've asked around all the usual fences that they know about. But I'm not stupid. I'm sitting on that necklace for now. I don't need to do anything to help lead them to Seamus. I'll sit on it for as long as I need to. I don't even want to risk breaking the necklace up and trying to shift some of the diamonds overseas. You find out who killed the toff first."

"I have one more thing to ask you about, the duke," Wolf said.

"What about him?" Mickey asked.

"We've heard rumours of his unnatural appetites."

"I don't bother myself with what you toffs get up to amongst yourselves," Mickey answered.

"But that's not all we've heard. There are rumours of very young girls, as young as 8, being sold by their families to Mrs Hutchins. We believe she may have delivered them to a brothel that the Duke of Somerset, the dead man, may have owned."

Mickey D looked genuinely shocked at this. "This is the first I've heard of it. I'm many things, but I don't dabble in whores, and certainly not children. If Old Ma Hutchins was involved in such a thing, she'll have to answer to me, don't you worry."

There wasn't much more to discuss, and he left soon after. Tabitha had made more fact and question sheets. "Question: was Annie's discomfort over the "coincidence of the butler being away" merely guilt that she knew that the boot boy had likely relayed that information to her family who had stolen the diamonds?"

"That certainly seems likely," Wolf observed. "Despite her best efforts, Mickey D had not only planted a mole in the household but, as far as she knew, he'd pulled off a theft that resulted in the duke's death."

Tabitha and Wolf again stared at the pieces of paper before them. "You know," Tabitha observed, "this is a useful way to think about this case, but we can't leave pieces of paper lying around the parlour. It will drive Mrs Jenkins to distraction. If only we could somehow stick them to a board in some way.

"I have an idea. Wait here a moment." Tabitha left the parlour and went to her bedroom, where she knew Ginny would be getting her nightclothes ready.

"Ginny, I want you to collect up all my small hatpins. Oh, and we need a bedsheet and your sewing skills." Ginny was intrigued, but a good servant didn't ask questions. She collected the requested items and took her sewing basket to the parlour. There she found Wolf and Talbot busy taking a hideous landscape painting off the wall. She glanced at her mistress, who explained, "I want you to sew the bedsheet around this picture frame, very taut so that we can pin pieces of paper on it using the hat pins."

Ginny now understood what she was doing, even if she didn't understand why. She knew that her ladyship would need some new hatpins if most of the ones she currently owned were to be used on this craft project. As with most ladies' maids, she was a fast sewer. Her almost invisible stitches quickly attached the bedsheet around the painting frame. Adding to Ginny's general confusion, once she had finished her handiwork, his lordship and the butler then hung the frame back up on the wall, except now the painting was covered by the taut bedding. Her mistress seemed ecstatic about this effect and started taking pieces of paper she had laid on the table in front of her and using the hat pins to attach them to the fabric.

"Oh look," Tabitha exclaimed, "this is just perfect!"

"Excuse me asking, m'lady, but perfect for what?" Ginny asked in bemusement.

"Come closer, Ginny, and take a look." Ginny moved over to where the painting hung and saw that each small square of writing paper had something about the burglary and the duke's murder written on it. Including the information she had found out from her tea with Annie. Ginny couldn't remember when she'd felt so proud. Clearly, her deductions had been deemed good enough to make it onto whatever crime-solving contraption this was.

Tabitha pointed at one of the pieces of paper now pinned to the board, then removed the pin and moved the paper to be near another group. "See! As we uncover more information and things seem more relevant to one discovery than another, we can move them over."

"You know what might help, m'lady," Ginny said, a little worried that she was speaking out of turn, "if I got some of my yarn and we used it to connect some of these pieces of paper. It could be pinned and moved. And instead of using all your hatpins, why don't you use some pins from my pin cushion?"

"Ginny, both wonderful ideas. Go and get your yarn now, and while you're gone, I'll swap the hatpins for your pins." Ginny left the room and returned a few minutes later with brightly coloured yarn. They quickly cut multiple lengths, and Tabitha used the strands to show the connections between the various pieces of paper. When she finished, she stepped back to admire her handiwork.

"From now on, as we discover anything, we'll write it on a new square of paper and pin it to the board. Ginny, can you make sure to add plenty of spare pins to the edge and cut extra lengths of yarn, please."

Wolf stood admiring their handiwork. "How much easier might all my work as a thief-taker have been if I'd been investigating using a board like this?" Tabitha positively glowed at this praise. She had always excelled in the schoolroom, but ever since becoming a debutante and a wife, it had felt like her brains were the least important part of who she was. It felt good to be contributing intellectually to something. And even better to have that contribution be valuable and appreciated. However, it wasn't lost on Tabitha that this board highlighted that they were no nearer to solving this case.

"Having it all laid out in front of us shows that there are many different threads to pursue, and we haven't been able to follow any of them fully."

"That's true. But it also shows our progress and the questions we need answering."

"Exactly!" Tabitha exclaimed. "Which is why you need to entertain my next suggestion, no matter your initial reaction."

Wolf narrowed his eyes, "What is your suggestion?"

"We need a way to get more information about the duke, the crowd he ran with, and who might be possible partners or clients in his nefarious venture. There's no better way to gather gossip than a ball; as luck would have it, you have been invited to one the night after next. I know you did not intend to attend, but I believe you should reconsider." Wolf was about to answer, but she continued, "Honestly, even if we weren't investigating this case, I'd advise you to attend. You cannot avoid society forever. These are the people that you need to know and they are intensely curious about you."

"I'm not attending a ball by myself. I'll only go if you accompany me."

"Wolf, you know why I haven't been invited and would not be welcome. And in addition, I'm supposed to be in mourning still. It would be quite unseemly for me to attend and be on the new earl's arm!"

Wolf smiled, "But isn't it a masked ball? You can be my mysterious companion." He knew that she could have no answer for that.

In response, Tabitha turned to her maid, "Ginny, go through my ballgowns and see which you can more easily alter to be less...well, more...I'm not sure what I want them to be," she admitted.

"A little less Lady Pembroke and a little more Lady Chalmers?" Ginny asked cheekily. Tabitha blushed but nodded. "I will get right to that first thing in the morning, m'lady."

CHAPTER 19

The next day was a slow one for progress in their investigation, but busy, nonetheless. At Tabitha's insistence, Wolf already had evening clothes, but she insisted that he needed something a little grander for a masked ball and had him try on some of Jonathan's fancy waistcoats. These then needed to be taken in a little. Tabitha wasn't sure why she had kept any of his clothes after his death, but now she was glad she had.

It hadn't taken Ginny long to choose which ballgown to modify; while Tabitha had owned quite a selection during her marriage to Jonathan, as with the rest of her wardrobe, most were too dull and conservative. However, there was one dress from when they were first married. It was a little out of fashion, but from early enough in the relationship that Jonathan hadn't totally brought down his iron fist to crush Tabitha's spirits. The dress was an iridescent blue, a wonderful complement to her chestnut hair. The dress also showed a little decolletage which meant less work for Ginny to make it slightly more risqué.

Ginny was pleasantly surprised to find that Becky had a very neat stitch and could help her with some of the less delicate alterations. Tabitha had asked Ginny to gain Becky's trust and to see if the girl was willing to share any other details about her time in the duke's brothel (or what they assumed was his brothel.)

Initially, Becky had been very quiet and nervous. But as they sat and sewed together, Ginny would start singing songs her mother had taught her when she was a child, and Becky was joining in before long. Becky had grown up in and around

Ginny's old neighbourhood, so they probably knew some of the same people. But Ginny didn't want to risk upsetting the young girl by discussing her family and prior life. It was more important to ease her into talking about what had happened to her since she had been sold to Mrs Hutchins.

Becky had a lovely singing voice, and joining in with the songs encouraged her to talk. Ginny commented, "Your sewing is very good. Very small, even stitches."

"I was responsible for a lot of the alterations," she paused, "there. The girls outgrew clothes quickly, and I was always needing to take down a hem and let out a waistband. My ma had taken in sewing, and so I learned at her knee." She paused again, "Of course, he didn't want us to grow too quickly, so we weren't fed much. I was always hungry. But even so, the girls did grow."

Ginny saw her opening and asked gently, "Who is the 'he' you mentioned?"

At first, she thought that the child wasn't going to answer. She stared down at the sewing she was working on and said nothing for a full minute or two. Finally, she said, "He was the main one. When a new girl arrived, he was always the first with her. I heard him say once that he took the risks and deserved the maidenhead." Ginny's stomach curdled, and she wasn't sure how much more she could listen to. But then she realised that if this poor child had to live through these tortures, the least she could do was provide a sympathetic shoulder to cry on. And if that meant hearing about unspeakable horrors, that is what she would do.

"Some of the men just wanted to play with the girls. Brush their hair, maybe kiss them. Maybe just have a girl touch them. Nothing else. Sometimes they liked to watch us play with dolls together. One man came at least once a week and liked to have two or three girls play at a doll's tea party. He wanted us to pretend that he wasn't there while we played. It was hard to pretend to be playing with my friends. But it was better than what some other men wanted, so we did our best. While we played, he would pull down his breeches…", the girl faltered.

Ginny put a hand on her shoulder and said, "Aye lass, no need to go on. I have an idea what he did. But what of the main man? Is that all he wanted you to do?"

At this, Ginny could see tears forming in the child's eyes and felt awful for pushing her. But she also knew that the more they understood, the more likely they could stop what was happening to the other girls. Becky wiped some tears that had started to fall and said, "He was gentle enough to begin with. He didn't like screaming, so they always gave the girl something to drink that made her not mind as much." Ginny assumed it was something laced with some laudanum. Not enough to put the child to sleep, but enough to make them more compliant.

"Then he would take all the clothes off the girl, and then…I'm sorry miss, I just can't."

"No matter child. No need to relive the horror of what he did. But what made him the main man?"

"Well, the other men came and went, but he was there most evenings, at least for a while. It seemed like it was his house. And he told Mrs Smith what to do. He was the only person she feared."

"Who was Mrs Smith?" Ginny asked. Though she assumed she was a cross between a madam and a matron. As Becky described the woman, Ginny could tell that her guess had been correct. She sounded like a cruel and heartless woman. But then, who else could stand by and watch children abused like that?

"Becky, I know this is all hard to talk about, and you're being very brave, but is there anything else you can tell me about this main man?"

"Well, Mrs Smith called him m'lord or his lordship. And we sometimes had gatherings in the drawing room where a group of the customers would drink, and all the girls would have to entertain them. When that happened, I heard the men call him Somerset."

Ginny's eyes lit up when she heard that. It was the first confirmation that the duke had been involved in running this brothel and had these unnatural appetites. She stopped pressing

Becky after that and instead started telling her stories of her childhood in Ireland.

When the alterations were finished, Ginny sent Becky into the nursery to help Mary with Melody. At this point, the girl's tasks were undefined and seemed totally within Ginny's discretion. Ginny put her sewing basket away, hung the dress up, and hurried down to find her mistress. Unable to find her in the sitting or drawing rooms, she timidly knocked on the study door. She entered to find Wolf and Tabitha hunched over some documents on his desk.

"Ah, Ginny. How is the girl doing?" Wolf asked genially.

"Well m'lord, she's a hard worker and a good enough seamstress that I'll easily find work she can help me with. And she's good with little Melody, so that helps Mary. But, well," she hesitated. "Well, she told me some things. Some of them so terrible I can't repeat them. But everything you imagined is true and worse. They drugged those little girls so they wouldn't scream and put up a fight."

Tabitha covered her mouth with her hand in horror but didn't say anything to interrupt her maid, who continued, "So then she started talking about the main man. The one who owned the house and ran everything. Everyone called him m'lord and when other men were there, they called him Somerset," Ginny finished with a dramatic flourish. Well aware that she had just provided a key piece of information.

"Ginny," Wolf exclaimed, jumping to his feet, "great work! I'm sure it wasn't easy to ask all those questions, but you've just provided the first definitive evidence of what the Duke of Somerset was up to."

Tabitha stood up and started moving towards the door. "Great work Ginny. Let's go and put a note on the board immediately." She walked towards the parlour, and Wolf and Ginny followed. She took down the piece of paper that asked the question: did the duke own a brothel to indulge other men with his unnatural taste and put a large checkmark and capitalised YES beside it.

Tabitha spent the rest of that day and the next catching up

on what she had neglected due to the investigation. Her priority was spending more time with Melly in the nursery. Tabitha was happy to see how well the child had settled. She was a bright little girl. Tabitha thanked Mary for doing an excellent job with her.

"Mary, this may seem an unusual question, but what else do Melody and the nursery need? You see, I was the youngest child and of course unable to have a child with the late earl. So, I find myself somewhat out of my depths as to the needs of a young child." Noticing that Mary was hesitant to speak up, she continued, "I will instruct Mrs Jenkins that you are free to order whatever you feel you need; toys, clothes, books, anything. You know far more about looking after children than I do, and I value your opinion and guidance."

Mary curtseyed and expressed her gratitude for this show of faith in her. Tabitha paused momentarily, unsure how best to phrase her next statement. "Mary, regarding Becky, I'm sure Mrs Jenkins has told you how I came upon her." Mary nodded, "What may not have been communicated is that I found Becky in dire circumstances. I haven't gone into details with the staff, and I trust you to be discreet. However, she will be spending some of her time in the nursery and hopefully can even help with Melody." She paused again, unsure what she was trying to say. "Mary, you seem to be a very kind and gentle girl. Certainly, I wouldn't have given you the role of caring for Melody if I didn't believe so. I would like you to be particularly kind and gentle with Becky."

"Of course, m'lady," Mary replied, "I understand." Tabitha thought the girl didn't fully understand the importance of the nursery being a safe haven for Becky.

Talbot had placed an advertisement for a tutor. Tabitha hadn't expected this to reap immediate returns, so she was pleasantly surprised when he informed her that he had a young man interested in the position who could come that afternoon if it worked for her ladyship. Keen to embark on her education project for Rat, Becky and whomever in her staff had interest,

Tabitha suggested that a note be sent to the young man asking him to come after lunch.

Wolf had spent his time trying to dig deeper into the ownership and management of the duke's suspected brothel. Now they had first-hand confirmation of his involvement in the enterprise, Wolf wanted to confirm his suspicion about the use of the unusual property purchase. He and Tabitha had decided that, regardless of whether it had anything to do with the duke's death, if they could confirm the activities, they would approach the new duke with the information in the hope that he would be appalled and quickly close the establishment down.

With a certain hesitance, Wolf had asked Tabitha over dinner the night before as they had discussed this, "Can we be certain that the new Duke of Somerset doesn't share his father's appetites?"

Tabitha assured him, "Anthony is nothing like his father in any way. Even before we discovered what the duke was, I knew him as a harsh man and a harsher father. As I told you, Anthony and I were childhood friends, and I saw first-hand his fear of his father."

"Fear doesn't mean he hasn't grown to share his father's predilections," Wolf pointed out.

"I have not spent much time with Anthony since we were grown. However, I would bet everything I own that he has not grown to be such a man. I don't believe that a boy as kind and gentle as he was as a younger man could mature into the kind of monster that his father was. I do not doubt that the new duke will be appalled to hear about his father's activities."

Wolf speared another roasted potato and replied, "Then let me gather all the evidence I can and then we will go and see him." Tabitha was thrilled to hear the 'we' again.

Wolf had sent Rat to watch the Holborn house for the evening. He reported the following morning that, over a few hours, he had seen a few well-dressed men entering and not leaving for at least a couple of hours.

"We need to get in that house, Rat," Wolf instructed when

Tabitha left the room.

Rat grinned. Wolf hadn't fully disclosed to Tabitha all the ways Rat had assisted him in his thief-taking capacity. He had assumed that she wouldn't take kindly to his use of the boy to break into buildings on occasion. But the boy was small, agile and quick-witted. He could enter through a small kitchen window and pad noiselessly through a house. And, as Rat had guessed, this was precisely what Wolf had in mind now.

"Her ladyship and I will be going to the ball tonight. I suspect that many of the patrons of the supposed brothel will also be in attendance, so it should be a quiet and early night. Take Bear with you, just in case there is any trouble. When the house seems to be abed for the night, I want you to enter, if you can, and see what you can find out. If you can bring any hard evidence, all the better, but even confirmation of the use of the house would be of help." Of course, Wolf did not tell Tabitha about Rat's errand. If the lad were successful, he would confess if he had to. But for now, he didn't want to argue with her just before their first major social outing.

The potential tutor, Mr James, had arrived after lunch. He seemed like an appropriately bookish young man. His clothes were well made but worn and spoke of a young man from a once prosperous family which had fallen on hard times. And indeed, this was the story that he told. Tabitha explained her plan to him. She had been worried that he would balk, both at the thought of teaching the servants, and at the elementary level of education that Melly and Rat needed. But Tabitha needn't have worried. Theodore James was desperate for a job, any job. Tabitha was prepared to pay a very generous salary and he would have been happy to train a dog to sit for a steady pay. Mr James had no ego around his Cambridge education being used to teach a 4-year-old and a bunch of illiterate servants how to read and write.

CHAPTER 20

It felt like a long time since Tabitha had dressed for a ball. Of course, during her debutante season, the preparation had been heightened with the anticipation of meeting eligible bachelors. After her marriage to Jonathan, social events such as balls had taken on a new pressure: showing Jonathan to as much advantage as possible. He had not spared any expense on her ballgowns or jewellery. He expected her to be dripping in diamonds, rubies, and sapphires. She announced to the world that he was a man of great wealth.

Only a few weeks after their marriage, when Tabitha was beginning to realise her mistake, Jonathan had been quite explicit in his expectations; she was to dress in the height of fashion but modestly. Her behaviour should be beyond reproach; there would be no flirting, no batting of eyelashes. He wanted his wife to be considered his finest jewel, but there should be no doubt in anyone's mind of her utter devotion and faithfulness. She should be demure and never forward in conversation. She would refuse to dance with anyone but Jonathan. He would dance with her for the first two dances and then the last. Besides that, she would either be by his side or his mother's.

After the first ball they had attended as a married couple, Tabitha reflected that she had never realised how dull a ball could be. She had changed from a young woman who couldn't wait for the next invitation to a ball to one who dreaded it.

This ball was different; she was no longer an ingenue giggling with the other young debutantes, eager to fill her dance card. But she also wouldn't be in terror of straying from Jonathan's severe rules and expectations and anticipating being punished at home after the ball if she seemed to fall short in any way. She was free to dress and behave as she saw fit. Of course, there was the small matter of her exile from society. What would happen if anyone recognised her, despite her mask? In truth, she didn't care. The new Earl of Pembroke was free to escort anyone he wished, and, besides the censure of people she neither liked and whose approval didn't matter to her, there was no reason for it not to be Tabitha. With that realisation, she felt a lightness that she hadn't for a long time and excitement at the prospect of wearing a beautiful ballgown and dancing with Wolf.

Dancing with Wolf. Now there was a thought. She assumed, and hoped, that dancing lessons had been part of his education as a gentleman. But, until this point, she hadn't considered what it might be like to dance with him. She remembered the thrill of dancing with a handsome young man before she was married. Even dancing with Jonathan had been exciting before their marriage. Of course, then, he had been charming and flirtatious. Her mandatory dances with him post-wedding had been quite a different matter. He had held her stiffly, barely spoke to her, and then deposited her back at her appointed post.

As she luxuriated in her rose-scented bath, Tabitha allowed herself to daydream and imagine what it might be like to be whirled around a ballroom by a man such as Wolf. He was tall and handsome. But more importantly, he was kind, and she sensed a real gentleness, despite the strength evident in his muscular forearms and broad shoulders. She thought of what it would be like to be in the arms of a man who respected her. She reminded herself that she had no romantic illusions about her relationship with Wolf but believed they had become friends somewhere along the way; friends and partners. Equal partners, she told herself. Tabitha admitted that she was excited to dance with such a man.

Tabitha might have been surprised that Wolf was in his bath, reflecting similarly. He had been unable to stop thinking of Tabitha's turn as Lady Chalmers. Ever since then, he had viewed her differently. He was still impressed with her strength and intelligence, to say nothing of her compassion and integrity. But now, those character assets were combined inextricably with her more physical assets; the luscious curves so well hidden by her mourning clothes but very evident in her Lady Chalmer's outfit. He hoped her beautiful hair would not be pulled back in its usual austere style tonight. And those eyes, those lovely, bright, intelligent eyes.

Wolf felt a little ashamed that he was thinking about Tabitha inappropriately, so he told himself that he wasn't thinking about Tabitha; he was thinking of Lady Chalmers. And it would be Lady Chalmers he held in his arms and danced with at the ball. Something to which he was very much looking forward.

Tabitha had communicated with Ginny, if somewhat hesitantly, that she wished her hair and makeup to be more Lady Chalmers than Lady Pembroke, at least to a point. Ginny had relished the chance to make her already beautiful mistress even more lovely. She had used a little powder and just a hint of rouge and lip salve, far less than Lady Chalmers had worn but more than Tabitha had ever worn. They had decided not to wear any of the large, gaudy showpieces with which Jonathan had insisted she accessorise herself. Instead, she opted for a simple garnet necklace with an elegant setting. The garnet was the perfect colour to complement her dress.

With her hair finished and jewellery in place, she looked at her reflection in the mirror and could only imagine how much Jonathan would have hated it. While her neckline was far from scandalous, it plunged far lower than anything he would have allowed his wife to wear. The garnet pendant drew the eye down to her milky bosoms swelling above the neckline of the ballgown. Ginny had done wonders with her hair, piling it up in a style that was both formal enough for a ball but with a softness to the curl that spoke of a woman who was still young and vibrant.

Tabitha found Wolf waiting for her in the drawing room. The look on his face told her everything about how she looked, but it was gratifying to have him add, "Lady Pembroke, you look beautiful." Tabitha noted how handsome and every inch the earl Wolf looked in his evening clothes. While his hair was as long as ever, he had at least managed to tame it, and he'd shaved! She noted that evening clothes showed off his fine muscular form exceptionally well. And then she was appalled that she'd even thought such a thing.

They collected their outerwear and masks, left the house, and entered the carriage. It occurred to Tabitha that, even with a mask, given the Pemberton crest on the carriage and Wolf's scandalously unruly hair, it was likely that he wouldn't be incognito for long. And, while there might be some initial speculation as to who the woman was on his arm, she didn't expect it to be long until tongues were wagging about her. She was sure that their unusual living arrangement had already caused wild stories to circulate, and by leaving her half-mourning and arriving at a ball on his arm, she was throwing fuel on the fire. But she found that she did not care a whit what was said about her. And she strongly suspected that Wolf cared even less about his reputation. But, to minimise the attention they might attract, Tabitha suggested they plan their arrival to be late enough to attract less notice.

As Tabitha stepped out of the carriage, she could hear the strains of music drifting through the air. The ball was at the palatial Mayfair residence of the Duke of Kensington. The event promised to be lavish, attended by all the best people in society. Which was exactly what Tabitha and Wolf were counting on.

The sounds of music and laughter filled the ballroom. The guests, decked out in their finest attire, waltzed around the room when not sipping champagne. At the centre of the ballroom was a magnificent crystal chandelier, which cast a warm glow over the proceedings. Elegant tapestries adorned the walls, and the floors gleamed underfoot. Wolf took a glass of champagne for each of them from a passing footman, and they joined the throng of guests, feeling the buzz of excitement in the air.

Wolf and Tabitha had decided to tour the various reception

rooms before deciding on their final plan of action. Off the main ballroom was a smaller room with tables heaped with an array of delicious foods, from platters of oysters to beautifully roasted meats and decadent desserts. People were standing in clusters nibbling on the food. Another room had a billiard table and a smoking room used by various well-dressed gentlemen.

So far, they hadn't spoken to anyone, waiting until they formed a better idea of which conversations they wanted to pursue and with whom. Wolf suggested that they dance; with the orchestra playing loudly, the dance floor was probably the place they could most easily have a private conversation without the risk of being overheard. Wolf led Tabitha onto the dance floor, sweeping her into a waltz.

As Tabitha waltzed with Wolf, she was surprised to feel a flutter in her chest. She had met Wolf just a few weeks ago, and while acknowledging that he was a handsome man, she had so far believed herself to feel nothing more for him than a cool, emotionally detached acquaintance. But as they danced together, she found herself drawn to him in a way she couldn't explain. His kind eyes and easy laugh made her feel at ease, and she wanted the dance to continue all night. Moving gracefully across the dance floor, Tabitha realised Wolf was more than just another handsome, titled and wealthy man. He was kind, caring and compassionate. And he was a man who took her seriously. So perhaps she was starting to feel something more for him than mere friendship. The thought filled her with excitement and trepidation, and she wasn't sure what to do with these new feelings. But for now, as they danced together, Tabitha allowed herself simply to enjoy the moment as Wolf spun her around the room.

For the first few minutes of the dance, it felt as if Wolf was also carried away by the moment and the music. He stared down into her eyes, and Tabitha met his look candidly. She believed that, in that moment, she saw her new feelings of attraction reflected in his eyes. He bent his head to whisper in her ear, and for a moment, she thought he was going to whisper words of love, and she surprised herself with her eager anticipation. Then he said, "How do you think we should start identifying likely suspects amongst the guests?"

Tabitha tried not to be disappointed and told him she had no more idea than he did. But then, as luck would have it, she saw the dowager countess holding court at the edge of the ballroom as they swept around the room. The older Lady Pembroke was sitting with a gaggle of cronies around her, probably judging and criticising the people walking by. Tabitha was sure that soon she would be the target of a lot of that censure if she hadn't been already. She answered Wolf, "I see the dowager countess over there. No one knows more about what is going on in society than she somehow manages to. I believe that she could steer you towards the duke's circle of acquaintances."

"Steer me?" Wolf asked. "I thought we were investigating together."

"And, so we are. But she has no reason to help me and is likely too consumed with outrage at my appearance here tonight to draw breath long enough to say anything else. But, as we know, you have charmed her." Wolf acknowledged this last argument. She continued, "It is also true that I would have no good reason for asking such a question."

"But I do?" Wolf said sceptically.

"Indeed, you do. You are still finding your way through society and the Pemberton business dealings. You will simply tell her that you found some records that indicate that Jonathan was contemplating a business deal with the Duke of Somerset and some associates. Your man of business has been unable to uncover anything more concrete, and you're hoping to make some discrete enquiries of your own tonight."

"That's actually a very good excuse and backstory if we find any of these so-called friends and associates," Wolf admitted as Tabitha blushed. "When this waltz is over, I will see you to the refreshment table and then go and pay my respects, which I'm assuming I should have done sooner rather than later anyway." Tabitha acknowledged the truth of that assumption. With this plan in place, she could enjoy the rest of the waltz. Wolf was a surprisingly good dancer, and Tabitha relaxed into her pleasure in whirling around the ballroom in his arms.

Wolf's feelings were remarkably similar to Tabitha's during the dance. The earldom had felt awkward and unnatural to him over the weeks since he'd inherited it. Still, that evening, walking into a duke's ballroom with a beautiful, intelligent, sophisticated countess on his arm, he felt every inch a noble for the first time. Tabitha made him stand taller, try harder, and want to be a better man. When he first received the news of his new status, he'd told himself there was no difference between Wolf the thief-taker and Wolf, the earl, just a fancier title and a nicer home. But now, for the first time, he glimpsed all that Wolf, the Earl of Pembroke, might be if he had the right countess by his side.

CHAPTER 21

Wolf accompanied Tabitha to the refreshment table and left her there, choosing between various delectable, sweet treats. There were tables scattered around the room, and she planned to position herself with a good view of the comings and goings in the room and observe while she ate.

Meanwhile, Wolf braced himself and approached the dowager. She saw him coming and struck a pose both regal and coyly flirtatious. Not for the first time, Wolf wondered how much her flirting with him was merely a game with her and how much he needed to be worried. She extended her hand as he drew near her chair, which he duly took and kissed. "Jeremy, you are a naughty, naughty boy!" she exclaimed. "How long have you been here before deigning to come over and see me?"

Wolf had never been at ease with this kind of drawing room banter but realised that the expectation was that he would say something charming even if untrue, "You tease me, your ladyship, for I'm sure you know that, if the choice had been mine alone, then yours would have been the first hand I would have kissed."

The dowager smiled benevolently at this charming flattery, and the ladies around her tittered appreciatively. Even if Wolf was unsure how to play this game, the circle of older women into whose lair he had stumbled had often played out some version of this scene. Everyone knew the part that each was to play. The dowager continued, "Pray tell me, Lord Pembroke, Jeremy," she added, looking at him from under her lashes as if she were the most demure of debutantes, "how was the choice not yours? I believe I saw you waltzing around the room with a statuesque beauty. Are you claiming that this was forced upon you?"

Wolf had no good answer to this and wasn't even sure what nonsense he was expected to return the rally with next. So, instead, he tried to turn the conversation slightly, "And how could one not notice you, no matter the charms of a dance partner? You look particularly beautiful tonight. If you are not careful, you will outshine all the debutantes here and steal the hearts of their beaus away." He could tell from the smug look on the dowager's face that this was an excellent reply. She smiled graciously while giving her circle of friends a look that claimed victory.

"Lady Pembroke," Wolf continued, hoping to press his advantage, "would it be possible for me to get you some refreshments and talk with you a little more privately?" Even as he said these words, Wolf had the awful realisation that the dowager and her friends could misconstrue his request. And if the look the dowager was giving him was any indication, she certainly wanted the ladies to construe it as such.

"Why Jeremy, you'll make me blush if you continue that way." Wolf was sure that very little could make the dowager blush, but he kept that thought to himself. "However," she continued, "I will allow you to fetch me a fresh glass of champagne, and when you come back, I'm sure these ladies will excuse us so we can have a cosy chat." It was clear that the dowager expected the women surrounding her to be the ones to leave. Indeed, as Wolf wandered off to find a footman with champagne, the ladies started to move away.

When he returned a few minutes later, the dowager had managed to get rid of any other potential rivals for Wolf's attention, and he seated himself next to her to begin his assault. He wasn't sure how to begin, so he determined just to come out and tell the story that Tabitha had suggested and make the request. This would satisfy the dowager on multiple fronts: it would validate her belief that she was at the epicentre of society, knew everything about everyone, and make clear that Wolf knew this fact. It would also put him in her debt, which was always useful.

As it happened, the dowager countess kept a very accurate and extensive mental list of the debts that people in society owed her, at least by her reckoning. She did not call in those debts for trivial matters but squirrelled them away for the day when she might get the best return on her investment.

When Wolf had finished his tale and made his request, she sat deep in thought for a few moments before answering. Wolf noticed that all flirtatiousness was gone from her manner and that she was all business. "I believe I can help you. Perhaps, the most expeditious way to achieve this is for you to give me your arm as we take a turn about the room. I will make some introductions as necessary. Whenever I introduce you as the charming new earl, you will know I'm introducing you to one of Somerset's cronies. Otherwise, just assume that it's someone I couldn't find a polite way to ignore as we pass."

As she finished her champagne and Wolf assumed they were about to stand up, the dowager touched his arm. She said, with a sudden noticeable chill to her tone, "One more thing, Pembroke," Jeremy didn't miss this switch from his given name, "please tell me that the lovely young woman you were twirling around the dance floor before is not my daughter-in-law."

Wolf had no idea what she wanted him to say. The dowager clearly knew that the woman was Tabitha, who herself had predicted that she wouldn't stay anonymous for long. But was the best move for this chess game to acknowledge the fact or try to deny it? He decided that trying to outfox a strategist as wily as the dowager was futile. She was always going to be a few moves ahead of him. Instead, he answered, "Trying to deny it would be pointless to one as eagle-eyed as you. Yes, Lady Pembroke was good enough to accompany me."

"Good enough? Poppycock! It is bad enough that she went into half-mourning after her husband had only been gone a few short months. But she has now even thrown that off for the most outrageously indecorous dress and is attending a ball with another man. I truly don't believe I have words to express how shocking this is." Wolf considered that she had already found plenty of words to express that but kept this thought to himself. She continued, "She may not care about society's censure for herself, but surely she could spare some consideration for how this reflects on me."

Wolf wasn't quite sure how any of this reflected on the dowager. However, he felt compelled to point out that the dowager attended the ball only six months after her son's death. She gave him a quelling look and replied, "When my husband, the late earl, died, I wore black for a full year and stayed in seclusion. I expected nothing less of Tabitha." This didn't answer Wolf's observation, but he wisely decided to let this go. "The girl has just caused one scandal after another. First, it was Jonathan's death, then coming out of full mourning after an outrageously short period. Then, of course, there's the fact that she continues to live in the same house as an unmarried man. And now, she's out dressed like a floozy, parading about on a man's arm, flaunting herself for the world to see!"

Wolf tried not to take offence at the role he was implicitly accused of playing, which filled the dowager with such horror. But he felt compelled to come to Tabitha's defence, "Lady Pembroke, with the greatest possible respect intended towards yourself, my understanding is that society has shunned the countess since her husband's death. I imagine that she has decided that the worst has already happened and that she might as well live her life as she chooses without considering the opinions of people who have already cast her out. How could it get any worse?"

"It could be worse for me!" the dowager exclaimed. "And let's not forget the fickleness of society. If that chit of a girl had just quietly stayed home and showed some appropriate humility, well, it may have all been forgiven and forgotten by now." She then patted Wolf's arm and assured him, "Pray don't concern yourself, dear Jeremy, that I in any way hold you responsible. I realise she had put you in an impossible situation by refusing to move out of Chesterton House." Wolf started to protest, but she continued over him, "You're too much of a gentleman to say otherwise, but the truth is clear to me. And to all of society. In fact. I made sure that this wouldn't in any way reflect poorly on you."

Wolf felt that this conversation was spinning quickly out of control. He wanted to remain in the good graces of the dowager, but he also felt that he needed to defend Tabitha. "Lady Pembroke, I must set the record straight and beg you to believe me when I tell you that the other Lady Pembroke has remained at Chesterton House solely at my request. Lady Pembroke has been gracious enough to remain to help me manage a household that I quite unexpectedly find myself the head of." The look on the dowager's face expressed her utter disbelief at this statement. Nevertheless, Wolf felt compelled to continue his defence, "Lady Pembroke also attended tonight's ball only to oblige me. If there is a fault, then it all lies with me."

Brushing off his refutations of her assured position on Tabitha's outrageous behaviour, the dowager finally stood up. Wolf followed her lead and offered her his arm. "So, Jeremy, let us tour the room, and I can make the appropriate introductions." Recognising a situation beyond his immediate ability to rectify, he held out his arm for the older woman, and they launched forth on their mission.

Tabitha had forgotten how entertaining people-watching could be at a ball. During her marriage, when she had only been allowed three dances and spent the rest of her time mostly in silence by her husband's side, observing the other guests had been the only way to fill the interminable hours until Jonathan decided they could leave. Tabitha's background and education had instilled an initial belief that the aristocratic circles she had been born into were the pinnacle of human society; that the uppermost class was inherently better in every way. But, after her marriage, she observed, most often at these balls, how a thin veneer of manners and sophistication masked behaviour that was no better than the most common guttersnipes.

A ball was the perfect social vehicle for bad behaviour. Loud, noisy and crowded, they were perfect for people inclined to liaisons in dark corners. Given the glances and gestures she observed, Tabitha used to amuse herself by anticipating which illicit couplings might be in the cards. She would watch young rakes disappear into the shadows only moments after merry widows or neglected wives had batted their eyelashes over their fans.

Sitting at a table eating a lemon ice, Tabitha found nothing had changed since she'd been out of society. Why would it? While unmarried young women needed their virtue beyond reproach, married women and widows could lead far freer lives. Of course, expectations were that societal conventions of discretion and good manners still be upheld, and the lineage of the heir and the spare must be beyond dispute. But past that, as long as affairs were constrained to one's social class and no scandal ended in the newspapers, a blind eye would typically be turned, both by the spouse and society. Except in the case of her marriage. She had been under no delusions that Jonathan would accept such behaviour from his wife.

Tabitha was so absorbed in watching a couple flirting outrageously in the corner of the room that she didn't realise that she was no longer alone and that a man had sat beside her. Her immediate assessment of the man was that he somehow managed to have all the regular features associated with a pale, handsome face, a strong jawline, an aquiline nose, and pronounced cheekbones. Yet there was something quite repellent about the man. He had strikingly cold blue eyes and a thin smile that made her shiver, and she just knew that this was a man capable of great evil. Tabitha was also shocked that he had sat down without asking her permission.

"Lady Pembroke, I believe. How good to see you back out in society," he said in a silky tone that held no warmth. There was something familiar about him and that voice, but she couldn't place it.

"I'm sorry, sir, but I believe you have the advantage if you know who I am," Tabitha replied coldly.

"Please excuse my manners. My name is Maxwell Sandworth, Earl of Langley. I was a very old acquaintance of your husband's and, in fact, attended your wedding. Jonathan and I belonged to the same clubs." Tabitha noted that he used the word acquaintance rather than friend. Her wedding had been a lavish affair, so many people attending the ball might have been guests. She had nothing to say in reply but merely nodded her head.

"When I saw you sitting here alone, I presumed on my relationship with Jonathan to come over and pay my respects." The explanation was reasonable, yet it all felt disingenuous and somehow off to Tabitha. There was nothing flirtatious in the man's manner, so why had he forced this introduction upon her? She was still wearing her mask, and yet he had recognised her. True, she hadn't made an enormous effort to disguise herself, yet this man who claimed only the passing acquaintance of a wedding guest had recognised her. And why had he bothered? Tabitha decided to keep her questions to herself and to see what he revealed.

"I saw you on the arm of the new Earl of Pembroke. Jonathan's cousin, I believe." Tabitha again merely gave a slight nod of her head in acknowledgement. "What kind of man is he? I heard it had taken more than six months to track down this prodigal son of the Chesterton family."

These words finally stirred Tabitha to a reply, "Prodigal son? That's an interesting choice of phrase. It implies that the new Lord Pembroke had been banished from the family in shame and is now returned."

Lord Langley laughed. Or at least Tabitha assumed it was supposed to approximate a laugh. Instead, it was a dry, rather forbidding sound. "Then let's call him the prodigal grandson, shall we? Indeed, from what Jonathan shared over the years, the new earl's father had been disinherited by the then patriarch. And from what I've heard, Jeremy, Lord Pembroke, Wolf to his friends, had been leading a quite interesting professional life until he inherited the title."

Tabitha wasn't sure what to make of this observation. Wolf didn't seem to particularly care what society thought of him and didn't seem to be making extraordinary efforts to hide who he had been previously. On the other hand, the man sitting with her seemed to have gone out of his way to discover details not generally known in aristocratic circles. And he seemed to be going out of his way to let her know he had discovered them. Why?

"Lord Langley," Tabitha said, deciding to speak plainly, "you seem to have come over to speak to me with a purpose. And I can't help feeling that the purpose is to cast aspersions on the new Lord Pembroke."

Langley laughed that disconcerting laugh again, "You do surprise me, Lady Pembroke, with your forthrightness. At least based on what I'd heard and seen of you during your marriage. And I am rarely surprised by people."

"Are you not?" Tabitha asked. "I find that people are rarely who they first seem to be and are constantly surprising. Take Lord Pembroke, for example. Despite what people might make of his professional background, he has shown himself time and again to be more of a gentleman than many who lay claim to the title," she said pointedly.

"Touché, Lady Pembroke. Consider me appropriately chastened. However," he continued, in a slightly quieter tone, "perhaps you should warn the new earl. I have heard that he may be attempting to continue some of his previous professional endeavours and has been enquiring into the finances of the late Duke of Somerset. Please remind him he's no longer in Whitechapel dealing with the dregs of society. He should be careful where he sticks his nose." With that threat hanging in the air, he stood, bowed, and excused himself.

Tabitha wasn't sure what to make of the conversation. Why did Langley care so much about Wolf's interest in the deceased duke's finances? How did he even find out about this? And what exactly did that threat mean?

CHAPTER 22

Tabitha continued to sit at the table, considering the conversation with Lord Langley. She allowed herself a slice of cake and another glass of champagne. No one else forced conversation upon her. She suspected gossip had circulated, and everyone knew she was in attendance and was determined to shun her. Fortunately, she was happy to be left alone with her thoughts. She would have enjoyed another dance with Wolf but recognised the danger there.

Eventually, Wolf came to rescue her. The dowager had been true to her word and had taken him around, making clear who had been a close associate of the duke's. She'd also shared titillating gossip about the various men, including which ones were rumoured to share some of the dead man's predilections. Wolf wasn't sure how the dowager came by such gossip and didn't want to pull on that thread. He felt guilty about leaving Tabitha alone for so long but knew she would understand. He harboured hope that he could dance at least once more with her.

Wolf indicated that his expedition with the dowager had borne fruit, and Tabitha said she had something to share. But they agreed that they were better off waiting until they were in the privacy of their own home to share.

On entering the house and handing their outer clothes to Talbot, who indicated that Bear and Rat were waiting in the study. Tabitha and Wolf hurried in. Wolf was worried there had been a problem with the mission to the brothel. On opening the door, they discovered Bear in an armchair sipping a glass of the earl's best brandy. Rat sat in another armchair with a cup of hot chocolate.

"Making yourself comfortable, I see," Wolf remarked. But his comment had no bite, and Bear and Rat grinned at him in reply. "Were you at least successful?"

Bear answered, "I'll let the lad tell you what he found."

"I'm not sure I want to ask where you were, Rat. Before we start," Tabitha said, "can I suggest we move to the parlour to write out all our findings and put them on the board? Also, I need to change out of this dress into something more comfortable. So, let us regroup in the parlour in 20 minutes or so. Bear, can you find Talbot and ask for more hot chocolate and perhaps snacks."

Getting out of a ballgown took a little more than 20 minutes, but before long, Tabitha was far more comfortable in a day dress and had taken her hair down. Wolf had never seen her hair anything but up and highly coiffured. Seeing it hanging down her back, thick with soft curls, he wished that fashion didn't dictate that she couldn't wear it like that all the time.

She took her favourite chair, grasped the cup of hot chocolate already waiting for her, and said, "So, who wants to start?" Wolf shared all the information he had gleaned from his time with the dowager. They wrote each man's name down on a notecard. Luckily, Wolf had an excellent memory for details. Under each name, he indicated any salacious gossip the dowager had shared. They added all these notecards to the grouping about the brothel. Unfortunately, however unpleasant, none of the dowager's gossip indicated a motive for murder.

Tabitha went next. On the carriage ride home, she'd reflected on whether her encounter with Lord Langley, however unpleasant, was likely to be connected to the case. But since he had explicitly mentioned Wolf's investigations into the duke's finances, Tabitha decided he had to at least be on the board.

As Tabitha replayed her encounter, Wolf sat in silence for a few moments and then said, "That threat sounds like it was quite personal rather than merely a general warning about meddling in the lives of my betters. But why? And I need to find out how word of our investigations has leaked out. Let's put it on the board, starting a new group, at least for now."

After Tabitha had written the notecard up, including the questions she had considered and that Wolf had just posed, she told Bear and Rat it was their turn. Rat was very excited to speak. He stood up and even cleared his throat. Wolf and Tabitha tried not to smile at the young boy's seriousness.

"Well, my lordship Wolf and yer ladyship, I got in the 'ouse no trouble." Tabitha raised her eyebrows but didn't interrupt. Rat continued, "You were right; with that ball going on, there weren't hardly any swells there that night. A peeler walked by once or twice, but then even they disappeared. Finally, I see through the window the Abbess putting out the lights, and then I wait. After a while, me and Bear go to the back like we planned. Bear stayed watching, and I went in through a window. Everyone was asleep, and I walked into a bunch of the bedrooms, and they were all young'uns. Some I even recognised."

Even though Tabitha had known intellectually that the brothel was likely using young girls, it was still shocking to hear confirmation that children were being taken from their families and sold into prostitution.

Rat continued, "So, then I was just going to leave like. But then, I came downstairs and saw that the 'ouse had a study just like yours Wolf. So, I went in, and there was a big desk, just like yours. So, I remembered all the important papers that you keep locked up in the drawer there and wondered what was in these drawers. So, I picked the lock, just like you taught me." At this, Tabitha shot Wolf a very sharp look, and he had the good sense to look chagrined. "And I found this book. I can't read what's written, but I know what a ledger looks like because ma used to keep one, so she knew who owed her wot for her sewing." And with that, Rat reached into his waistband and, with a dramatic flourish, produced a medium-sized black, leather-bound notebook.

Wolf took the book from him and started paging through it. "Well done, lad! You're right; this is a ledger. But keeping track of what?"

"Clients of the brothel? Don't you think that's the most obvious answer?" Tabitha asked.

"Yes, it's the obvious answer. But I'm not sure it's the right one. Apart from anything else, it doesn't seem like a record of money paid. Look, see what you think." He brought the book over to Tabitha, and she flicked through it.

"So, a column seems to indicate a person. That's clear enough. Then the next column has the word photo by some of the initials, but by others, more cryptic text. This is interesting; you'll never guess whose name I found here. Langley." Everyone looked up at this information. "By his name, it says 'Anthony'. Whatever can that mean?"

"Who's Anthony?" Wolf asked.

"Could that mean Anthony Rowley, the new Duke of Somerset? What on earth could that be about? And then there's another column that seems more freeform. The final column just had some check marks."

Wolf took the book back and continued to look through it. After a few minutes, he looked up and said, "Bannister. That's the name of one of the men the dowager indicated was in Somerset's circle and may share his unnatural urges. And here's his name with the word 'photo' next to it. I believe this Bannister is high up in the government, but the dowager didn't know what he actually does. The next column says 'uniforms', and there's a check next to it. Rat, what else was in the drawer where you found this? Any photos?"

"Nuffink. I did look to see if there was anything else worth taking, but there didn't seem to be."

"Wolf, what do you think this all means?" Tabitha asked.

"Well, we may have found some people with motives at last. I think that what the duke was cataloguing here was blackmail. Given that we have reason to believe that Bannister could be a client of the brothel, it seems plausible that the duke found a way to take compromising photographs of him and other patrons. He was then blackmailing them, though I'm not entirely clear for what gain."

Tabitha interjected, "But even if that is the case, and I agree it makes sense, what about the entries that say something other than a photo?"

"Well, we have to assume that the duke was an all-purpose blackmailer holding other things over those men's heads. What this does give us is a whole lot of people with motives. Including, so it seems, your Lord Langley."

"And while I normally decry judging a book by its cover, I have to say that it's hard to imagine a man more suited to being the villain than Langley. Everything about him screams cold-blooded murderer," Tabitha said. She created a new notecard entitled 'Blackmail' and put it on the board. She then moved Langley's card and those of all the men Wolf had met at the ball to this new group. She also wrote on Langley's card, 'What was he being blackmailed over?'

When she finished reorganising the notecards, Tabitha took a biscuit off the tray before her, sat back down and considered the board. "We seem to have gone from no suspects to too many. What is our next move?"

Wolf considered the question, "I think the first thing we must do is close that brothel down. We're assuming that your friend Anthony, the new Duke of Somerset, has no idea what he has inherited, and we must rectify that as soon as possible. Nothing is more important than stopping what is happening to those girls."

Tabitha agreed, "Tomorrow, you will send a note requesting a meeting with Anthony. I suggest that you ask him to attend you here. If you and I appear at Rowley House to meet with Anthony, it will only cause unnecessary speculation amongst the women of the house."

Wolf paused, unsure how to answer this, "Tabitha, you know that you are an integral part of this investigation at this point, but are you sure I shouldn't meet with the new duke alone?" He saw that she was about to object and raised a hand to be allowed to continue, "This is not about your talents, it's far more basic. What we have to tell him is shocking enough. Or so we're assuming. To hear it from another man will be bad enough. To hear it in front of a woman may be unbearable. Our objective is not to shame him and certainly is not to anger him. But rather, it's to inform and encourage him to do the right thing immediately. I agree that asking him to wait on me here is the better idea. But I do think that I need to handle this alone."

Everything in Tabitha wanted to refute what Wolf was saying. But she couldn't because she knew he was right. Anthony was a gentle, sensitive soul. There had been a time when she had even felt a passing fancy for him. But he had never shown any sign of feeling anything but friendship for her or any debutante so far. She could only imagine how mortified he would be when hearing the depths of depravity to which his father had sunk. Having her witness to his mortification would be unbearable for him, and she should save him that added pain if she could.

"You are right, of course. But will you tell him everything? Even about the blackmail?"

"I think we must. Even if this is not why his father was killed, he needs to know what was afoot. He may have enemies he is unaware of because of his father's schemes. Let's not forget that we believe it's his name in this book. Though why would the duke use information about his own son to blackmail someone? And let's not forget that the evidence that his father held still exists and which the new duke needs to find." Wolf considered what he had just said and added, "I don't know that the evidence needs destroying; it depends on what we find. But it does need to be managed. And the new duke needs to be the one to manage it.
"

They agreed on the plan for the following day. By the time they had finished, Tabitha had realised that Rat had fallen asleep in his chair. She felt terrible. She knew that Mrs Jenkins had the boy doing household chores that required him to be up with the maids in the early morning hours, and now they had kept him up until past 2 am. She made an impulsive decision and said to Bear, "Carry the boy up to the nursery. There's a spare bed in there. I'll leave a note for Mrs Jenkins telling her where he is and that no one is to wake him tomorrow."

She saw that Wolf was about to say something, and anticipating it, she added, "Yes, I know that this could be seen as the kind of special treatment that I promised he wouldn't receive. But at this point, he is doing double duty in the household staff and additionally as part of this investigation. No other servant besides Bear is asked to do this, so it is already a special situation." Wolf knew Tabitha would not be swayed, so he told Bear to carry Rat upstairs.

CHAPTER 23

The following morning was a busy one. Wolf sent his note to the new Duke of Somerset, who said he would happily meet with the Earl of Pembroke at 2 pm. Meanwhile, Talbot had reminded Tabitha that the tutor would be starting the next day and that she still needed to make her offer of education to the servants. After breakfast, Tabitha descended to the kitchen where Mrs Jenkins had gathered the entire staff. While there was serious doubt that Fred, the gardener well past his middle years, would be interested in learning to read or read better, Tabitha was determined that everyone would receive the same offer.

After explaining that the tutor would come daily, Mrs Jenkins proposed a schedule that accommodated anyone on the staff who wished to attend an educational hour three times a week. Tabitha made a point of explaining that there was no expectation that they would make this hour up. Mrs Jenkins had informed Tabitha that if a significant number of the staff under her control chose to take up this offer, she wasn't sure how to cover the lost time. But Tabitha had assured her that she and Wolf were prepared to adjust their expectations and be inconvenienced if necessary. Maybe the maids dust the rooms every other day. Or perhaps the newspaper didn't get ironed (something that Wolf continued to think was an absurd waste of time.)

While not all were interested in taking Tabitha up on the offer, she was pleasantly surprised. All the maids had raised their hands. Bryans, the footman, had also expressed an interest in improving his reading. Ginny could already read but expressed an interest in working on her arithmetic. As expected, Fred, the gardener, had shaken his head and mumbled about how he knew enough to prune the roses and what else did he need?

Tabitha had then left it to Mrs Jenkins and Talbot to work out an appropriate schedule. The tutor would come daily to allow enough time to minimise the impact on the servant's schedule. In addition, Rat, Melly, Becky and Mary would sit with him every day. While Mary did know her letters, her reading skills were very elementary. Tabitha had decided it was important that she be able to read well because she needed to keep up with Melly.

On leaving the kitchen, Tabitha had gone up to the nursery to spend time with Melly. Mary and Becky had stayed behind in the nursery while Tabitha talked to the staff. It had already been determined when they would work with Mr James, the tutor. When Tabitha entered the nursery, she found all three involved in an elaborate game involving the two older girls sitting on the floor singing a nursery rhyme while Melly ran between them, plopping in their laps. There was a lot of giggling involved.

It made Tabitha so happy to see Becky laughing and singing. Knowing what Becky had been through for the last few years, that she could be sitting here playing just like any other little girl, was nothing short of amazing. It was amazing how resilient children could be.

The girls stopped singing when they saw Tabitha enter, and the older girls jumped up to curtsey, but Tabitha gestured that they should sit back down. "Please don't stop your game. I just came by to see how everyone was doing."

Melody ran up to her, tugged her skirt and said, "Come and play Tabby Cat. You sit down between Becky and Mary, and we'll teach you the song."

Sitting on the floor in corsets wasn't the easiest or most comfortable thing, but Tabitha somehow managed it. The song they'd been singing was Oranges and Lemons. Melly explained earnestly that as the song ended, she had to sit in the nearest lap, at which point, the person whose lap she was on would tickle her. She seemed thrilled to have three laps to run between now.

Tabitha lost track of time. The game became sillier and sillier as Melly started making up absurd rules. Tabitha remembered playing silly games like this in her nursery with her nanny. Her mother had never lowered herself to join in. She couldn't remember a time when her mother visited the nursery.

Tabitha was so busy laughing and singing along that she didn't notice Wolf standing in the doorway. But Melly did and rushed up to him crying, "Wolfie, Wolfie, come join in." Wolfie? When had that nickname stuck? Tabitha could see that Wolf didn't know how to resist the little girl but wasn't sure about being included in the game.

After a few moments, he inevitably lost that battle and allowed himself to be dragged into the nursery and onto the floor. "Melody, I'll play for a few minutes, but then I must drag....," He paused, not sure how to refer to Tabitha at this point, and then again giving into the inevitable, "Tabby Cat downstairs to do some work with me." He gave her a pointed look as he said that, and Tabitha assured Melly that the game could continue but that she and Wolf, 'Wolfie', needed to leave after one more round of the game.

Wolf was totally out of his depths in the game. Tabitha did wonder what he had played in his nursery, probably soldiers. When the singing began again, he didn't join in but did clap his hands. But Melly was having none of that, and walked over to him, put her little hands on her hips and said to him very sternly, "Wolfie, you must sing the rhyme, or you're not playing the game. And you promised you'd play." After that, he joined in, hesitantly at first, his deep baritone and surprisingly good voice gradually becoming louder and more confident.

Tabitha was certain that Melody had deliberately run in such a way that she ended up in Wolf's lap when the singing stopped. She applauded the little girl's powers of manipulation. She'd be a force to be reckoned with in a few years. The look on Wolf's face as the child sat herself down on him was priceless. "Wolfie!! Play the game. You're supposed to tickle me now." Tabitha didn't think she could be more amused by Wolf's discomfort with the situation he found himself in, but this stern order from a 4-year-old girl and his reaction to it was one of the most entertaining things she'd ever witnessed.

Wolf was a large man with large hands. She was sure those hands were very deft when handling a gun or picking a lock. But he had no idea what to do with them when called upon to tickle. Initially, he waggled his fingers near Melly's abdomen, but she cried, "No, more. More! It's not even tickling." The finger waggling became more intentional encouraged by the child's increasing giggles.

As amused as Tabitha was watching a 4-year-old imperiously command Wolf, a part of her was suddenly nostalgic. Could she feel nostalgia for something she'd ever actually had? Looking at Wolf and Melly, she imagined a similar situation if she'd been able to have a child of her own. And instead of Wolf, the man playing happily with the giggling little girl was Jonathan. Except, it could never have been Jonathan, could it? Even if she had managed to conceive and carry a baby to term, he never would have been this kind of father because he wasn't this kind of man.

The more she thought about it, the more Tabitha realised that perhaps it was for the best that she had been unable to have Jonathan's baby. At the same time, a tiny part of her wanted to believe that being a father might have softened Jonathan, making him a different man. But the larger part of her realised what a fantasy that thinking was. The most likely scenario was that the child would have been someone else for Jonathan to bully and torment. Even in the best-case scenario, he would have used Tabitha's love for the child as a weapon to bully and torment her.

So no, she couldn't feel sad that she and Jonathan had never been blessed with a baby. She couldn't, in good faith, wish her deceased husband as a father for any child. She knew that however much love she had lavished on a child, it could never have compensated for all the harm Jonathan would have inevitably caused.

The tickling might have continued for much longer, but Tabitha decided to rescue Wolf, "Okay, Melly, Wolfie and I have to go and work now. You can keep playing with Mary and Becky."

At this, Melody stood up and gave a surprised Wolf a big hug and a kiss on the cheek, "Thank you for playing with me, Wolfie. Will you come and play again sometime?"

Tabitha could have sworn that the man had blushed. He looked unexpectedly touched by the little girl's affection and hugged her back, "Thank you for letting me play, Miss Melly. I'd love to come back and play another time." He disentangled himself from the child and stood up.

"Next time, we can have a doll's tea party," Melody exclaimed. Tabitha made a mental note not to miss that sight for anything.

Leaving the nursery, they descended to the ground floor, and Wolf led Tabitha to the parlour. She took her customary seat and asked with great curiosity, "What did you need me for, Wolf? I assume it must be serious if you were prepared to hazard the nursery to track me down." Wolf made a face, and she laughed and teased, "But I think you ended up having fun despite yourself."

Wolf smiled sheepishly and replied, "I want to prepare what I will say to Somerset when he arrives this afternoon. Luncheon will be soon, but I need you to coach me through how I will talk to him."

"Coach you?" Tabitha asked with genuine surprise.

"Yes, you know the man. I want to understand the best way to approach this. There is no good way to tell someone that his father was not only a child molester but the owner of a brothel that catered to other child molesters. Oh, and by the way, he was also blackmailing various men in society, and, in one case, the blackmail had something to do with you. However," Wolf continued, "there are different ways to say this, and I'd like your advice on how best to say it to a man you know well."

"Well, I'm not sure I know him well, at least as a man. But I used to know him well, so I'll tell you what I can based on that information." Wolf's deference to her opinion genuinely touched Tabitha. “As I told you, Anthony, or at least the Anthony I knew as a child, is a gentle, sensitive soul. I don't doubt he will be horrified by what you tell him.”

“Do you believe that he will doubt me?” Wolf asked. He had started pacing the room and seemed more worried about the upcoming conversation than he had let on.

“Wolf,” Tabitha said gently but firmly, “you don’t have to be the one to do this. Or you don’t have to do this alone. We can change the plan, and I can join you.”

Wolf shook his head and gave her a strained smile, “Thank you for saying that. But I know that I must be the one to do it. However difficult a conversation it may be.”

“Then let me share some information that may help. When we were children, Anthony was afraid of his father. It wasn’t so much what he said but how he shrunk back whenever the man came near. As I’ve said, Anthony was a sweet, gentle, sensitive boy, and clearly, this was not the kind of son and heir his father wanted.

"Anthony confided in me that his father once took him hunting and was so frustrated at his 11-year-old son’s unwillingness to shoot a gun that he snatched it from him, and Anthony felt he would have beaten him with it if there hadn’t been servants as witnesses. Instead, he sent him back to the house in disgrace and, let me try to remember the words Anthony had said he used.” Tabitha paused as she dug through memories, finally saying, “I believe that Anthony had told me that his father had spat at him, ‘I curse the day I accepted such lily-livered spawn.”

Wolf stopped pacing and asked, “What did Anthony think he meant by that?”

“I don’t think he examined the sentiment too deeply. Instead, he took it as another indication that he was a profound disappointment to his father.”

“Are there any siblings?”

“Well, there weren’t for a long time, which I’m sure added to his father’s frustrations. Finally, another child was born, but she was a daughter. Hannah. She's probably about 8 or 9 now. Too young for me to have known her when I was a child myself."

"So, if I'm interpreting what you're telling me correctly, it won't be a huge fall off a pedestal for a beloved and revered father?"

"Exactly," Tabitha confirmed. "While I'm sure he'll be shocked and horrified at the depths to which his father had plunged, it won't be a shock that his father was not a good man. He was already well aware of that.

Wolf sighed, "That is some kind of relief, then. Though he had his faults, my father was a kind and loving parent when I was a child. Much of my trepidation at having this conversation with Somerset was borne of imagining how I would feel if I had been told such news. But knowing that he didn't hold his father in the same esteem I held mine makes my anticipation of this meeting a little easier. Thank you."

"You're very welcome. I hadn't considered that telling this news might feel so personal to you. I will add this, for all his gentleness and sensitivity, I believe that Anthony is a man of strong moral fibre and great decency. His father thought him weak, but he is not. His strength is just different from that respected by men like his father. He will appreciate the unvarnished truth, told plainly and directly. He won't shy from it, and I believe that, as hard as it may be for him to hear, he won't doubt it."

With Wolf comforted as much as Tabitha was able, they adjourned to the dining room to eat a hearty meal to fortify Wolf for the afternoon ahead of him.

CHAPTER 24

Over lunch, Tabitha and Wolf had agreed that she would stay out of the way during the duke's visit. Once she'd acknowledged the wisdom of Wolf's suggestion that she not be in the meeting, she realised that she needed to avoid Anthony totally during the visit. She'd decided that the safest place was up in the nursery, overseeing Melly's lessons.

As he sat at his desk waiting for his visitor, Wolf reflected on the strange circumstances over a mere few weeks that had left him an earl waiting to have a challenging conversation with a duke. During his thief-taker days, he'd certainly had some interactions with the higher echelons of society. In fact, a part of Wolf's value to his clientele was that he was a well-spoken, well-educated man who could fit in with the upper classes when needed.

However, nothing he had done before had prepared him for the conversation he was about to have.

When Talbot announced the duke, Wolf's first impression was of a slight, delicate young man. He was about average height, but his frame was slim, and his entire being had almost a femininity about it. His facial features were almost pretty, and long and fair lashes framed his striking blue eyes. Wolf hadn't met the new dowager duchess, Lady Cassandra Somerset, but he could imagine that if her son favoured her, she must be a great beauty.

Wolf hadn't realised how young the new duke was. But then he considered that the man had been a childhood friend of Tabitha's, and she was barely 22 years old. Even so, Tabitha had some inner strength that shone so clearly that it seemed to give her maturity beyond her years. The man standing uncertainly in his study seemed younger than his years.

Wolf stood, walked around his desk and shook the other man's hand. Then he indicated that they should both take an armchair. Without asking the duke, Wolf asked Talbot to pour them both a brandy. While it was early in the afternoon, Wolf knew the other man would need a stiff drink shortly.

The drinks poured and handed out, Talbot excused himself. Wolf took a sip of his brandy, unsure how to begin. He was surprised when the duke took the lead and nervously asked, "Pembroke, you asked to speak to me on a matter of some delicacy. Let us dispense with pleasantries and get straight to it."

Realising that he could procrastinate no more, Wolf launched into his tale. He had already decided there was no point in being vague about his past. Perhaps making himself more vulnerable would help ease the shame of what Anthony was about to hear.

Wolf told him briefly about his upbringing and how he became a thief-taker. He told him about his surprise at inheriting the title. The duke listened closely, but he could also see his eagerness for the story to move on to whatever was important to his life. "I know that it seems that I am spending too long on my own story and that you are eager to hear why I asked you hear today," Wolf explained. "But I feel you need to understand my role in this."

Tabitha and Wolf had discussed over lunch how to address the question of Mickey D. They didn't want to tell the duke that they knew who stole his mother's diamond necklace. But they also need to explain how they had become involved in the case in the first place. They'd decided that they would focus the case on the brothels. They would say that someone from Wolf's prior life had alerted them to young girls taken from their families and that, as they investigated, the duke's involvement had become clear.

Wolf ran through the story as they'd discussed. As Tabitha had predicted, the young duke was horrified to hear about his father's activities. But not so shocked that he denied that a man such as the late duke could have done anything so heinous. In fact, to the contrary, the son immediately believed all that he was told about his father's crimes. Wolf was surprised that there was no resistance to what he said. It led him to believe that the son had, for some reason, his own prior suspicions about his father's unnatural urges.

When he came to the part where they had found the book listing the blackmail victims, this seemed more shocking to the son. As they'd planned, Wolf then planted the mere suggestion of the possibility that the father's murder might not have been as it seemed, but instead be somehow related to one of the men blackmailed.

"But how could that be?" the duke inquired. "Someone broke into the safe and took the necklace."

"Well," Wolf explained carefully, "there are a couple of possible explanations. One is that the necklace's theft was an elaborate ruse to cover a murder committed for another reason. Or there's always the possibility, however unlikely it may seem, that the two crimes were wholly unconnected."

"Unconnected? What do you mean?" The duke's confusion was clear on his young face.

"I mean that they happened coincidentally on the same evening."

"Excuse me for questioning your reasoning, but you are clearly an educated man, so I will mention Occam's Razor; while it is physically possible that the two crimes are unrelated, it is far from the simplest, most likely suggestion."

Wolf decided not to press this point and instead to press on the other possibility, of the ruse, "You are, of course, correct, Somerset; that is an improbable scenario. However, the staging of the theft by someone determined to get their revenge on your father or merely to stop his blackmail seems less contrived a scenario.

I understand that the police have yet to discover the necklace or hear whispers of its sale through their usual channels."

"Indeed, but from what they have shared with me, they are not surprised by this. A necklace as distinctive and valuable as my mother's wouldn't have been easy to, what's the word they use?"

Wolf interjected, "Fence. A thief usually uses a fence as a middleman."

"Yes, it wouldn't have been easy to fence. The police inspector on the case suggested that even without the complication of murder, he would have expected the thief to either try to get the necklace out of the country or not to move it for some time to let the trail get cold."

"Indeed," Wolf agreed, "both are the most likely scenarios in my extensive experience of such crimes. Your father's murder would have made any smart thief bide his time before trying to sell off such a necklace. After a while, the best bet would probably have been to break down the necklace and try to get rid of the stones.

"And so, you are correct; the lack of evidence that the theft was part of a normal burglary gone wrong does not point to anything in and of itself. But the clear evidence of your father's crimes and a rather long list of people with motives to want him dead does raise questions. At least in my mind."

Wolf felt that he had belaboured this idea enough. His real purpose in having this meeting wasn't to convince the duke about the murder but to make him aware of the brothel and the blackmail and enlist his help in finding the blackmail materials. To this end, he had one final uncomfortable revelation to make. "Somerset, there is one more thing that I need to tell you. I don't know what it means, but you should know."

The younger man's eyes widened at this news, no doubt wondering how much worse this conversation could get. "In the book, we discovered where your father seems to have listed his blackmail victims. We found a listing with your name, Anthony, next to it. While this could refer to someone apart from yourself, we... " Wolf paused here, not sure that he should reveal Tabitha's part in this, "That is my associates, and I felt that, to the point of the simplest explanation being the most likely, it is highly plausible that it refers to you."

"Are you asking if my father was blackmailing me?" the duke asked.

"Not at all. Your name was not listed as the person blackmailed but rather as the cause of the blackmail," Wolf explained gently.

"Then who was being blackmailed?"

"Maxwell Sandworth, Earl of Langley." Wolf noticed that the young man visibly paled at this information. Yet again, his instincts told him that there was something about this news that was not wholly a surprise.

The duke didn't reply for a few moments, then he seemed to compose himself and said, "I barely know the earl and have no idea why my name would be associated with his." His tone when he said this was so hesitant and nervous that it led Wolf to believe that the duke had an excellent idea why their names might be linked and cause blackmail. But he decided not to pursue this yet.

Instead, Wolf redirected the conversation back to what he needed to request, "Somerset, I believe that as your father's only heir, you are now the owner of this establishment." Wolf felt the fact hadn't sunk in previously; he continued, "May I make some suggestions as to your course of action?"

"Please do, sir. I am as appalled by all this as you might expect. Still, I am at a loss as to how to proceed."

"I suggest that your first action is to go to this house, get rid of all the adults 'supervising' and immediately halt the heinous trade."

"Do you believe I should attempt to return all the girls to their families? I'm happy to take whatever steps are necessary to do so."

"Unfortunately, it's unclear that this would be the best course of action. At least for all the girls. As far as we can tell, their families sold them to a madam who procured them on your father's behalf." The duke winced but didn't interrupt. Wolf continued, "While we can't know for sure, it does seem that at least some of the families may have reason to suspect what they were selling their daughters into but did so anyway. I can't imagine returning to such a situation is in those girls' best interest.

"I believe that, at least for the time being, the best course of action is to leave the girls in the house, watched over by someone you trust to be gentle with them. Do you have such a woman? If not, perhaps I can help. I know some honest, kind-hearted women from my past who would be appropriate caretakers for these children." The duke indicated that would be the best scenario. Wolf rang a bell, and when Talbot entered the room, he asked him to find Bear and send him to the study.

The woman Wolf had in mind was Bear's mother. She was a plain-speaking, honest woman. Her son had inherited his size, at least in part, from his mother. She stood taller than Wolf himself and had shoulders almost as broad. She was a gentle, kind woman for all her intimidating size. She had raised seven children and now lived comfortably, thanks to Wolf's new fortune. She didn't need the work, but Wolf hoped the situation would rouse the compassionate woman to action and that she wouldn't refuse the task.

While he waited for Bear, he continued, "I believe that once we are sure of the girls' comfort and safety, you need to go through your father's study in that house. We have reason to believe he kept the blackmail materials in that location. There must be a safe somewhere in that room."

"But," the duke asked with a quizzical look on his face, "even if we find it, how would we open it? I certainly have no idea what the combination is."

Wolf considered how to answer this. He was more than capable of getting the safe open. He knew a lot of good safe crackers, not the least of whom was Mickey D. But it would be more prudent to try to get the safe opened in a manner less likely to raise awkward questions. "I'm assuming there is a safe at Rowley House. Do you know the combination to that one?"

The duke nodded, "Yes. When I reached my majority, my father showed me where all his important papers were and gave me the combination to the safe. Why do you assume there is a second safe?"

"Because we know that he had blackmail materials, and it's precisely because he gave you the combination to the one at your home that it makes sense that he kept those materials in another, secret location. The obvious place is in his study at the brothel."

The duke flinched at the word brothel but only remarked, "I'm assuming that your guess is that he used the same combination for both?"

"Most people would." At that moment, there was a knock at the study door, and Bear entered the room. The duke looked up and was visibly startled to see the mountain of man before him. Wolf made the introductions and asked Bear if he thought his mother would agree to help them, at least in the short term.

"I believe she would," the enormous man answered in a gravelly voice that, to the duke's ear, sounded like it came from the belly of a bear. "In truth, I think she's a little bored since our Margie got herself wed. She's a woman who has been used to working all her life, and the retirement I've been able to let her enjoy just isn't who she is."

"Good!" Wolf exclaimed. Would you please go and ask her and, assuming she does say yes, have her gather up some possessions and meet us over at the brothel. Take a hackney cab both ways. I want you to be there when the Duke of Somerset and I go to take possession of the property. Do you think that you can meet us there within two hours?" Bear assured him that he could and left to collect his mother.

"What is the lady's name?" the duke asked. "I'm assuming she isn't Mrs Bear."

Wolf laughed. He did know Bear's name, but he hadn't used it in so many years that it took him a moment to recollect it. He had long called Bear's mother, Mother Lizzy and had to think hard to remember their family name. "Caruthers. Mrs Elizabeth

Caruthers. Yes, that's what it is."

"I must ask you," the duke began, "while I don't doubt anything that you have said, do you have physical proof that I own the house in question?"

"Yes, I do. Please don't ask me how I came by it. However, that is a very good point. What I have is merely a copy of a deed. I suggest that you call on your father's, well now your, solicitors and get the actual deed as proof. Perhaps even bring your solicitor with you."

"That's an excellent suggestion. I have my carriage here and will make haste to their offices immediately," the duke looked at his pocket watch and added, "I will meet you at the address, if you'll give it to me now, in two hours."

Wolf gave him the address and said, "Wait in your carriage when you arrive. I have no idea what men your father may have on staff to secure the property. We shouldn't attempt anything until we have Bear with us. I'll also bring my footman. He's a strapping young lad."

With the plan in place, the duke thanked Wolf, "I can only imagine how hard it must have been to speak so frankly with me about these matters. I appreciate both your candour and your discretion. I will not forget these favours, Pembroke."

As he said these words, Wolf felt like the young man had visibly aged since he first entered the study. Such were the kinds of trials that did force an expedited maturity on a man, Wolf reflected.

CHAPTER 25

After seeing the Duke of Somerset out, Wolf rushed to find Tabitha. Finally, he tracked her down in the nursery, writing playful, colourful letters for Melody to learn. Seeing him enter, she jumped up and exclaimed, "How did it go?"

"Actually, better than I thought it would. I believe that at least some of what I had to tell him wasn't a total surprise."

Tabitha reacted with shock, "Are you saying he knew about the brothel? Surely not."

Wolf quickly reassured her, "Not at all. That news was as terrible a shock as you might imagine. But his father's preference for very young girls, I don't think that was entirely new information. I also believe he has some inkling about what his father might have been blackmailing Langley. The young man must be terrible at the gaming tables. His face is utterly transparent." Wolf continued, "He and I will meet there in less than two hours. With Bear, " he quickly added when he saw the worry on her face.

Wolf quickly told her his plan for Bear's mother and the girls still in the brothel. "I think I should come with you," Tabitha exclaimed forcefully. Seeing a no forming on his lips, she passionately continued, "I know what we discussed. But at some point, Anthony will have to find out that I know everything. And those young girls are going to be terrified. Their experience to date has been that when supposedly upstanding men enter that house, it hurts them in some way. You need another woman there, beside Bear's mother, to help reassure them."

A little voice piped up from the corner of the room. Tabitha had forgotten that Becky had been helping Mary put Melly down for her nap in the little bedroom off the nursery. She must have overheard the conversation. "Excuse the interruption, m'lord and m'lady, but I would like to come with."

"Becky, we can't ask that of you. You suffered greatly in that house. We can't make you go back there," Tabitha said reassuringly while going over to the girl and wrapping her in her arms.

"But the other girls know and trust me. I'm the only one they will trust of all of you. They'll believe me if I tell them how kind you've been to me. I will be upset returning, but you rescued me from all those horrors. The least I can do now is to help rescue my friends."

Tabitha had tears in her eyes as she held the young girl, "You are right, my dear. Of course, you must come and help us rescue everyone else. You are very brave and very kind." Tabitha directed a very determined look at Wolf over Becky's head. She knew his first instinct was to refuse to allow the young girl to join them. But Tabitha's glare made it clear that she and Becky would be part of the expedition that afternoon.

Wolf raised his hands in surrender and said, "I will meet you both downstairs in just over an hour. We will take the carriage to Holborn, where the duke, Bear and his mother will meet us. Oh, and I plan to take Bryans with us." Tabitha quirked an eyebrow at this piece of news, and Wolf answered her unspoken question, "We have no idea what we're going to encounter there. We need as much manpower as we can muster."

With time to spare, the entire group of Wolf, Tabitha, Bryans, and Becky, set off for Holborn. Tabitha held Becky's hand the entire journey. She wasn't sure if she was trying to reassure the girl or herself. Probably both. Tabitha was scared about what they'd find at the house. Intellectually, she knew what they'd find; young girls turned into whores. But even though she had found Becky in similar circumstances, the girls they were rescuing were even younger. Some would be only a few years older than Melly, and Tabitha wasn't sure how she would manage when confronted with the reality of that.

They stopped down the street from the house. Wolf got out and returned a few minutes later with Bear and a woman who looked like Bear in a grey wig and a dress. But she had the kindest smile Tabitha thought she had ever seen. Bear introduced his mother, Mrs Caruthers, to Tabitha. "Call me Lizzy luv. Or Mother Lizzy if you prefer. Most everyone does."

"Then you must call me Tabitha."

The older woman's eyes crinkled with pleasure, and she answered, "But now aren't you a grand lady. I'm thinking I'm supposed to call you my ladyship or something like that."

Wolf replied in Tabitha's stead, "And are you going to start calling me your lordship? Because I don't think that's going to work for me."

The old woman cackled, "You? No. I've cleaned too many scrapes and bandaged your forehead too many times to call you anything but Wolf. But she's a real grand lady."

"And what am I?" Wolf asked laughingly. He went over to Mother Lizzy and kissed her on the cheek, which made the woman blush like a young milkmaid. "Thank you for coming. I know that you didn't have to."

"Of course, I had to. Once Albert explained the situation, I had no choice." Now it was Bear's turn to blush.

"Mother! I've asked you not to call me that. At least in public."

"It's the name you were baptized with, and if its good enough for Jesus, it's good enough."

Bear continued to protest, "But you're happy to call Wolf by his chosen name. It's not like you call him Jeremy!"

"Jeremy? That's his name, is it? Well, I do say."

"You know it's his name, mother."

As amused as he was by this banter, they had important work to do. While they'd been standing talking, the duke had appeared with a little, stooped, older man at his side. Introductions were made all around, and the stooped man was revealed as the duke's solicitor, Mr Eames. Mr Eames did not look happy to have been dragged along. But when one of your richest, most prestigious clients insists you accompany them, you have no choice.

Wolf went through the plan with everyone. The duke would approach the house with Mr Eames. Wolf, Bear, Mrs Caruthers and Bryans would accompany them but hang behind. Once the duke had successfully claimed the house, he would immediately banish whatever adult was in charge. They assumed that the servants knew what had been happening in the house but had decided to leave them in place, at least for the time being. Mrs Caruthers could determine which staff to replace as necessary.

With the madam ejected, Tabitha and Becky would follow the others into the house to comfort the girls.

The whole plan went remarkably smoothly. It was clear that, with the duke dead, the madame had been expecting something like this for a while. She packed her stuff quickly enough to have had most of it packed for a while.

There hadn't been any children on the lower levels of the house, so Mrs Caruthers, Tabitha, and Becky had gone upstairs. They finally found the children living in what must have been the nursery once. Beds were lined up dormitory style, and the girls were sitting, mostly silently, on their beds. There didn't seem to be anything at hand for them to do. No toys, no books, assuming any of them could read. Some sat two on a bed, braiding each other's hair. Others lay in their beds, maybe sleeping, maybe too traumatised to do much else.

When Tabitha and the other two women entered the room, there wasn't any immediate reaction. It seemed the girls had just assumed that servants had come upstairs. But once they saw Becky, the girls got off their beds and gathered around her. Girlish voices filled the room as everyone wanted to talk to her, question her, and in many cases, hug her.

In turn, Becky seemed overwhelmed to see her old friends. A few younger girls hung back, and Tabitha assumed they hadn't been there when Becky had been. Looking at those girls broke Tabitha's heart. She locked eyes with Mother Lizzy and saw that the older woman was as affected as she was, with tears filling her eyes.

Becky quickly answered all the questions by explaining that Tabitha and her friends were good people who had come to rescue them all, just as they had rescued Becky. They were all safe now. Girls did ask if they were going home. Becky looked over at Tabitha, not sure how to answer. Tabitha said, "Girls, we know you've all had a horrible time here. But we want to keep you here for just a short while more until we can determine the best thing for each of you. Would that be okay with all of you?"

The girls all nodded, too shocked to do more than agree with the grand lady who had suddenly appeared out of nowhere.

The rest of the visit was handled very efficiently but gently, mostly due to Mrs Caruthers, who proved to be a highly competent and compassionate manager. The decision was made that the girls would continue to sleep in the nursery; Mrs Caruthers's wise observation was that the bedrooms on the floor below likely held some unpleasant memories.

In an aside with the duke, Mrs Caruthers and Tabitha suggested that the current house was not the best place to house the girls for anything other than a short time. The house held too many awful associations for the girls to thrive. Given that no one had a plan for what should ultimately happen to the children, the house in Holborn would have to do for the time being, but the duke promised that he would find a better alternative as a top priority.

The matter of the existing servants solved itself; on descending to the servants' quarters, Mrs Caruthers found that the housekeeper and cook had quietly packed their bags and left with the madam. The remaining maids were nervous, anxious creatures who seemed to have themselves been victims of intimidation and abuse.

CHAPTER 26

With the girls left in Mrs Caruthers's capable hands and Becky happily reunited with her friends, Tabitha, Wolf, and the duke went to the study to find the safe. The duke's claim to his property unchallenged, Mr Eames had returned to his offices. Bear and Bryans had returned to Chesterton House.

Anthony, the young Duke of Somerset, was initially shocked to find Tabitha to be part of their expedition. But he was so overwhelmed by the evidence of his own eyes as to what his father had been up to that he didn't have the presence of mind to question her involvement and knowledge of the affair. Tabitha decided not to say anything to comfort him or highlight the shame of the situation. But instead, she would just claim her place as part of the investigation as if it were the most natural thing in the world.

This wasn't Wolf's first time locating a hidden safe, but he wasn't sure he was ready to make that skill known to the duke. While he had been reasonably candid about his previous life as a thief-taker, he had erred on the 'taker' part of the name and glossed over some of the more illegal activities the job had sometimes entailed.

However, upon entering the room, it became immediately apparent that assuming the safe was in the study, there were only a few places it could be. This was so evident that Tabitha asked, "Could it be behind one of the paintings?" Of course, that's precisely where it turned out to be, a 'hideaway' so obvious that Wolf questioned whether the dead duke was a criminal mastermind or a bumbling villain.

Finding the safe was easy. But, if it didn't have the same combination as the other one at Rowley House, Wolf was left with some difficult choices. He had some skills as a safecracker, but those were minimal and not necessarily talents he wished to highlight. He decided to cross that bridge when they came to the safe. He breathed a sigh of relief when the safe swung open.

That relief was temporary, however, because he now realised they would have to deal with whatever they found in the safe. At the front were some stacks of money. Behind them was a stack of papers bound together and another of photos.

Wolf and Tabitha had deferred to the son to be the one to claim the evidence of his father's crimes. The young man took out the papers first, handling them with such nervousness that it seemed he felt they were physically toxic. He quickly put them aside. Yet again, Wolf wondered how much the duke knew about why his name had been in that book of blackmail victims.

The duke took the photos out and very briefly glanced through them, disgust evident on his face. "They're exactly what you expected to find here. And some of the men involved are society's more illustrious members. I can only imagine the power my father wielded with his possession of such photos. Now, my question is," he paused and looked at Tabitha and Wolf for answers, "what do I do with them?"

Wolf carefully considered his choice of words, "Somerset, I realise that your first instinct might be to destroy the photos. Blackmail is a vile crime. But some of the people your father blackmailed, as these photos show, are not innocent victims. The only innocent victims here are the children upstairs." At this reminder of his father's catalogue of crimes, the duke fidgeted with discomfort and began wringing his hands. But he didn't dispute Wolf's statement.

"I believe we must keep these photos, at least for now. Apart from anything else, as I've mentioned, one of these people may have murdered your father, and these photos are evidence of possible motives." The duke accepted this with a nod of his head. They spent some time searching the study for anything else pertinent to the duke's various illicit activities. Still, Rat had thoroughly searched the deck drawers, and there was nothing more to find.

Tabitha observed that the afternoon's activities had worn down her old friend. He sat slumped in his father's old desk chair, staring vacantly as if unsure what his next actions should be. Tabitha went and stood behind him and put a gentle hand on his shoulder, "Anthony, none of this is your fault. Your father's sins are not yours."

He turned his head, and his startling blue eyes were wet with tears, "It may not be my fault, but it is now my responsibility. These girls," he waved his hand towards the ceiling to indicate the children living on the floor above, "are my responsibility. My responsibility is to have evidence and knowledge of crimes some of my peers have been engaging in perpetuating. The weight of all that lays heavy on my soul."

Tabitha sighed, "Anthony, it lays heavy on your soul because you are not the same man as your father. You are a good, decent, compassionate man. It is terrible to confront evidence of such sin in your own flesh and blood, but it doesn't reflect on you. Not in my eyes, Wolf's, or any decent person's."

Anthony sank his head into his hands at these last words and openly wept. At this startling display of emotion, Tabitha bent beside his chair and pulled him into her arms. Finally, he pulled away from Tabitha's embrace and shocked her by saying, "He was not my flesh and blood."

"What?" Tabitha and Wolf exclaimed at the same time.

"I am not the natural son of Martin Rowley." He sat back down, and Tabitha and Wolf both claimed armchairs in shock, ready to hear an explanation of this extraordinary statement.

"How do you know such a thing to be true?" Tabitha asked.

"Because my mother told me so, when I was 11 or so. After a particularly brutal interaction with my father, one I believe I told you about once, I was sobbing in my mother's arms. At some point, I asked her why my father had cried that he cursed the day he'd accepted me. Initially, she tried to soothe me with platitudes, but I could not be soothed. The look on my father's face and the hatred with which he'd spat out the words had affected me too deeply.

"Finally, she confessed that he was not my natural father. She didn't go into details at that point. But a few years later, after another such incident, I pushed her for more information. She told me she had married my father, not realising she was pregnant. Somehow, at some point, he suspected I was not his child and confronted her with the fact. She acknowledged the possibility, but in the absence of any other male child and the unlikeliness of her providing him one at that point, she begged him to continue to accept me as his son."

"Well," Tabitha observed, "after so many years, the law was on your side. You were born in wedlock, and it was long past the time when he could have disputed your parentage. You were his heir by all rights."

Anthony corrected her, "I was the heir to his title and the entailed property. But most of his fortune was his to dispose of however he wanted. And while he might have no choice but to accept me as his heir, he didn't need to acknowledge me. His ability to turn my mother's life and reputation upside was something he was well aware of. If he had cut me out of his will, he would have left me an empty ducal title and an estate I could not maintain."

Tabitha was shocked by her friend's admission. Wolf was less surprised. He had suspected some of this for a few days. He was surprised that the young duke was aware of the circumstances of his birth, though, and asked, "Do you know who your father is?"

"No. My mother would not tell me that. She said that the man could never acknowledge me as his child, and so it could not benefit me in any way to know the truth. But, of course," and at this point, he indicated towards the stack of papers from the safe, "there is good reason to suspect who it may be."

Wolf answered for him, "Lord Langley, I presume?"

The duke nodded in acknowledgement of the likely truth.

"Why else would my name be next to his as a subject of blackmail? I don't know what my father wanted from him, but I'm assuming that the threat was to fulfil his promise to disinherit me to the extent he was able and to tarnish my mother's name to all of society."

"If this is true, it gives Langley as very strong motive to want your father dead before he was able to follow through on his threat," Wolf observed. "But I wonder how he discovered that Langley was your father."

"Perhaps he beat it out of my mother," the young man suggested reluctantly.

"Or perhaps it just became obvious as you matured," Tabitha replied. She continued, "I've only talked to Langley once, the other evening, but now I think about it, your eyes are a perfect match for his. Yours have a warmth to them that his are lacking, and your colouring favours your mother, but now I know the truth, I wonder how I didn't see it before. You are clearly his son. You certainly don't favour the old duke in any way at all. Something that I'm sure was a constant irritant to him as it reminded him of the truth of your parentage."

"We need to talk to Langley," Wolf began to say. Anticipating the duke's answer, he added, "Tabitha and I need to talk to him. You may feel the need to have your own conversation with the man, but we need to decide if he had the opportunity to murder your father."

Anthony winced at the word 'father' but said nothing about it. However, he asked with curiosity more than anything, "I still don't understand why you are so adamant that my father's death was anything other than a by-product of the burglary. Moreover, I don't understand why you care to prove or disprove that. Is there something about all this that you're not telling me?"

Tabitha and Wolf exchanged glances, and with a quick, almost imperceptible shake of his head, Wolf indicated that they would not share the entire truth of the story with the man. Instead, he replied, "Do you not want to know the truth? If one of the men being blackmailed by the late duke caused his death, shouldn't he be punished?"

Anthony shook his head in doubt, "Yes, indeed. If this was why my father was killed, the murderer should be brought to justice. But I still don't understand why you believe this was the case."

"Just indulge us," Tabitha said gently. "We have some reason to suspect this may be the case. We won't drag you into our inquiries. And once we have exhausted this line of questioning, we will let it go. Won't we, Wolf?"

Wolf nodded his agreement. After all, it was possible that Seamus did kill the duke when he stole the necklace. All Wolf had committed to was investigating to the best of his abilities. Once he had done that, he would consider himself free of this debt to Mickey D.

There was one more request Wolf needed to make of the duke, "Somerset, I must ask for your indulgence; I need to interview everyone in your household, including your mother and grandmother."

"Whatever for?" the younger man demanded. "Surely, there can be no need for anything that intrusive."

Tabitha silently indicated to Wolf that she should manage this situation, "Anthony, we realise how hard this has all been on you all, but if someone else was in the house that night and murdered your father, that person must have been witnessed by someone. Perhaps a servant who doesn't realise the importance of what they saw or heard."

Anthony shook his head, "As I've stated, I see no reason to believe that the death was a result of anything other than a burglary gone wrong, and yet you're asking me to allow you to interrogate my entire household. Including my grieving mother and grandmother. Tabitha, how can you ask such a thing of me?"

In answer, Tabitha stood up and walked back over to where her old friend was sitting. She rested her hand on his arm and said as kindly as she was able, "Anthony, surely you can see that with everything we've discovered," as she said this, Tabitha waved her other arm to indicate the house, the girls, the photos and the letters, “that there may be more to the duke’s death than just the everyday theft of a necklace.

“He was a man who had woven a web of evil and dark secrets around himself. It is entirely plausible that he finally found himself caught in this web. We will be as discreet and sensitive as possible, but if you are all to put his wicked legacy behind you fully, we must shine the full light of truth upon his life and death.”

Anthony sighed in resigned acknowledgement of the wisdom of her words, “I will let the household know to expect you tomorrow and will tell everyone, including my family, to be as open and candid with you as possible.”

CHAPTER 27

They had left the house in Holborn in Mrs Caruthers's capable hands. Bear had stayed behind to help her. The little girls were initially wary of such a huge man, but he sat on the floor and started talking with them, and by the time Tabitha and Wolf had left, Bear had become a clear favourite.

"It is astounding that they can trust another man," Tabitha marvelled. "To see them up there, chattering away to Bear, it felt like they were any normal group of little girls. I'm sure there are scars which they may carry for their entire lives. And I'm sure that as time progresses, we will encounter inevitable mental wounds caused by what they've endured, but it makes my heart a little lighter to see that they're not totally broken."

Wolf nodded in agreement but secretly wasn't convinced that the girls' trauma wasn't severe. He wasn't sure what they could do to help them put their horrors behind them, but he suspected the children would never be able to heal fully.

They had also left Becky behind. The young girl begged to stay with her friends. The pull of friendship seemed greater than the memory of horrors. Tabitha was happy to let Becky do whatever gave her the most comfort. While the plan for the girls' future was vague, Tabitha was confident education would be a part of it. So, if Becky decided to stay with the other girls permanently, Tabitha would support her choice.

Anthony, Duke of Somerset, had also stayed. Wracked by guilt at what his father had done to the girls, he was unwilling to leave Mrs Caruthers behind and wash his hands of the situation. He wasn't sure how he could help her, but he expressed a willingness to do whatever she needed, however lowly the task.

Tabitha and Wolf discussed their next move in the carriage on the way home, "I know you will fight me on this, but I need to see Langley alone," Wolf stated, ready for an argument.

Instead, Tabitha laid her hand on his arm and replied, "I agree." Wolf expressed his amazement at her immediate capitulation. Tabitha laughed, "Am I so contrary that you always expect the worst from me? Indeed, I can imagine why you would expect me to demand participation, but you forget I have met Lord Langley. It wasn't hard to get the measure of the man. He won't respond well to my presence." Wolf could only agree.

They decided he would drop Tabitha off at home and then head straight over to Lord Langley's house to catch him in before he headed out for the evening. While Tabitha had no idea where the man lived, she correctly suspected that Talbot would. Servants knew all sorts of things.

As it happened, Langley didn't live far from his own house, so Wolf decided to walk over. He hoped that some fresh air and exercise would help clear his head and inspire him as to how to approach this conversation. On reaching the house, one slightly less grand than his own but nevertheless impressive, Wolf knocked on the door. It was opened by a man who looked like he could be his own butler's twin brother. As it happened, Wolf had discovered when he'd asked Talbot about the other earl's address that this man was his first cousin. His name was also Talbot.

Wolf asked to speak with the earl and was being brushed off by this other Talbot when the earl, Lord Langley, appeared in the hallway. "What is it, Talbot? I thought I heard the door."

"Your lordship, this gentleman requests an audience with you. I was just telling him that you were unavailable."

Langley walked over to the door, and recognition spread over his features, "Pembroke, isn't it? I remember you from the ball."

"Yes, Langley. I only need a few moments of your time."

The other man answered in an icy tone, "Well, I'm afraid that I'm on my way out for the evening, so this will have to wait."

The conversation so far had been conducted on the doorstep,

with Wolf left standing like a common merchant come to peddle his wares. Wolf decided that only boldness would work with this man, so he stepped into the house, causing the butler to step backwards or collide with a peer of the realm. "Really, Pembroke, this simply won't do. You arrive at my house without notice and then force your way in. I realise that you were not born and raised within society, but even so, this is beyond the pale."

Initially, Wolf had planned to be discreet and sensitive about the matter he had to discuss, but this constituted a throwing down of the gauntlet, and he said, with no regard for who could hear him, "I would like to discuss your son with you."

Langley was a fair-skinned man, yet he visibly paled at this statement. He paused for a moment and then indicated that Wolf should follow him. He led the way to his study and indicated that Wolf should sit. He then sat down behind the desk. "As is well known, I am unmarried, and I can assure you that I have never fathered a child on either side of the blanket."

Wolf was a good chess player and knew a weak opening move when he saw one, "And yet you let me in when I mentioned a son. Surely a man who was sure he was childless would not have capitulated so quickly."

Langley didn't answer, but he did get up and pour them each a glass of brandy. After handing one to Wolf, he sat back down and began to swirl the drink in his glass, gazing into the amber liquid as if hoping to discover the best next move in its depths. Finally, Wolf continued, "Let us stop playing games. Neither of us has the time or patience. At least I know I don't. I know the new Duke of Somerset, Anthony Rowley, is your natural son." Wolf held his hand up to prevent whatever denial was coming next and said, "And he knows as well. His mother told him quite a few years ago that Somerset was not his father."

"Never! She would never do that."

"And yet she did. I also know that the former duke was blackmailing you with this information. I don't know what he wanted from you, and I don't know what he was threatening to do beyond revealing a fact that wouldn't have changed who the title passed to, but I do know that blackmail was taking place."

The other man sighed, sipped his brandy and then decided. "Cassandra, the now Duchess of Somerset, and I were in love. We were both 18 and had met at a ball. She was the most beautiful creature I had ever seen. We met secretly for weeks, but eventually, she convinced me that I needed to ask her father for her hand in marriage."

"Why all the skulduggery? You were an earl or at least the heir to a title. Wouldn't you have been seen as a good prospect?"

The other man laughed sardonically, "Back then, I was neither an earl nor the heir to the title. I wasn't even a second son, but a third. Cassandra's father was a marquess, and while her family might have deigned to have her lower herself to marry an earl, they certainly weren't going to throw her away on a nobody. But we were young and in love and hopeful. And so, I built up my courage and asked for her hand in marriage. Her father all but threw me out of the house.

"By the next week, Cassandra was betrothed to Somerset, then Viscount Rowley. But, with the help of a soft-hearted lady's maid, we managed a last meeting. Anthony was conceived during that last tryst. We were both innocents, and neither realised the import of what we had done and the likely consequences."

Langley paused, took another sip of brandy to fortify himself, and continued, "She was married three weeks later. When she found herself pregnant, she genuinely believed it was her husband's. But he knew it wasn't."

"How could he have been so sure of that?" Wolf asked incredulously.

"It turned out that Somerset was unable to consummate the marriage. Over the years, I've heard whispers in the clubs, mere slivers of ephemeral gossip, but enough to make me believe that his tastes ran to other, how can I say it, younger flesh. At almost 19, Cassandra was too old to rouse her husband's desire.

"Cassandra, in her innocence, had no idea that her marriage had not been successfully consummated. She happily informed her husband of the impending birth when she first missed her courses. "

"When did he inform her of the truth?" Wolf asked.

"You have met Anthony, The Duke of Somerset, correct?"

"Yes, I met him the other day for the first time," Wolf answered.

"What was your impression of the man?"

Wolf wasn't sure how to answer this. Was it a trick question?

Langley saved him from having to answer by continuing, "I'm assuming it was obvious he is, what is the best word to use? Delicate, yes, that's the word. I'm assuming it was clear how delicate he is." Wolf didn't refute this assumption, and Langley continued, "Somerset was what might be called a man's man. Hunting, riding, boxing, drinking heavily, and gambling were how he spent his leisure hours. But his son liked reading, liked music. Once, he caught the boy learning to sew from Cassandra and could barely restrain himself from thrashing them both. Anthony was not the son and heir he wanted. The fact that he knew that he wasn't his son only exacerbated his frustrations at the boy's perceived failings. Finally, he couldn't stop himself from throwing this fact in Cassandra's face.

"When did her husband realise that the child was yours?" Wolf couldn't help but ask.

"Cassandra's marriage to that man was a deeply unhappy one. I had stayed away from her. In fact, had gone to the continent for more than 12 years. Anything, so I didn't have to witness her marrying another man. While I was gone, my older brothers died, one in a hunting accident and one of a lifelong sickness.

"Suddenly, I was called back from abroad and found myself an earl. Inevitably, Cassandra and I were thrown together socially, and eventually, we found our way back to each other. It didn't take long for Somerset to become suspicious. Of course, such affairs are not uncommon in our circles and are usually tolerated as long as the parties are discreet. And as the boy matured, the resemblance to me must have been sufficient to make him suspicious. He was incensed at being made a cuckold.

The man paused again, took another sip, then looked directly at Wolf and said, with a little apologetic shrug of his shoulders, "And then there were the letters."

"Letters? What letters?"

"Somerset intercepted letters between Cassandra and me and then confronted her with them. He had been spying on our correspondence for some time, waiting for the most damaging letters. One day, Cassandra referred to our child, and this was the letter he finally used against her.

"He made clear that the only way she could ensure he wouldn't disinherit Anthony and use the letters to divorce her for adultery was if she broke off all contact with me. That was when he approached me, and the blackmail began."

Wolf was curious, "What did he blackmail you for?"

Langley's face contorted with hatred, "That is the sickening part of all this; he needed nothing from me except to stay away from his wife. But he was a sadistic bastard; the pleasure of blackmail for him was not in any material gain he could make but in knowing his hold over someone. He made it clear that he might ask me for something at any point. Maybe money, some kind of help, maybe my vote in the House of Lords. He wasn't sure what it might be. But when he asked, he expected me to jump to attention. He liked to remind me of his hold over me regularly."

Wolf laid his cards out in front of this man, "It seems you were not the only person he was blackmailing. He had compromising photos of some very eminent men. Photos that would undoubtedly bring disgrace and perhaps even ruin. Would you imagine that he behaved similarly towards them? That the hold he had was the true reward he sought?"

Langley agreed with that assessment, "Somerset was a bastard. From just the snippets I heard around my club and the House, he was likely involved in various business dealings that were, at the very least, of a shady nature. If you have his heir's ear, you should encourage him to audit all his holdings thoroughly. Anyone involved in such businesses likely often needs a favour from a judge or someone in the government to turn a blind eye. So, I'm sure he sometimes called in the 'favours' he was due. But, I doubt I was the only person he took enjoyment from torturing."

Now, Wolf had come to the most difficult part of the conversation. He paused, then said, "There is reason to believe that the deceased duke's death was not merely the result of a botched robbery. It is clear that everyone he had a hold over," and at this, he looked the other earl directly in the eye, "everyone had some motive to want him dead."

"Are you suggesting that I murdered the man?" Langley asked with a wry, hollow laugh.

"I'm suggesting that you, amongst others, had a motive. In fact, you had more motive than most. You were in love with his wife and watched him treat her and your natural son with great cruelty. He threatened to disinherit your son and disgrace the woman you love. It would be almost unnatural if you didn't wish the man dead."

"You are right, of course. I harboured great ill will towards the man. I tried to get Cassandra to leave him. Even if he could have divorced her and left her penniless, I would have married her."

"And yet she wouldn't?" Wolf asked.

"She could have lived with the disgrace for herself but not for her son. Society can be vicious, and he is a sensitive soul. She could not do that to him. And then, of course, there was Hannah."

Wolf couldn't help but ask, "Is Hannah also your child?"

"No, she is not. After twelve years of an unconsummated marriage, Somerset became so incensed by what he saw as Cassandra's mollycoddling of his son that he got blindingly drunk one day and attacked her. Apparently, the thrill of assault overcame whatever performance issues he had previously suffered. Hannah is the result of that night. If her husband had divorced her for adultery, he would have gained sole custody of their daughter, and Cassandra could have been prevented from seeing her child."

"You must see that this all gives you even more motive to kill the man, " Wolf pointed out.

"Yes. I can see how it might look that way. I can only tell you that I didn't kill him. I might have wanted to and won't pretend to be sorry that he's dead. But I wasn't the one to commit the crime."

"Do you have an alibi for the night in question?"

"I would have to check my diary, but if I wasn't out at my club, I was likely home for the evening. My household staff will be my alibi." They both knew how likely it was that the man's servants would say anything other than that he was home all that night, so Wolf didn't press the matter.

However, he did reply, "I would appreciate you checking your diary, nevertheless, at your convenience." With that, he stood up, thanked the earl for his time, and excused himself. As he was about to leave the study, he turned and asked, "Langley, what will you do now?"

"About what?" the man replied.

"About the duchess. About your son."

"Ah, yes, that is the question, isn't it? Cassandra will mourn the full year, I am sure. And when that year is up, I will ask her to become my wife. I have every reason to believe she will accept. At that point, her son will become my stepson, at least in the eyes of society, and I hope we can form a close relationship." He paused, then added, "Just because I didn't kill the man doesn't mean I don't intend to take advantage of his death." Wolf nodded in acknowledgement of this and left.

CHAPTER 28

Tabitha held dinner until Wolf returned, waiting impatiently for him in the drawing room, sipping on a sherry to calm her nerves. When she heard the door, she jumped out and ran into the hallway to meet him. She could barely wait for him to remove his outerwear before pulling him back into the drawing room with her.

"Tabitha, I realise you're anxious to hear how the meeting went. But can we move the conversation to the dining room? I'm famished."

They alerted Talbot that they were ready to eat and settled at the dining room table. "Now, tell me how it went," Tabitha demanded. "He is so clearly evil, don't you agree?"

Wolf laughed, "Tabitha if you want to be successful at the investigation game, you'll have to find a good balance between trusting your instincts and not judging a book by its cover.

I agree that Lord Langley is difficult to like, at least initially." Tabitha was curious about that choice of words but didn't want to slow down his story with questions. "Rather than being a textbook villain, the man has led a life of disappointments, which has hardened him." He then told her Langley and Cassandra's love story, Somerset's discovery of Anthony's true parentage, and subsequent threats against the mother and son.

When Wolf arrived at the part where Langley claimed that the duke had derived a sadistic pleasure from threats he held over the heads of others, Tabitha couldn't help but exclaim, "The duke was a thoroughly despicable man, wasn't he? I've concluded that no matter who killed him or why, they did the world a great favour by removing such evil."

Wolf couldn't disagree and continued, "Langley denies he murdered the man, even while acknowledging that his life will be greatly improved with him gone. He certainly has a motive. He may well have had the opportunity, and yet," he paused, considering what he wanted to say next. "And yet, my instinct is to believe him. I'm unsure why I do, yet there it is."

They didn't linger over dinner; they wanted to retire to the parlour and put everything they had discovered on notecards and the board. They were in the middle of this when Mickey D entered the room. Tabitha was so used to the man entering the house by stealth and just appearing in their midst she didn't even bother commenting on the fact.

"Mickey, what can we do for you?" Wolf asked.

"Well, for a start, you can tell me you've discovered who killed the duke." Mickey retorted. "Bruiser gave me a heads up that the peelers had a tip-off that my lads were involved in the burglary and that they'd be paying me a visit tomorrow. I've had to get Seamus and the necklace out of the country quickly."

Tabitha couldn't help but ask, "How do you know they won't just assume it's another one of your gang?"

"Bruiser says they've found a witness who can identify a man seen leaving the back of the toff's house. Honestly, I don't know if they do, but it's better to be safe than sorry."

"I have to point out, Mickey, that if they have a witness, then Seamus could have been arrested for the burglary whether we find the supposed murderer or not," Wolf stated.

"There's a big difference between being found guilty of theft and murder. If it's murder, he'll hang." As far as Tabitha was concerned, a lengthy prison sentence didn't seem like such a wonderful alternative, but she kept this thought to herself. Mickey continued, "But it's more than just the lad Seamus; I have a reputation in London. I'm not a murderer, and neither are my lads. Peelers like Bruiser deal with me when they have to because they know there are far worse than me out there." That at least made more sense to Tabitha.

Mickey D stood up and looked at their board. He said nothing while he read all the evidence they had collected. Tabitha was impressed that the man could read. Finally, Mickey turned back to them and asked, “So it seems that duke was a nasty piece of work if ever there was one.”

Tabitha and Wolf couldn’t disagree, and so said nothing. Mickey continued, “Not that my lad Seamus did kill him mind, but if everything you have here is true, he’d have removed a real evil from this world if he had. Not that he did, ” he added.

“So, what are your next steps?” Mickey asked.

“I was just about to tell her ladyship that tomorrow, the new Duke of Somerset has given us leave to question his entire household, including his mother and grandmother. Someone must have seen or heard something.” He paused momentarily, then asked Mickey, “Did Bruiser tell you who came forward as the supposed witness?”

Mickey laughed, “Bruiser is happy to play both sides, but he’s not stupid enough to set me on a potential eyewitness.”

They didn’t have much more to share with Mickey, and he let himself out once it was clear he would not be offered any brandy.

The next morning, they had a light breakfast and left for Rowley House. Wolf had sent a note to Anthony alerting him to their arrival time. Tabitha said it was essential that the duke, as the new head of the household, be present to ensure everyone’s cooperation.

Anthony received them in the bright, modern drawing room. He was sitting with his mother and grandmother, neither one of whom looked at all happy. There was also a young woman Tabitha didn’t immediately recognise. She must have been at least ten years older than Tabitha but had a childishness to her look that made her seem younger. She was very pretty but with the aura about her of a cornered animal, scared and looking to escape. She had lovely dark brown eyes that were wide with some emotion. Was it just nervousness? Was it fear?

Tabitha continued to think she recognised the woman but wasn’t sure. Luckily, Anthony made the introductions, “Lady Pembroke, Tabitha, I believe you know my grandmother, the

Dowager Duchess of Somerset, and my mother, the duchess. And I'm unsure if you remember my aunt, Fannie, Lady Fannie." He gestured towards the young woman who looked, if possible, even more nervous about having attention called to herself.

"Of course, I remember you now, Lady Fannie. We met many years ago when I was just a child, climbing trees and scraping my knees at your country estate with Anthony. " So, this was Fannie. Tabitha was wracking her memory for what she knew about the late duke's much younger sister. She was clearly still unmarried. She realised she would inevitably have to call upon her mother-in-law again if she wanted the full story.

Her attention was drawn back as Anthony's grandmother, the dowager duchess, stood up and said imperiously, "Anthony has insisted that we all talk with you. But, I would like to state my opposition. We all gave our statements to the police when Martin was killed in what was clearly a burglary gone wrong. I have no idea why you two, or my grandson, believe you know better than a police inspector. However, Anthony insists, so I will sit for your questions. But I am not happy about this. Not happy at all."

Wolf stepped in and said as gently and graciously as was possible, "Your Grace, well, both Your Graces, in fact, and Lady Fannie, I assure you that we would not be inconveniencing you if we didn't believe it possible that a gross miscarriage of justice might take place without our involvement.

"To inconvenience you as little as possible, why don't we talk with you all first and then talk to the rest of the household staff?" the dowager duchess made a harumphing sound but didn't disagree. Wolf turned to Anthony, "I assume you have a study here. Would it be possible for us to use it for our interviews?" Anthony assented and stood to take them there.

"Lady Fannie, why don't you go first?" Wolf said.

The young woman turned panicked eyes to her mother, who said, "I will be present when you interview my daughter. I will brook no argument about this." Obviously, this wasn't a fight they would win, so they accepted the inevitable and followed the dowager duchess to Anthony's study.

Wolf took the chair behind the desk, and Tabitha moved an armchair next to it so they could both fully view their interviewees. The dowager and her daughter settled on the last two chairs, which Wolf had turned towards the desk before sitting down.

"Lady Fannie," Wolf began, "if you can take me through your movements on the evening of your brother's death. I apologise for making you recount such unpleasant memories, but I believe this is important."

The woman acknowledged his words and began, "We all had dinner together as usual. Then Cassandra, Mama and I retired to the drawing room, leaving Martin behind with his port. When we don't have guests, we ladies usually go to our beds early. However, Martin has always been a night owl. Often staying up reading in his library until the early morning hours sometimes."

"Did the late duke follow you into the drawing room after his port?" Tabitha asked.

"Yes, briefly. Cassandra likes to play the piano of an evening, and mother and I often play cards. Martin had no patience for either activity and usually came in briefly and then removed himself to his study."

Wolf picked the questioning back up, "And just for clarification, this room is the study and is where the duke would spend most evenings?"

The younger woman shivered at the realisation that she might be sitting in the very chair her brother was murdered in and answered, "Yes, this room was Martin's sanctuary. Mother and I rarely entered it when he was alive, and I believe the same is true of Cassandra."

"Which floor is your bedroom on?" Wolf asked.

"My bedroom is on the floor above, with the rest of the family's rooms."

"Given that this study is on the ground floor, is it reasonable to say that if your brother had guests in the evening, you would be unlikely to know about it?"

At this, the dowager interrupted, "We have a staff who keeps me informed of all comings and goings."

"Except that," Wolf pointed out, "your butler was off that night and, by all accounts, your upper footman may have been," Wolf paused, trying to find a delicate way to phrase what he needed to say, "indisposed. Is that correct?"

The dowager replied, "We may have been somewhat light on staff that night. However, we would have known if someone had knocked on the door and been admitted."

"What if they didn't knock?" Tabitha asked. "What if they arrived at an appointed time or even entered by force?"

Again, the dowager answered, "Well, we know someone did; the burglar. I'm not sure what the point of rehashing the obvious is."

Wolf asked, "Did you hear the burglar enter the house?"

"What kind of absurd question is that?" the dowager demanded. "Do you think we would have cowed in our rooms if we'd known someone was breaking into our house?"

Actually, neither Tabitha nor Wolf couldn't imagine what else this elderly woman and her frail daughter would have done if they'd suspected their house had been broken into. Still, they refrained from pointing this out, and instead, Wolf asked, "So, if you didn't hear the burglar, why would you have heard if another person had also entered the house, perhaps also breaking in?"

The dowager had no answer for this but deflected and asked with a voice dripping in sarcasm, "So you are asking me to believe that our house was the site of not one, but two break-ins that night? That is quite the coincidence, Lord Pembroke!"

"I agree that this isn't the most straightforward solution, but I instead wanted to make the point that if you didn't hear one break-in, there might have been another visitor of whom none of you were aware that night." The dowager's silence conceded the possibility.

Accepting that there was no way to question Lady Fannie without her mother's interjections, Wolf decided to make the most of having them together, "Your Grace, was your evening in any way different than your daughter's?"

Tabitha noticed something flick across the older woman's face. She wasn't sure exactly what it was, but she believed they were about to be lied to, "My evening was the mirror of my daughter's. I retired to bed no later than 10. My maid helped me prepare for bed, and I was asleep I'm sure by 10:30 and didn't stir until morning." There, that was the lie. Tabitha was sure of it. As she said this last statement, her eye twitched very briefly.

Tabitha glanced at Wolf, but it was impossible to tell from his face if he had noticed the same thing. He continued questioning, "And who discovered your son's body the next morning?"

The dowager answered quickly and confidently, "Annie, my personal maid."

Something in this answer was too sure as if it was rehearsed, and it didn't make sense to Tabitha, "Your lady's maid? Why would she be the one to come into your son's study?" The dowager didn't answer. Tabitha continued, "At least in my household, one of the housemaids would come in first thing and make up the fire. Certainly not my lady's maid."

The dowager hesitated, clearly trying to decide how to answer, "Perhaps I have that wrong. Perhaps one of the housemaids had come in first." Her previous confidence in answering contradicted her statement.

"They'd come into the study, make up the fire and somehow not notice their master bludgeoned to death in a chair by that very fire? That surely strains the bound of credulity," Wolf said.

The dowager had no reply, and Wolf and Tabitha realised that this conversation was at a standoff. But Tabitha had one more question to ask of the very nervous Lady Fannie, who had been anxiously picking at her cuticles through most of the conversation, "Lady Fannie, just one more question; did you like your brother?"

This was clearly not a question she was prepared to answer, and her mother's eyes immediately flashed with anger as she asked, "What kind of question is that, Lady Pembroke? And to ask of a woman in mourning."

"I apologise if this line of questioning is painful, but I need your daughter to answer. I know what it is to go through the mourning rituals for a man I had nothing but personal distaste for." The dowager duchess' eyebrows raised in surprise at this statement, but she did not comment.

"So, I ask again, Lady Fannie, did you like your brother?"

With tears forming in her eyes and beginning to roll down her cheeks, the duke's sister admitted, "I hated him. He was not a good brother, son, husband or father. My brother was cruel and took great pleasure in inflicting pain on those around him. I believe no one in this family truly mourns his death." The dowager looked as if she were about to refute this statement, but her daughter reached out her hand and lightly touched her mother's. "Mama, it is but the truth, and we can ignore it no more. Martin was a brute, and all our lives are better with him gone."

With this dramatic statement made, Tabitha and Wolf didn't have much else to ask the mother and daughter and asked them to send Cassandra into the study.

The deceased duke's wife was composed and thoughtful in her answers, which stuck so closely to the story told by the dowager that, again, both Tabitha and Wolf sensed a coordination of the two stories. And just as with the dowager, when she came to the part where she had fallen asleep and heard nothing, telltale expressions on her face indicated an attempt to deceive.

Tabitha glanced at Wolf, and an unspoken agreement passed between them that Tabitha would pursue the next, more delicate line of questioning. "Your Grace, you were quite a few years younger than your husband, is that correct?"

"Indeed, but that is hardly unusual in society."

Tabitha played her next card, "Was it a love match?"

The other woman laughed humourlessly, "Was your marriage a love match, Lady Pembroke? How many love matches are made in our circles? Martin was to be a duke. It was a very eligible match as far as my father was concerned."

Tabitha hated herself for having to interrogate this woman on painful issues she had such personal experience of, but she had no choice, "Were you in love with someone else perhaps?"

Cassandra, the Duchess of Somerset, sat up a little straighter, if that were possible, looked Tabitha squarely in the eye and said, "Langley sent me a note this morning. Please don't dissemble; we both know I was in love with another. And we both know the truth of Anthony's birth." She continued, "I know that you believe Langley a prime suspect in my husband's death, and I can even see why you would think that.

"As I'm sure you've heard, my husband was a viciously cruel man. The only time our marriage was consummated was through an act of brutal assault on my person. Langley may have had every reason in the world to want my husband gone, but I can assure you, Maxwell would never stoop to murder."

"How can you be so sure?" Wolf asked.

"Have you ever loved someone, Lord Pembroke?" The question caught Wolf off guard, and he wasn't sure how to answer. "What about you, Lady Pembroke? It is common knowledge that your husband was no kinder than mine. You surely felt no love for him. Have you ever had strong emotions towards another, perhaps?" Before she could help it, Tabitha glanced at Wolf, only to find him looking at her.

The duchess' sharp eyes caught the exchange, "So that is how it is? Interesting. Then let me ask you when you love someone deeply, do you believe there is a side of them of which you're unaware? Or do you believe that you understand each other fully and completely, and that is what true love is: seeing each other's flaws and loving anyway?

"I know Maxwell. He is a complicated man. Our separation over these twenty or so years has hardened him and made him uncharitable to the world. But he is a gentle man at his core and could not resort to such a brutal act, even for my sake."

Wolf let this all go. Having met the man, he was not convinced of his inherent gentleness, but this was not a point worth debating. However, he had one final question: "Your Grace, how would you characterise your late husband's relationship with your daughter?"

The immediate reaction on the woman's face was so extreme that even though she worked immediately to rearrange her features to hide it, she knew it hadn't been quick enough. "As I have already said, Martin was not a kind man. That extended to his children."

The conversation ended shortly after, and the interviews of the staff began. The butler confirmed that he had been out of town when the murder happened. He explained that his mother was ailing. He had requested time off to return to his village to visit her. The upper footman, when pressed, admitted to spending the evening in the butler's parlour drinking the man's brandy. He acknowledged that he was probably asleep by the time the family went to bed and would have been highly unlikely to have heard anyone entering the house.

Penny and Ginger, the housemaids, couldn't explain why Annie, the lady's maid, had been in the late duke's study. They agreed that laying the fire in every room was part of their daily duties. They could think of nothing special about that morning that would cause Annie to rise even earlier than they did and enter the room. They were just grateful that, whatever the reason, she had done so and saved them from finding the body.

CHAPTER 29

Annie, the dowager's lady's maid, was the final person they questioned. Tabitha guessed the woman was in her mid to late thirties. She fancied that she could see something of the woman's relation to her own maid Ginny in her face, but perhaps it was nothing more than the apparent Irish heritage both women had.

What was clear was that Annie was not happy about the interview. She entered the room with an obstinate, sullen look that did not bode well for the conversation ahead. Tabitha had decided that she didn't want to break Ginny's confidence with her cousin, and so had decided to ask the same question Ginny had over tea and see for herself what the reaction was.

"Annie, isn't it?" Tabitha began. She hoped to ease the woman into the conversation and win her trust. "I believe you know, indeed, are friends with my maid Ginny."

The maid nodded her assent, but the hard look on her face never wavered.

"I'm assuming that, just like Ginny, you grew up in Whitechapel."

"Aye, I was born in Ireland, but we moved to London when I was a wee lass."

Wolf stepped in, "Before ascending to my title, I spent a lot of time in Whitechapel. I wonder if you know Mickey D." At this name, the woman's eyes opened in what could only be interpreted as panic. She licked her lips, obviously trying to determine how much Tabitha and Wolf already knew about her connections in Whitechapel.

Finally, making some kind of decision, Annie answered

briefly, "Aye. I know the man."

"How do you know him?" Wolf continued.

Recognising the futility of evading the question, Annie answered, "As it seems you may already know, the man is my uncle for my sins."

"That's an interesting way of putting it," Wolf observed.

"How would you put it if your mother's family was one of the most notorious gang of criminals in London?"

Wolf considered how to frame his next question. He was sure Mickey D hadn't warned Annie, but she was obviously suspicious about how much they already knew. He'd rather see what she volunteered before showing his hand. "My understanding, from Mickey himself, is that he tries to install young people in some of the great houses of London. Young people who are perhaps willing to be of service to him."

Annie snorted, "Of service? That's a nice way of putting it. He installs spies and accessories to his crimes. And no, before you ask, I am not one of them. My mother has always been dead against her brother and his ways, and I have too much loyalty to m'lady to go against her family in any way."

Wolf decided it was time to show his hand, "And yet, there is a young boy, installed in this house by Mickey, and by my understanding of it, you are aware of the fact."

The maid looked incredibly discomforted by this statement. Still, she hardened her features even more and demanded, "And where would you be hearing such a thing from?"

"From Mickey D himself," Wolf answered. He wasn't sure what Annie had expected, but it wasn't to hear this. "According to Mickey, you were not only aware of the boy but warned him that you would be watching him."

Wolf could see that Annie was about to try to sputter out some explanation. Still, he held up his hand and continued, "And yet, despite all this, even though you knew that a notorious gang of thieves had installed someone in this house, you never made mention to the police or the dowager duchess of the fact after the burglary. How could that be?"

Annie licked her lips again and said, "I'm no snitch. I'd warned the boy off, and my ma had warned off Mickey. I had no reason to think they hadn't heeded the warning, so I assumed another gang took the necklace."

The absurdity of that statement was so self-evident that Wolf didn't bother to push on the subject. But he did move to another line of questioning, "Annie, one more question; do your daily duties involve making up fires in the morning."

Before she could consider what she was saying, the woman said indignantly, "I'm a lady's maid, not a parlourmaid."

"Indeed. That was what Lady Pembroke and I assumed. So, why were you in the deceased duke's study well before the parlourmaid?"

Again, it was obvious by how the woman chewed on her lip that she was considering how to answer. Finally, she seemed to land on something plausible, "M'lady had sent me to find a book."

Tabitha couldn't help exclaiming incredulously, "A book? At that early hour? I find it hard to believe the dowager duchess is even awake at such an hour, let alone ready to sit down to read. What was the book?"

Stumped by this question, Annie answered, "I don't remember."

Tabitha had a thought, stood and went over to the bookcases lining one wall in the study. "Annie, can you join me over here for a moment." The woman stood up reluctantly. She joined Tabitha, who said, "Can you read me these book titles, please." After a few hesitant attempts to sound out the names, Tabitha took pity on the woman and said, "Thank you, Annie, you may go."

Back at the house, Wolf and Tabitha gathered Bear, Ginny and Rat for a war council. These three had been such important parts of the investigation so far that Tabitha and Wolf felt obligated to share with them all they had learned over the last couple of days.

As Tabitha wrote out more notecards, Wolf explained all they had discovered. When it came to their interview with Annie,

Wolf reluctantly told Ginny, "I'm sorry to say this because I know the woman is a friend, more than a friend, but she's lying. The duchess and the dowager are lying as well, of course. Whatever reason Annie had for going to the study that morning, it wasn't because she was retrieving a book. She can barely read. Even allowing for the absurdity of the dowager rising before dawn and desperately desiring a particular book, there was no way for Annie to tell if she had found the correct book."

Tabitha raised her head from writing, took a blank notecard and said, while she wrote, "Why was Annie in the study so early?"

Rat piped up, "It's like she knew she was going to find something there, ain't it?"

Wolf and Tabitha nodded, agreeing, "You're right, Rat. That's exactly how it looks. For some reason, she knew what she would find and, perhaps, wished to ensure that she found the body before the other maids."

Reluctantly, Ginny asked, "Do you think that she knew about what the thief had done?"

Wolf answered, "That's certainly one likely scenario. We know she has links to Mickey D's gang. We know that she knew he had a boy installed in the house. Perhaps, she knew more about the planned burglary than we realise."

Ginny was very anxious to defend her friend, "Maybe she had a suspicion about the burglary, but how would she have known about the murder?"

"I don't know," Wolf acknowledged, "but it's the only thing that explains why she went into that study, let alone so early. It seems as if she wanted to ensure she was the first to witness what had happened. For that to be the case, she had to have had some idea that a crime had occurred."

Tabitha asked, "What do we make of the duchess and her daughter-in-law lying about their activities that night? Or, at the very least, lying about whether they heard anything?"

"I don't know," Wolf admitted, "but I observed that as well. In fact, between the ladies of the house and their maid, the only person I am convinced was telling us the unvarnished truth, at least she saw it, was Lady Fannie."

Tabitha agreed, adding, "I'm also convinced that Anthony is innocent of any knowledge. Would you agree, Wolf?" He did agree. Tabitha pinned the new notecards on the board and arranged them to reflect their new discoveries. She sat back down, and they all sat in silent contemplation. After a while, Tabitha said, "Much as I hate to say it, I must visit the dowager countess tomorrow." Wolf raised an eyebrow in surprise, and she continued, "Alone. As much as the dowager is quite a fan of yours, I believe what I must ask her will be answered with more candour, woman to woman."

Tabitha stood in front of the board with all the notecards attached to it and groups, contemplating it for a while. Eventually, she turned to the group and said, "Something that's been said repeatedly during this investigation is the unlikely coincidence of two unrelated crimes happening in the same house on the same night."

No one said anything, unsure where her reasoning was taking her. She continued slowly, as if trying to work out the jumble of her thoughts, "Every time someone states this, it's been with the underlying assumption that the primary crime was the theft of the necklace and that the murder of the duke was ancillary to the completion of the burglary. The assumption has been made that Seamus entered the study to steal the necklace, was surprised by the duke sitting there drinking his nightcap, and that Seamus killed the duke with the candlestick and escaped with the necklace."

Everyone nodded in agreement, but still, nobody said anything. "Early on, we observed that the duke was murdered while sitting in his chair, but that makes no sense. If we play out the scene, Seamus presumably enters through the study window. He begins to make his way to where he believes the safe is. Meanwhile, the duke sits in his armchair in front of the fire. We were in that room today. Wolf, you had to move the armchairs away from the fireplace so that we could sit at the desk and interview everyone.

The room's layout is such that the window is behind the desk, bookcases are on the wall in front of the desk, and the fireplace and chairs are to the left. Thinking about that room, the most likely place for the safe is on the wall to the right of the desk. There were two paintings on that wall, so I expect the safe is behind one. We should confirm this with Anthony."

Wolf nodded in agreement and said, "I believe you're right. Unless the safe is in some particularly clever spot, such as behind a false front in the bookcase, it must be behind one of the paintings. We know Seamus found the safe, so it's reasonable to assume it wasn't cleverly hidden."

"Exactly," Tabitha continued. "So, Seamus enters through the window behind the desk. At this point, the duke sits with his back to the window. Those chairs had high backs. Seamus wouldn't have seen anyone sitting there, so he had no reason to cross to that side of the room.

"The duke hears Seamus enter. Why would he stay seated? We've already observed that the likely action is for him to stand up. Not just stand up but walk towards the intruder. Now let's consider the candelabra. Rowley House, just like Chesterton House, has gas lighting, but it's believable that the duke preferred to read late at night by candlelight. So, the candlestick is by his chair. Why would he not pick it up to see who had entered? If he had picked it up and Seamus had wrestled it away from him and killed the duke with it, as we've been led to believe, then the body would have been found on the floor."

Ginny interjected, "Seamus could have moved the body to the chair."

"Yes, he could have. But why bother? Surely, at that point, all he was concerned with was taking the necklace and leaving as quickly as possible. Everyone said they heard nothing, but wouldn't the duke have called out? Wouldn't he yell for help if he came upon an intruder? After all, he didn't know the footman was drunk and asleep.

"None of it makes sense if the underlying story is as we've

been led to believe. And, as I've said before, why was the light off in the room? Mickey D said Seamus waited for the light to go off before he broke in. But if the duke was there reading, why was there no light?"

"But what else could it be, m'lady?" Bear asked. Everyone else was waiting, intrigued to see where Tabitha would take her conjecture next.

"What if murdering the duke was the plan all along? If he was killed in his armchair, then this explains why he never stood up. And why wouldn't he stand up if he heard a noise? And if he'd been asleep in the armchair, Seamus would never have known the duke was in the room and would have opened the safe, taken the necklace, and left. For the duke to sleep through all that, he must have been in an incredibly deep sleep."

Wolf suddenly saw where Tabitha's thinking was going, "Or he'd been drugged."

"Exactly!"

"M'lady, I apologise if I'm too slow to keep up," Ginny said. "But why would someone drug him? Even if they knew that the burglary would occur, there could have been no way to be certain that Seamus would kill the man. Unless Seamus is lying and had intended to kill the duke all along."

"You're not slow at all, Ginny. You're exactly right. One possibility is that Seamus lied and was hired to murder the duke in his study, making it look like a burglary had gone wrong. Of course, we only have Mickey's word that Seamus didn't kill the duke."

Wolf said carefully, "I'm disinclined to believe this version of events. I've met Seamus. He's a smart lad. I'm not saying he couldn't be paid to murder a man; everyone has their price. But this strikes me as a dumb way to go about it. After all, as we've seen, it didn't take long for the police to focus on Mickey D's gang because of the burglary. Killing the duke in the one way that was most likely to lead back to him just seems like something Seamus was too savvy to sign up for. Why not kill him another way? Attack him on the street, for example?"

"And we're missing something; if, as we've posited, the duke must have been drugged and if he didn't wake when Seamus entered the study, then someone in that house is the most likely candidate to have added something to his food or drink," Tabitha pointed out. At this point, she was pacing the room, her thoughts whirling around in her head so quickly that she was having a hard time keeping them all straight. "But, if his food or drink was drugged, why not go further and poison him? Why complicate the scenario with the whole burglary?"

Wolf answered her, "Because whoever drugged him wanted to ensure that the finger of blame was pointed firmly outside of the household."

"So, are we saying that someone in Rowley House killed the duke?", Ginny asked.

"Well, I believe it's still possible that someone other than Seamus entered the house that night and was the person who bludgeoned the duke. But I believe they must have had help from someone within the house who drugged him. But, as the earl and I have discussed, the simplest explanation is often right. And in this case, the simplest explanation is that the person who wanted the duke dead is someone in the man's household.

"By all accounts, he was a despicable person. If his own sister has no love for him, I can't imagine that his household staff cared much for the man. It's not hard to imagine all sorts of motives people might have to kill him."

Ginny asked, "Would you like me to try to find out if any of the maids seem to have suddenly found themselves in the family way? If he'd been messing with the maids, perhaps someone killed the duke to avenge her."

Tabitha considered this and answered, "Under normal circumstances, I would agree. But we know that the duke had very particular tastes. Ginny, are any of the maids young enough to be of interest to such a man?"

"I don't believe so, m'lady. When I was there the other day, I met the scullery maid, and she's at least 15. And a large, strapping girl at that."

"Well," Tabitha concluded, "I believe that it's now even more imperative I talk with the dowager countess tomorrow. The Rowley family has secrets, and that much is clear. The dowager duchess and her daughter-in-law were lying about something. And they'd coordinated their stories, I'm sure of it. If anyone knows their secrets and what they're hiding, it'll be my mother-in-law. I'll send a note around now asking for an early audience. I'll tell her we need her help. That will undoubtedly intrigue her enough for her to agree."

CHAPTER 30

As Tabitha had anticipated, the dowager was intrigued enough by her note to suggest Tabitha call in the morning. Tabitha dressed as conservatively as possible. While not happy to concede so much to the dowager that she put her full mourning clothes back on, she did dress in the darkest half-mourning dress she owned and pulled her hair back into the simplest chignon. She wanted nothing in her attire to trigger her mother-in-law in any way. Given this, she was shocked on entering the dowager's drawing room to see the woman herself had thrown off full mourning. In fact, she had skipped half-mourning altogether and returned to the bright colours she had always adored.

Seeing Tabitha's outfit, the dowager snorted and observed, "Hoping to get on my good side, are you, girl? You think that dress is enough?"

Tabitha didn't answer but couldn't help looking at the dowager's dress. Some of her thoughts must have been reflected on her face because the dowager continued, "If his wife cannot be bothered to mourn Jonathan properly, I see no reason why I should depress myself and those around me by wearing that awful bombazine." There was no good answer to such a preposterous statement, so Tabitha schooled her face and said nothing.

"Come and sit, girl. What was so important that you made me rush my toilette this morning?" Again, Tabitha kept her own counsel. She hadn't been the one to propose the time she should call.

"I need your help, Mama," Tabitha stated in a voice she tried to make as docile as possible.

"So, you said. Let's not beat around the bush any longer. What do you need to know?"

Over dinner the previous evening, Tabitha and Wolf had discussed how best she should phrase her questions. They needed to find out as much as the dowager knew about the Rowley family without letting her know any of their suspicions. But the older woman was no fool; she would know there was a good reason Tabitha was questioning her. They needed a plausible explanation without telling her the whole story.

"As you may know, Anthony Rowley, the new Duke of Somerset, is a childhood friend of mine. While he was reviewing his late father's papers, some concerning items came to light. Not knowing where to turn, he came to me and asked for my advice. I suggested that we include the Earl of Pembroke in the conversation. I'm not sure what the earl has shared with you, but before ascending to the title, he had engaged in business that has given him experience dealing with some of the less salubrious parts of society."

Tabitha had suspected that this titbit would be tantalising to the dowager. Hopefully, so tantalising that she would focus on that and not unpick the rest of the story too much. The dowager narrowed her steely grey eyes and contemplated Tabitha, "You're asking me to believe that a peer of the realm, a duke nonetheless, had no one better to turn to for advice than you, a mere chit of a girl? Really, Tabitha. I'm not in my dotage yet."

Tabitha was worried that the dowager would so discount her story that the meeting would end almost before it had begun. But she needn't have worried. "As absurd as this whole story is, I'm intrigued enough to let this clear fabrication go. What do you need from me that you would go to the trouble of creating such a fiction?"

Relieved at her temporary reprieve, Tabitha told the dowager what she wanted to know. "The earl and I met with the entire Rowley household yesterday." The dowager raised her eyebrows at this but didn't say anything. Tabitha continued, "It is clear that his family does not much mourn the late duke."

At this, the dowager made a sound that Tabitha couldn't interpret, but again, the older woman said nothing. Tabitha paused and said, "I met the late duke's sister, Lady Fannie. I understand that she is unmarried and quite the recluse." The latter had never been said outright. But given that Tabitha had no memory of ever seeing the woman at any society event, it was a fair assumption to make.

Finally, the dowager spoke, "Yes, poor, dear Fannie. My youngest, Jane, had been great friends with Fannie when they were children, even though she was a couple of years older. I had come out at the same time as Catherine, the dowager duchess. We became firm friends, which lasted through our marriages' early years. Catherine was a great beauty in her day, and it was no surprise to anyone that she managed to secure a duke's attention. Though, my impression was that he turned out to be a husband much in the mould of my own and that she wasn't a happy woman."

The dowager looked pointedly at Tabitha and observed, "However, much as I was, Catherine was a model of rectitude and patience and bore her lot in life with a grace and forbearance that not everyone seems able to aspire to." The look she gave Tabitha as she said these last words dispelled any doubt, not that there had been, that this was meant as a direct reproof of Tabitha's behaviour.

"Anyway," the dowager continued, no doubt confident in making her point, "it was only natural that our children should play, and we encouraged the nannies to bring them together as much as possible."

"What was Lady Fannie like as a child?" Tabitha asked with genuine curiosity.

"Fannie was a delightful child. Always singing and laughing. Of course, I did not get many opportunities to see her for myself, but whenever I asked Jane, she would always say how much she loved Fannie for how sweet tempered and joyful she was. And then, one day, that all seemed to change."

The dowager paused and wrinkled her brow as if trying to remember those days, "Yes, I remember that poor Catherine confided in me that she had no idea what was wrong. She took the child to one of the top doctors in London, who could find nothing physically wrong with her. And yet, it was as if all the life had drained from her. Overnight it seemed she had gone from a happy, carefree little girl to a melancholy, sullen child who barely spoke.

Now, Tabitha had to ask the most important questions, which she was most nervous about asking, "I understand that the late duke, Fannie's brother Martin, was quite a few years older than she was."

"Yes," replied the dowager, "almost sixteen years older. Catherine had experienced great trouble conceiving and carrying a baby to birth, not unlike your own troubles." The dowager said this last statement without any of the compassion one might expect such an observation to engender. "When she managed to deliver a healthy son, her husband was ecstatic, and there was little expectation she would manage to do so again. So, you can imagine everyone's surprise when Fannie came along."

"With such a great age gap between the siblings, it seems unlikely they would have much to do with each other," Tabitha said.

The dowager agreed, "For most of Fannie's life, Martin was at Eton, then Cambridge, then on his Grand Tour, and then living in his rooms in London, as far as I understood. Though it was interesting, and I remember quite vividly Catherine saying this at the time that suddenly, Martin started spending more time at Rowley House.

"Catherine wondered why Martin had suddenly been so keen to spend time with his family. She had put it down to a newfound desire to spend time with his dying father, and she was grateful to see her son exhibiting so much family feeling. He had been a wild young man during his time at Cambridge and even beyond. Catherine had heard stories of gambling, excessive drinking and the like. Of course, much of that is to be expected as a young man sows his wild oats. And Catherine understood this and appreciated this evidence, at least as she saw it, of her son maturing and becoming ready to take on the title."

Tabitha found this story increasingly interesting, "So the late duke was suddenly at home much more and, presumably, spending at least some time with his much younger sister?"

"Indeed, Catherine was quite touched, as I recall, that he seemed so interested in spending time with the child. She had no expectations that a 24-year-old man would take any interest in an 8-year-old girl." Tabitha's ears perked up at this statement.

The dowager continued, "Poor Fannie was so much younger than her brother that it was almost as if she were an only child. It warmed Catherine's heart to see Martin devoting so much time and attention to her. He took her out for rides in his carriage and to the theatre, just the two of them enjoying the family box."

"Did he? That seems almost excessive attention for a grown brother to lavish on a young child," Tabitha observed.

The dowager concurred, "I felt so at the time. Indeed, even by Catherine's telling of it, Fannie seemed overwhelmed by his attention. Still, it was to be expected that she would be in awe of her sophisticated, handsome older brother. But Catherine was forever raving about her wonderful son and how he doted on his younger sister."

"So, when did the change in Fannie begin?" Tabitha asked, even though she was beginning to think she knew the answer.

"It was a long time ago, and so I'm unsure of the exact timeline, but I do remember that it was around the time when Jane was suddenly of an age when Fannie suddenly seemed to be far too young for a playmate. In fact, overnight, Jane felt too grown up to play with anyone and started acting like the young lady that, at 11 or 12, she probably was ready to be. So, if Jane was that age, then Fannie was probably 8 or 9 by this time.

"Catherine was beside herself. After trying multiple medical interventions, it was finally decided to send her to sea for fresh air. Catherine had a sister who married a viscount from the south coast. Not Brighton, but one of those kinds of places. She and Fannie went to visit for some months, and, if I remember rightly, even though Catherine returned to London, Fannie ended up staying there for more than a year.

"When she finally returned to London, Catherine confided that the child had improved. However, she had lost the light in her eyes. She never sang any more, barely ate, and jumped at the slightest sound. When the time would have come for her season, Catherine felt she was too delicate and of a nervous disposition.

"Catherine made an attempt the next season, but it was a complete disaster. To say she didn't take would be an understatement. Season after season, Catherine had hoped that her daughter's nerves and temperament would improve, but they never did. Finally, the family gave up all hope, and Fannie was forever more the spinster sister. While still reserved and nervous, the expectations of marriage now removed, Fannie became a little gayer and revealed herself to be an excellent companion for her mother."

This conversation had been far more informative than Tabitha had possibly imagined. Still, she had one more question, which she tried to phrase with great delicacy, "Lady Pembroke, Mama, did Catherine, the dowager duchess, ever wonder if there was anything to be worried about in the attention the late duke showered on his sister?"

The dowager's mouth pinched, and Tabitha was sure she was about to be reprimanded for speaking such an outrageous thought out loud, and then the dowager's shoulders seemed to slump a little, and she said sadly, "She had alluded to some sort of concern, at one point. It was when Fannie's behaviour had become so worrying. Catherine was in my drawing room sobbing and pouring her heart out to me, the poor woman.

"She confessed that her husband had been away, and she had been out for the evening at a dinner I was hosting, as it happened. She recounted coming home unexpectedly early with a terrible headache. She went up to her bedroom and encountered Martin leaving Fannie's room late at night in a state of partial undress. He had said that he had heard her crying out and had quickly put on clothes and rushed to comfort her. Catherine had entered her child's bedroom to find her daughter in an almost catatonic state, curled up in a fetal position. Fannie's behaviour had never been the same again. Martin stopped spending as much time with his family and seemed to have returned to his bachelor ways."

The dowager was an intelligent woman and, indeed, had been the person who had told Wolf the whispered rumours about the late duke, so Tabitha felt no qualms in asking her, "Did the duchess never connect Fannie's supposed illness with whatever happened that night?"

The dowager countess gave her a sharp look but replied, "If she did so, she never mentioned it to me."

"And as you tell me the story now, what connection do you make?" Tabitha asked.

"From your tone, I presume Jeremy told you what I shared with him about the rumours that swirled about Somerset?" Tabitha nodded. "Then, I can imagine that you have made the same connection I made, though I will admit I did not make back then: the duke's unnatural interest in young girls began with his sister."

With the grotesque conclusion finally said out loud, Tabitha was momentarily speechless. Throughout the story the dowager had told, Tabitha had a growing suspicion, but to hear the other woman put that suspicion into words, brought the true horror of it home.

Tabitha did not stay for much longer. She had much to think about and wanted to gather her thoughts before she wrote the notecards and told Wolf what she had discovered.

CHAPTER 31

Tabitha was deep in thought during the drive home. She was so deep in thought that she failed to hear what Talbot said when opening the front door for her, "I'm so sorry, Talbot. Did you say something?"

"Yes, milady. I merely wanted to inform you that the tutor arrived promptly this morning, and so far, the lessons are going smoothly, from what I can tell."

"Thank you, Talbot. I had completely forgotten that it was today. Is Miss Melody behaving for Mr James?"

Talbot chuckled, "I must admit to wondering that myself, milady, and so I took the liberty of peeking into the nursery. It seems that the young man has quite a way with children. From what I could tell, he has combined learning her lessons with a doll's tea party. He was sitting at Miss Melody's little table and working on her letters with her. For every letter she read correctly, she was allowed five minutes to serve tea and then teach the letter to her doll. I must confess, it was quite amusing to watch."

This made Tabitha smile. After the morning she had been through, the thought of Melly trying to boss her Cambridge-educated tutor around was just what she needed. "I need to speak to his lordship, Talbot. Do you know where I might find him?"

"I believe he was hungry and unsure when you'd be back. He asked for luncheon to be served, milady."

"Thank you, Talbot. I find I have little appetite, but I will join his lordship."

Tabitha made her way to the dining room. While she'd

learned much from the dowager, she was still unsure what it all meant. The man had molested his sister when she was a child, and it was now clear why she hated him. From what the dowager had said, it was unclear if Catherine, the dowager duchess, had known the truth back then. And even if she hadn't, did she now? Had Fannie killed her brother?

It was hard to imagine the delicate, almost childlike woman having the physical strength and mental fortitude to commit murder. And, if they were correct, this wasn't a crime of passion but rather a premeditated murder. Unless Fannie was a different woman than she seemed, it was hard to imagine her concocting and executing such a cunning plan.

Having run through some of these thoughts in the carriage, Tabitha articulated them to Wolf over lunch. Well, over his lunch. As she had said to Talbot, Tabitha found she had no appetite. Wolf was as appalled as she was, and he expressed the same doubts about Fannie's ability to kill her brother; however horrific her treatment had been at his hands.

"Why now? She's lived in the same house as her brother her entire adult life. While that couldn't have been pleasant, she somehow managed to do so. Why snap suddenly? We have every reason to believe that Lady Fannie has held no unnatural interest for her brother for many years. So, why now?"

"Something about this case is off," Tabitha said in frustration, "and I can't put my finger on exactly what."

"I agree", Wolf concurred. "When Bruiser first told me that Mickey D wanted me to investigate this case, he said that Mickey was worried he had a mole in his gang. I'm assuming he believed that because if the burglary was to cover up the murder, there would have to be someone in his gang who had helped coordinate it. How else could the murderer have been sure when the theft would occur?"

"It seems to have been so convenient, doesn't it?" Tabitha mused, finally having enough appetite to pick at some of the excellent game pie they'd been served. "The butler has the night off. The footman is drunk. The jewels are in the house for a mere couple of nights. The perfect time for a burglary, if there ever was one. How did Mickey's gang get so lucky, for want of a better word?"

"I think it's time I visited Whitechapel. He said he's worried about a leak from within the gang; perhaps I'll have more luck flushing the mole. And I'd like to ask some questions around the neighbourhood. We've been letting Mickey dictate the rules of the investigation for long enough. It's time to get some answers."

"I agree," Tabitha said, "we need to talk to his people. To understand the sequence of events that led to the decision of when to stage the theft."

Wolf looked at her, making sure he had heard what he thought he had. The determined thrust of her chin and the stubborn look on her face assured him he had heard what he had thought he had. "Let me be clear, Tabitha; this expedition has no 'we'. Bear and I will be visiting Whitechapel alone."

"When you wanted to talk to Anthony alone, I agreed because I could see the wisdom in him hearing about his father's evil from another man. Talking to the dowager alone made equal sense because she finds you charming and barely tolerates me. I was happy to step aside both those times because it was in the best interests of the case. But you don't want me to come to Whitechapel with you only because you are being overly protective of my person."

Wolf sighed and tried to explain, "Tabitha, you are a strong, independent, intelligent woman, and I have no doubt that this case has progressed as quickly as it has because of your involvement. If I had any doubts about including you initially, consider those doubts utterly dispelled. However, Whitechapel is no place for a titled lady, no matter how fearless she considers herself. And Mickey D's boys will show no respect for your money, status or gender. I cannot allow you to be exposed to all that."

Tabitha had anticipated all his arguments and had decided that she would brook no refusal, "Wolf, as you say, I'm an independent woman and may go where I please. You can take me with you, or I will follow you, but either way, I will be going to Whitechapel today. The only choice you have is whether I go alone."

"Tabitha, is there no way I can talk you out of this? I know you believe that you are no delicate high society lady who will faint at the slightest thing, and overall, I agree with that assessment of your character. But you have no idea what you are proposing I agree to."

Wolf was exasperated at her insistence. He was reasonably sure that there was nothing he could say to talk her out of accompanying him, but he had to try. When she said nothing more but merely sat with the same determined look on her face, he finally shook his head and said, "Fine. It seems I cannot talk sense into you. But you cannot wear your normal clothes. Bear and I will change into our old clothes, and you need to find something to wear to blend in somewhat better."

"That is a perfectly reasonable request. I'm sure that Ginny will be able to help me with something." Wolf was secretly sceptical that any dress was plain enough to mask Tabitha's status. She had an inherent poise and graceful deportment that would need more than a ratty dress to disguise.

Wolf had informed her that he was planning on leaving at dusk. He wanted to catch Mickey D and his gang together, and he knew they usually gathered early in the evening to eat together. That left Tabitha with a few hours to try to come up with a sufficient disguise.

After lunch, Tabitha decided to visit the nursery before going to find Ginny. She was happy to see Rat eating his midday meal with his sister. She had understood Wolf's concerns about Rat living in an awkward betwixt and between position, not quite a family member, but with privileges beyond most of the servants. So she was relieved that any such awkwardness hadn't deterred the boy from taking her up on her offer to spend time with Melody.

Both children looked up as she entered the room, and Melody squealed, "Tabby Cat, look, Matty came to play." Rat looked a little embarrassed at his sister's use of his given name but said nothing. It was clear that the little girl's imperiousness extended to her older brother.

Tabitha went and joined them at the table while they ate. After a few minutes, Rat said, "M'lady, what's up? Seems your mind's away with the fairies. Ma used to say that to me lots of times."

Tabitha's instinct was to assure the boy it was nothing, but it occurred to her that he knew Whitechapel and could perhaps help her. Despite her reluctance, he was already drawn into this case so much that it seemed pointless to leave him out now. "His lordship intends to visit Whitechapel to visit Mickey D and his gang. I have insisted that I be allowed to join him."

Rat's expression as she said this was very similar to Wolf's when they'd discussed this over lunch, "Pardon me, m'lady, but a fine lady like wot you are shouldn't be going there. It's not right. What is his lordship Wolf about letting you go?"

"I go where I please and let his lordship know this. But, as you've pointed out, dressed as I am now, I will be far too conspicuous."

"What's consickuous?" Rat asked.

"Conspicuous is the word. It means, I'll stick out like a sore thumb."

"That you will m'lady," Rat agreed.

"I am going to see if Ginny can help me find an outfit that will blend in."

"Fair enough," Rat considered for a moment, "but even in an old dress, you don't look like any of them Whitechapel birds. I'll tell you right, it's not a good place for a lady likes you."

Tabitha considered the boy's words. As determined as she was to accompany Wolf, she didn't want to hinder the investigation in any way. "You're right Rat. I have an idea, but I need you to help me find Bear. Can you do that? I'll stay here with Melly for a while. Ask him to meet me up here, please."

Rat jumped up, eager to be of help. He kissed his sister on the top of her head, and ruffled her hair, and rushed out of the room. Mary had been busy tidying up the nursery while Tabitha had talked to the children, and with Rat gone, she came over to answer Tabitha's questions about how the lessons were going so far.

Mary confirmed Talbot's account of the young tutor's success in enticing Melly to learn. The blush on Mary's cheek suggested the child wasn't the only one he had won over. "So, you found him to be patient with you as well, Mary?"

"Oh yes, m'lady. Mr James is a wonderful teacher. He didn't get angry when I got some words wrong. He was so kind."

"That's wonderful to hear, Mary. " Tabitha reflected that at least this endeavour was going well so far.

Melly finished her meal, and Tabitha read to her for a while. Eventually, she heard a sound and saw the huge bulk of Bear standing in the doorway. Even Melody seemed a little in awe of the giant of a man. Tabitha decided she didn't need sharp little ears overhearing her conversation and bade Melly farewell.

Indicating to Bear that he should follow her into the hallway, she shut the nursery door behind her and told him what she needed and why.

Bear's initial reaction was shock. But when Tabitha explained she would accompany them to Whitechapel no matter what, and Wolf and Rat's observations that it would be hard for her to disguise her class and status, he reluctantly agreed to help her. He agreed to liaise with Ginny to provide the requested items.

Less than an hour later, Ginny met Tabitha in her bedroom. "Some of his lordship's clothes may work, but as tall as you are for a woman, he's a tall man. I may be able to hem the trousers and take them in enough. Let's see what Bear managed to gather and then I'll know what I have to work with, m'lady," Ginny announced, ever the picture of practical efficiency.

Within a few hours, Ginny had worked her magic, and Tabitha stood in front of her mirror disguised as a man. Ginny had pulled her hair back to fit it under a broad-brimmed hat. The hat also cast some shadow over Tabitha's face. Ginny had explained how to bind her breasts. Tabitha didn't ask why Ginny had this knowledge.

Ginny reached for a little bowl on the dressing table filled with what looked like ashes, and she used her fingers to smear some on Tabitha's face. Ginny had used the ashes subtly and strategically, and Tabitha had to admit, they gave her face a more masculine look, hinting at the start of beard stubble.

"You won't past muster on close inspection, but of an evening I think you'll pass as a young man well enough. Of course, your voice will give you away, so I suggest that you hang back, don't call attention to yourself, and try not to speak." Tabitha had to smile at the stern, almost commanding manner with which her lady's maid spoke to her. While Ginny was hardly a picture of docile obedience under normal circumstances, her involvement in the case seemed to have given her more license to speak freely to her mistress. Tabitha was not sorry about this change.

CHAPTER 32

Tabitha was waiting, in her disguise, in the hallway. Wolf came down the stairs and, with her face at an angle and her shabby clothes, assumed a strange vagrant was in the house, "Sir, who are you, and why are you loitering in my hallway?" he demanded.

Tabitha turned her head, and Wolf exclaimed, "What on earth are you playing at? And are those my clothes?" he asked, as closer inspection revealed the outfit's familiarity.

"They are. My apologies for taking them without your knowledge and for whatever alterations Ginny has performed."

"You can't possibly imagine that getup will enable you to pass as a man?" Wolf sputtered, reaching the bottom of the stairs and inspecting her up close."

"You thought I was a man, " Tabitha pointed out.

"For a moment, when I couldn't see your face fully, " he answered.

"It is still day, and this hallway is well-lit. But by the time we get to Whitechapel, it will be early evening, and I doubt that anywhere we go will be as well-lit as this house." Wolf's silence confirmed her expectations. "I do not need to pass for a boy under close scrutiny. I need merely to pass for one at a casual glance. I will hang back and won't speak unless it's necessary."

Tabitha continued, "Rat confirmed your feelings that Whitechapel was no place for me to be as a lady. And so, this is my solution."

Wolf ran his fingers through his hair in exasperation, "So, my word on the subject wasn't sufficient? It had to be validated by a child?"

Tabitha laughed harshly, "Interesting that you're happy to assure me that Rat is experienced and savvy beyond his years when you're justifying involving him in this case, but now I'm at fault for taking advantage of that experience."

It was clear to Wolf this argument was going nowhere. He looked Tabitha over more closely and had to admit that her disguise was a good one. The strategically placed ashes gave her normally alabaster skin a roughness that gave the illusion of some beard stubble, even if it didn't bear close inspection. She could probably pass for a young man if she kept her hat low. It was certainly safer walking through the streets of Whitechapel in this outfit than as a woman.

"Fine! Again, it seems I have little choice in the matter," he conceded.

They were joined at that moment by Bear. He had known what Tabitha's plan was but, even so, was initially surprised to see a scruffy young man talking to Wolf. That surprise only lasted a few moments, and then a huge smile broke out over his normally quite formidable visage, "M'lady, I almost didn't recognise you. The clothes worked out better than I'd expected.

"You knew about this?" Wolf demanded angrily, "In fact, you abetted it? Whose side are you on?"

"There are sides?" Tabitha asked. "Since when?"

"Since I find myself ignored, overruled and manipulated at each turn in my own house."

Tabitha wasn't sure whether to be amused or outraged. Reflecting on the various times recently when she had persuaded Wolf to agree to something against his better judgement, she conceded the point to him and landed on amused. "Please don't blame poor Bear. If you are helpless against my machinations, how can you expect the poor man to be more immune to my charms?" She smiled brightly as she said this, and Wolf shook his head helplessly.

"Let's just go, shall we?" he said resignedly.

They managed to hail a hackney cab quickly and made their way to Whitechapel. As before, Wolf had the driver drop them on the outskirts of Whitechapel. While a hack wasn't a carriage, it still would draw unwanted attention.

Whitechapel was a place of contrasts. A bustling hub of commerce and industry where factories, markets, shops and pubs thrived, it was also a slum of poverty and misery, where overcrowded tenements, filthy streets, disease and crime prevailed.

Cramped tenement buildings leaning precariously towards one another lined the narrow, winding streets. The air was thick with the smell of human waste and rotting garbage piled high on the curbs.

The sound of horse-drawn carriages echoed through the streets, mixed with the chatter of people from all walks of life. The area was known for its poverty and crime, with gangs of pickpockets and thieves lurking in the shadows, ready to pounce on unsuspecting victims.

As the sun set, the streets took on an even more intimidating atmosphere. Gas lamps flickered to life, casting an eerie glow over the already dark and shadowy alleys. Prostitutes, known as "unfortunates," took to the streets, hoping to make a living for the night.

On reflection, Wolf realised Tabitha's disguise, while not perfect, had been a wise plan.

Mickey D lived and worked out of a townhouse that was in quite respectable shape, given the neighbourhood. Every evening, his wife, or at least common-law wife, Angie, made a large meal, and the gang members were welcome, perhaps even expected, to turn up more evenings than not. Mickey used this time to catch up with his people, plan upcoming jobs, and generally try to keep spirits up and loyalty tight.

Wolf had been part of these large, boisterous meals on occasion and had a deep fondness and respect for Angie. She was a formidable woman who brooked no nonsense from the gang members or Mickey himself. He might be feared on the streets of Whitechapel, but there was no doubt who ruled in their household.

Angie was a plump, rosy-cheeked woman, rarely seen without a wooden spoon in her hand. Cooking for her family of seven children plus the growing gang was hard work. But her food was legendary, and if fear of Mickey wasn't enough to make his men join the evening meal, Angie's cooking was.

Wolf knocked on the door a little before 7 pm. Angie opened it and, on seeing Wolf, exclaimed, "Well, I never! From what I hear, you are the last person I expected to see on my doorstep now that you've become a toff." With that, she clasped him to her plentiful bosom in a hug that almost squeezed the breath out of him.

"Come to see himself, are you? And Bear, good to see you too." The large man got his own hug, and Angie then turned to Tabitha. "Who have we here?"

In the hack, Tabitha had chosen the name, Will. "It's in honour of William Shakespeare and all his cross-dressing heroines!" she announced.

"Luckily, I'm sure that literary allusion will be lost on Mickey and his boys."

'Will' was introduced to Angie. Tabitha greeted the woman with as firm a handshake as possible while trying to avert her face as much as possible. The lamp above the door was bright, and Angie looked suspiciously at the young man before her but didn't comment. She led them into the house and towards the large kitchen at the back.

The kitchen table seemed to be a few large oak tables pushed together. Her youngest children fed earlier, Wolf recognised Angie and Mickey's oldest son, Paddy, sitting at the table with at least ten other men. He hadn't seen Paddy in some time and was shocked that the lad was now grown up, or at least grown up enough to be part of the gang dinners. Wolf wondered if he was also now part of their criminal activities.

Everyone looked up when Wolf, Bear and Tabitha entered. They were already enthusiastically eating Angie's mutton stew with soda bread. Mouths were full, so there were some grunts of welcome, and a few head nods in acknowledgement.

On seeing the trio enter, Mickey put down his spoon and said in surprise, "I didn't expect a visit from you, Wolf. Or should I say your lordship these days?"

"I've told you before; Wolf is just fine. I have some questions to ask, and I want to ask them of the group," Wolf answered.

Giving Tabitha a curious glance, Mickey stood up and indicated that Wolf should follow him into the hallway. Leading his guest into a cosy parlour, Mickey closed the door and asked, "I told you that I have some concerns about how tight the seal is with my boys. Isn't that why we agreed that I would come to you?"

"Yes, I know what you said. And that made sense in the beginning, but now I need more information than I believe you can provide alone. There's a missing piece of this puzzle."

"And what might that be?" Mickey asked.

"I believe you're right. I think the burglary was a set-up to cover the murder. But I don't understand how it was set up."

"I've told you; it could only be a leak in my gang. How else could it have happened?"

"But even that doesn't make sense. Someone had to know the burglary would take place that night. We think the duke was drugged, which is why he didn't awaken when Seamus broke in. Someone drugged him, knowing what was going to happen. How is that possible?"

"Well, the young lad working as the boot boy was the one we heard about the necklace through. He'd overheard about it from the servants talking and had come and told his older brother, Paul, who is in my gang."

"Is the boy still employed at the house?" Wolf asked.

"Of course. If he had left after the burglary, it would have pointed the finger too obviously in the direction of Whitechapel," Mickey explained. I've been at this game too long to make those mistakes. "

"Is this Paul here tonight? I'd like to speak to him."

"He is. I can send him in. I'm assuming I should also send in Bear and your," he paused and winked, "young friend. Who is he again?"

Wolf shook his head, aware that Mickey had seen straight through the disguise. "You know quite well who it is, I believe."

"A beautiful woman. She even makes a fetching young man," Mickey teased.

Sighing deeply, Wolf said, "She forced me to bring her with, against my better judgement. And then she concocted that disguise and tried to convince me no one would see through it."

"It takes more than a headstrong lass to pull one over on Mickey D," the man chuckled. "Tell her that next time she wants to wear that outfit, she'd be better off with some false facial hair. I can let her know where to find something suitable. Oh, and perhaps pad the shoulders of the jacket some."

"I will tell her no such thing. This will be the last time she wears such an outfit."

Mickey laughed again, "I always wondered who the lass would be who could tame you, Wolf."

"I take offence at the notion that I need taming and that, if I do, anyone has succeeded. Lady Pembroke and I are friends, nothing more."

"Aye, if you say so, lad. I'll send them to you. and I'll send Paul. Do you want Ang to send some food or drink in?" the man offered before opening the door.

"I would say no, but I would hate to offend Angie. So, if she has any of her famous ginger biscuits around, I'd be happy to take some of them."

A few moments later, Tabitha and Wolf entered the room, followed by a thin, sullen-looking young man. Wolf assumed he was Paul. Wolf indicated that everyone should take a seat. As they were doing so, Mickey D re-entered the room with a plate of biscuits, "Angie said you've made her very happy by specially requesting these."

Mickey sat himself down. Wolf raised his eyebrows. Mickey stated, "I'll not be letting one of my boys be interrogated without being present."

Wolf took one of the biscuits, closing his eyes in appreciation at the juxtaposition of the buttery texture with the spiciness of the ginger. Then he began, "Paul, I believe your brother works in the household of the Duke of Somerset."

Paul's face became, if possible, even more sullen-looking, "What if 'e does. Our Billy's a good lad, a 'ard worker."

"I'm sure he is. However, Mickey has already told me that your brother, Billy, was the one to tell you about the duchess' diamond necklace being taken out of the bank and put into the duke's study for just a couple of nights." Paul didn't answer, so Wolf continued, "How did Billy come to know this information?"

Paul looked to Mickey, who nodded, "'E told me he overheard it like."

"Who did he overhear and how?"

"'E said it was one of the maids. The stuck-up one who thinks she's better than all the other maids just because she gets to wipe the old duchess' arse." Paul laughed at this. Wolf glanced over at Tabitha in apology for the boy's coarseness.

"He was sure that's who he overheard speaking?" Wolf asked.

"Yeah, 'e made a point of saying that 'e was surprised she was even being friendly with the other maids. Normally, she'd go below stairs with 'er nose stuck up in the air like she was the toff. But this time, she sat down at the table when the maids were having a quick bite to eat and started chatting. So friendly, she was."

"Where was Billy during all this?"

"Well, they call him the boot boy, but they 'ave him doing all sorts of jobs that no one else wants to do. One of the things 'e 'as to do is to wait on the other servants during their meals like they're the toffs."

"And Billy does this every meal?"

"As far as I can tell. We don't see 'im much anymore, 'ave 'im working day and night they do. But 'e gets time off on Sunday mornings to go to church and comes 'ome 'ere to go with our ma. That's why 'e told her about the necklace and told 'er to let me know. I'm not much for church these days," Paul explained.

"Thank you, Paul. That was very helpful."

"And our Billy won't get into trouble, will 'e?"

"I can't condone what he did, and I certainly hope that he means to reform, or I will have to tell the new duke," Wolf looked at Mickey when he said that. The man nodded his acceptance of these terms.

Paul left the room, and Wolf ate another ginger biscuit and took another couple in his pocket, "You don't suppose I could persuade Angie to share her recipe for these with my cook?" Wolf asked.

"Now, why would she be giving that away for free? What about if she sends you a batch every week? For a hefty fee, of course."

"Of course. They would be most gratefully received. I'll tell my housekeeper to expect the first batch tomorrow. Will that be okay with Angie?"

"Aye, that'll be fine. Do you have all the information you need?"

"I have one more question. Maybe less a question than a confirmation. It was Annie, your niece from whom you indirectly heard of the open position of boot boy?"

"It was. But as I told you before when she suspected that Billy was one of my boys, she had her ma, my sister, come and warn me off. But I also told you, Annie's no snitch. She might have suspected the lad was one of mine, but she kept that to herself."

Wolf had all the information he needed, and with farewell hugs to Angie from Wolf and Bear, the three left Whitechapel.

They had missed dinner, but while they were all hungry by the time they returned to Chesterton House, no one felt like a formal dinner. Talbot rustled up some game pie, cheese, freshly baked bread and cold cuts of meat. Bear included, they sat in the parlour, Tabitha still in her disguise, and ate their cold collation while discussing their evening.

Tabitha was trying to eat and write notecards, "I'd never realised how comfortable men's clothes were. No corset, petticoat, or voluminous skirts. I may have to dress like this more often," she said.

"Just don't use my clothes next time," Wolf commented while

helping himself to a second plate of food. "So, what do we think we know?"

Tabitha started, "It seems quite the coincidence that Mickey heard about the boot boy position because of Annie. And then Billy, the boot boy, learns about the necklace also from Annie. For someone who is supposedly so opposed to her family's criminal activities, she was, if nothing else, rather free with the information she shared around them. It's hard to believe she didn't know Billy was one of Mickey's lads. And even if she didn't know for sure, we know she had strong suspicions. So, why not be more careful around him?"

"Even more than just being sloppy, it almost sounds like she went out of her way to go below stairs to announce the news about the necklace at a time when she knew Billy would overhear it," Wolf continued.

Tabitha finished her notecards and wrote on the final one, 'Did Annie scheme to get one of Mickey's boys in place and then intentionally plant the information about the necklace?' She pinned the notecards on the board and said, "I think the most obvious answer is, yes, that's exactly what Annie did." Tabitha sat back down.

"And the necklace is only there for two nights, but the butler is only off one of those nights, so there had to be an excellent chance that news would get back to Mickey. And a reduced male staff would increase the odds of a successful burglary. Was it just a coincidence that the butler had that day off?' Wolf pondered.

Bear hadn't said anything so far, but he chimed in, "For what it's worth, all of this," he waved at the board, "is starting to feel very intentional, even where we thought there were coincidences."

Tabitha and Wolf agreed with him. The three ate in companionable silence for a while. Tabitha finished eating first, put down her plate and stood back up. She went and stood in front of the board and looked at all the notecards. She did some rearranging and regrouping. Then she stood back and stared at it all.

"It's starting to make some sense. At least, we strongly suspect how someone ensured the burglary would occur. They drug the duke and leave him sleeping in his study. The burglary happens, and Seamus leaves. The duke could have been bludgeoned before or after the theft."

"Yes," Wolf pointed out, "except, surely it wasn't a hundred percent certainty that Mickey's gang would break in. At least, we're assuming it wasn't. And in that case, the murderer wouldn't want to risk killing the duke until they were sure the necklace was gone."

"Why go to all this trouble? Why not stage a burglary?"

"This is so much more believable," Wolf took a sip of wine and considered her question. "There's even a witness to Seamus escaping. Whoever killed the duke probably didn't have a full understanding of what happens to jewellery that's stolen. Perhaps they thought it would be traced more quickly than it has been and recovered, providing the ultimate red herring. It's likely that not many people knew the combination to the duke's safe. How could the murderer even get to the necklace? But the safe wouldn't pose a problem to a bunch of crooks. It was an elaborate plan in many ways, but also a very clever one."

"So, who is the murderer? This Annie?" Bear asked.

"She's certainly the number one suspect. If nothing else, she was an integral part of the plan, even if she didn't do the deed. But what's her motive? Fanny on the other hand has a clear motive. It's just so hard to imagine her wielding a candelabra and killing her brother, however much she may have wanted to. "

Bear said, "Perhaps Annie did it for Lady Fannie?"

"That is certainly a very sound theory. We've heard about Annie's much vaunted loyalty. Perhaps that loyalty extends past the dowager to her daughter. But we still don't know the answer to one key question, 'why now?' Fannie's abuse was a long time ago. Why would she wait until now to avenge herself?"

Wolf brushed some crumbs off his sleeve, stood up and said, "Let's all sleep on this. We've put together so many pieces of this jigsaw puzzle, but it still feels as if we're missing something important. "

CHAPTER 33

Tabitha slept badly that night. Tossing and turning, she found that sleep wouldn't come. She tried to clear her head and count sheep like her nanny had taught her. Eventually, she fell asleep. When Ginny came in the following morning to draw back the curtains and bring her a cup of tea, it felt like she had barely slept.

"If you don't mind me saying so, m'lady, you look awful," Ginny confessed.

"I feel awful. I'm sure I barely slept for more than two or three hours last night," Tabitha answered sleepily. "Can you run me a bath and get some coffee rather than tea, please?"

A bath and two cups of coffee later and Tabitha began to feel somewhat human. She decided to go to the nursery straight after breakfast. This case had started feeling so ugly that she felt a strong need for Melly's sweet innocence.

The old schoolroom, next to the nursery, had been set aside for the lessons for the staff. Tabitha could hear Mr James talking with one of the maids as she walked by it. She thought it was Jane, previously the scullery maid, now promoted to the second chambermaid.

Entering the nursery, Tabitha found Melly playing with some building blocks with Mary. Becky hadn't returned from the Holborn house, and Tabitha wondered if she would choose to stay there. She made a mental note to talk to Anthony about his plans for the girls.

Melly looked up as she entered and said, "Tabby Cat, I'm building a house for my dolly. Can you help me?"

Yet again, Tabitha lowered herself to the floor, despite the constrictions of her corsets. She and Melly spent a delightful hour building a very elaborate home for the doll.

As Melly chattered happily, Tabitha reflected, how could someone hurt a child? The duke's molestation of all his victims had begun when they were only a few years older than the little girl in front of her. As awful as it was to contemplate, Tabitha forced herself to imagine Melly in a few years, taller, golden curls hanging down her back, being abused by a grown man. The thought was sickening.

She pulled Melly to her and hugged the child. She realised that she would do anything to protect this little girl. Anything. She'd even kill for her. She said it to herself again. She'd even kill for her.

Tabitha jumped up, "Melly, I must go. I'm sure that Mary will keep playing with you."

Tabitha rushed downstairs and burst into Wolf's study. "I know what the missing piece is," she announced triumphantly. "I know why the duke was killed. I know what the trigger event was."

Wolf looked up in surprise when she entered the room. Tabitha's manners were always genteel, and she usually knocked before entering. He didn't mind that she hadn't; he was just surprised to see her exhibit anything other than her usual composure.

"Sit down and catch your breath," Wolf told her.

Tabitha threw herself into one of his chairs and said, "It's Hannah."

"Remind me who Hannah is," Wolf asked.

"The duke's daughter. Anthony's younger sister. She's around 8 years old. He must have started abusing her or led someone to believe the abuse was about to begin."

Wolf considered what she said, "That would explain why now. But it still leaves us with as many suspects as before. Anyone could have wanted to protect her, even the servants."

Tabitha acknowledged the truth of what he said but added, "It could have been anyone, but I don't think it was. We've already discussed how improbable it is that Fanny committed the murder. But Cassandra, the girl's mother, or even Catherine, the dowager duchess, I could see either of them become a ferocious lioness in the defence of an innocent child."

"The dowager duchess? Do you think she has the strength to have committed the murder?" Wolf questioned.

"Why not? She's no frail old lady. She has health and vigour and is quite sturdy in build. And the victim was asleep, so she could take her time."

"Even so, your theory is that either the man's wife or mother killed him. It stretches the limits of credulity. Don't you think?"

"No, I don't. We know he was a cruel husband. I doubt his wife would have any qualms about choosing her daughter over him. We know that he assaulted his sister for several years and that she has never been the same. Catherine had seen what had happened to her daughter; how could the dowager duchess possibly let history repeat itself with her granddaughter?"

As Tabitha had spoken her theory out loud, she became increasingly sure she was right. Melly had not been in her life for a month, yet she was sure she would do anything to keep her safe. She couldn't even imagine how ferocious a mother would be of her child. Her only question was whether his mother or wife knew the full extent of the man's evil. Had Fannie ever spoken about what happened? Despite these questions, given the facts they did know, this was undoubtedly the simplest explanation.

"It's still possible one of the men he was blackmailing killed him," Wolf pointed out. It wasn't that he didn't give Tabitha's theory a lot of credence, but he had learned over his career to be careful of jumping at the first, seemingly obvious answer.

"We must talk with the dowager duchess and her daughter-in-law." Tabitha announced firmly. "Tomorrow, we must talk with them. And we need Anthony in the room."

Wolf paused, unsure how to phrase his next thought. He had been a thief-taker for almost ten years. He'd had a front-row seat to the vagaries of the legal system, particularly when it came to members of the aristocracy. Tabitha was an impressive woman, but she was young. She had led a sheltered life until he came into it. He did not doubt that she saw the world unambiguously as made up of good and evil.

"Tabitha, I'm not saying we shouldn't do what you suggest. But I want us to think through how this will play out. Let's start with this: if you are correct and the deceased duke's mother or wife killed him to prevent him from molesting his daughter as he did his sister, what do you think the appropriate justice is?"

Tabitha looked as if she was unsure what the question was, so Wolf elaborated, "I'm not talking about what the legal system might or might not do to an elderly dowager duchess. I'm asking what justice looks like in this situation. Justice for Fanny. Justice for Hannah. Justice for all the little girls in Holborn whose childhoods were stolen."

"Are you implying that the results of our storied legal system may be other than justice?" Tabitha asked, genuinely curious.

"I'm not implying that. I'm stating it outright. It cannot be news to you that our legal system functions differently for the rich and connected than it does for the disadvantaged members of society. Let me put it another way, I believe we both consider that the violent death the duke suffered was deserved." Tabitha was a little horrified to find herself agreeing with such a proposition, but she nodded in agreement anyway.

"As you said, he was a cruel man. More than cruel, he was an evil man. He ruined young lives for his own pleasure. The only regret we can have is that someone didn't kill him sooner.

"You've also expressed sympathy for why his wife or mother would kill him to protect the innocent 8-year-old Hannah. So, the world is beyond dispute, better off without this man in it. Whoever killed him did a great service to all the other little girls who would have certainly fallen into this man's clutches over future decades.

"Not only was the murder of general utility to the world but that the murderer should be the particular person we believe her to be and have the very personal motive is wholly and utterly understandable."

Tabitha had been nodding along with all this. Finally, Wolf arrived at his summation, "If all this is the case, then what do we believe should happen to the person, to the wife or mother, who killed such a monster?"

Tabitha sat in silence, pondering his question. Eventually, she answered, "I don't believe justice is served by this person being arrested and hung for the crime."

Wolf smiled at her answer. "Do you not agree?" she asked anxiously.

"I agree completely. And I'm happy to see that you do understand the difference between the law and justice."

"So, what do we do? Just ignore what we know?"

"Under other circumstances, I might just do this. However, while the murder might be forgivable, their plan had another victim. Seamus. They set him up for murder and if he had been caught, he would have hung."

Tabitha could see this but pointed out, "Seamus was hardly innocent. He did commit a crime."

"He did. And I'm sure that's the story the killer told themselves. But the punishment for theft is very different from that for murder. Particularly when the murderer is a poor Irish immigrant, and the victim is a duke. And then we come to the next complication. Mickey D. He is going to want an answer. What do we tell him?"

Tabitha's eyes widened suddenly, "And what about Annie? I'm assuming her uncle would not take kindly to learning she had setup one of his gang."

"Not taking it kindly is an understatement," Wolf agreed.

"I have an idea," Tabitha said thoughtfully. "Let me say it all out loud before you tell me it's crazy." Wolf agreed to hear her out. If only because he had no plan of his own.

"We haven't told Mickey any of our suspicions that it was Annie who Billy overheard. And we certainly haven't told him we believe she went out of her way to get Billy hired and then to have him hear her conversation. In fact, Mickey still believes

Annie is loyal to her family and that's the only reason she hasn't gone to the police with whatever suspicions she might have."

Tabitha continued, occasionally pausing to think through what she wanted to say, "What about if we tell Mickey someone in the family killed the duke and it was a complete coincidence that it was that night. We can even tell him why. Would he believe that?"

"He might. He doesn't know what we do about the layout of the study and the impossibility of the duke having been disturbed and then killed. If we tell him that we now believe the duke was already dead when Seamus broke into the study, why would he question the story? But what about Seamus? He's in exile abroad and likely won't be able to come home anytime soon. Particularly, if another suspect isn't found. Which we have no reason to believe they will be."

Tabitha smiled and snapped her fingers, "I have the answer. Anthony will provide for Seamus to build a new life for himself, wherever he wishes. Perhaps he should travel to America. It's not as if he had a particularly rosy future if he'd stayed here."

"That might work," Wolf conceded. "I think the whole plan might work. And if it does, justice would have been served. I will send around a note to Somerset tomorrow and we will lay this all out before him."

CHAPTER 34

The following morning, they had barely finished breakfast, and Wolf had not sent his note to the Duke of Somerset yet when the dowager countess graced them with a visit. When Talbot announced that he had taken the dowager to the drawing room and had called for tea and cakes, Tabitha raised her eyebrows and said, "At this hour? What on earth is she doing here now? I'm shocked she can ready herself to leave the house before 11 am, at the earliest."

She was intrigued to find out what had brought her mother-in-law out at what Tabitha was sure the older woman would normally describe as "an unholy hour to be anywhere but your own bed."

They found her settled with a cup of tea and a slice of seed cake. She looked up as they entered the room. "Mama, how surprising to see you. And so early in the morning. Is everything alright?" It occurred to Tabitha there might be a real emergency, but she couldn't imagine why she would be the first person to whom the dowager would turn. Though on reflection, she could see that Wolf, dear Jeremy, might be.

Only then did Tabitha notice the dowager held a newspaper. The older woman gestured to it and exclaimed, "I assume you both know something about this?"

"Something about what?" Tabitha said in genuine innocence. She noticed that Wolf didn't look quite as surprised as she was.

"The old duke and the children. And also, those other men. Apparently, there are photos! I know this must have something to do with all the questions you two have been asking, and I want to know what!"

Reaching for the newspaper, Tabitha and Wolf read the salacious headline "Murdered duke ran child brothel!" The article said that the newspaper had received photos of highly prominent men, all named, who had patronised the brothel. Thankfully, the newspaper had not published the full photos but had published all the men's names.

When she finished reading, Tabitha sat down in amazement and asked Wolf, "Did Anthony go to a newspaper with the photos?"

A little shamefaced, Wolf sat and said, "He may have."

Tabitha stared at Wolf, and the dowager demanded, "Will someone please tell me what all this is about."

Leaving out Mickey D, the theft, the murder, and Hannah part of the story, they told her about their suspicions about the young girls taken from Whitechapel to a house in Holborn. A house owned by the duke. If she wondered why they'd had cause to have those suspicions in the first place, the dowager kept those thoughts to herself. They told her about going to the house with Anthony, saving the girls, and finding the photos. They also omitted all mention of the new duke's parentage and that piece of blackmail.

Given her suspicions about the duke and his sister, the news was less shocking to the dowager than it might have been. When they had finished the story, she asked, "But how did the story and the photos end up in the newspaper?"

"Yes," Tabitha said with an edge to her voice, "I'm curious to hear that as well. Wolf, I can tell you know something about this, and I can't believe you kept whatever it is from me." Tabitha sounded genuinely hurt, and Wolf regretted that he had caused her to feel anything less than fully part of the investigation. But, as he told her, this hadn't been his decision or story to tell.

Wolf admitted that shortly after finding the photos in the Holborn house, Anthony had written to him asking what his next steps should be. His first inclination was to turn the photos over to the Metropolitan Police, but he wanted Wolf's opinion. Wolf had considered how to phrase what he wanted to say. Wolf had been sure that, like Tabitha, the new Duke of Somerset held the legal system in far higher regard than he did.

Finally, he'd told Anthony that he believed the men in the photos were so high in society and the government, so influential that it was unlikely the police would bring charges against them, ultimately. The entire incident would be swept under the rug. Instead, Wolf suggested Anthony take the photos and story to a journalist for whom Wolf could vouch. He knew the man would write the story in such a way as to ensure justice was served. At least a form of street justice. Whether or not the police would then follow up and take any action against the men, their reputations were tarnished in society, business, and government.

What Wolf hadn't suggested was that Anthony would reveal the key role of his own father in the brothel. It was quite amazing he had chosen to do so, and Wolf expressed this to Tabitha and the dowager, "He could have told this story and omitted the role his father played in this. I wouldn't have thought any less of the man if he had chosen not to drag his family name into this."

"Anthony is not that man. He is too honourable to make things easier on his own family than this article and the scandal it will ignite will have on the other men's families. Their wives, children, and mothers will all be caught up inevitably in the sordid gossip from such a salacious news article. As much as his instinct might be to protect his mother, sister and grandmother wherever possible, I believe he would not protect them at the expense of doing what he feels is the right and honourable thing."

Wolf nodded. While he had known Anthony for a very short time, he had taken the measure of the man and was sure Tabitha was correct. The truth was, he was a duke, his mother and grandmother were duchesses, and the scandal wouldn't stick to them for long. It would be far easier for society to view them all as unfortunate victims, which they were. And once society's sympathy had been galvanised towards the Rowley family, it could hardly not be directed towards the other men's innocent family members.

Before leaving the drawing room, the dowager had turned, haughty and imposing, as if she were the queen herself, and said, "Jeremy, you have neglected me. I shouldn't have had to rouse myself at an ungodly hour to be kept informed of events. With the season in full swing now, I will need an escort to Lady Ramford's soiree. I will expect you to collect me on Thursday at 7 pm."

The outrageousness of the dowager believing she had either the authority or the right to demand where an earl should spend his evenings and with whom stunned both Tabitha and Wolf enough to allow his silence to stand for an affirmation. With a sly smile, the dowager swept out of the room, satisfied she knew more about the whole story than anyone else in society, perhaps even more than the Dowager Duchess of Somerset herself.

Tabitha would have asked her to be discreet. Still, in this case, she realised that the dowager wagging her tongue throughout society about how honourable Anthony had been could only help plant the seed of the hoped-for sympathy towards the family.

With the dowager gone, Tabitha turned to Wolf, "Why didn't you tell me about your correspondence with Anthony?" She asked in a very hurt tone.

"Tabitha, I wasn't keeping anything from you intentionally. The man asked for my advice and I gave it. I had no idea whether or not he would take it. In fact, I doubted he would. I haven't spent a lot of time around truly honourable men, or women, in my life. I never would have expected him to include his own father's role. The duke is an extraordinary man."

"He is," Tabitha conceded, "I would have expected nothing less of him. If I'd been consulted," Tabitha added. But there was no edge to her voice now. She accepted Wolf's explanation. He had shown himself ready to accept her as a full partner through so much of the investigation that it seemed churlish to take offence at this one small omission. But she had to ask, "Do you really believe that going to the newspapers is the best way to ensure justice is served?"

"Yes, I do," Wolf answered. "As you know by now, I believe that a legal remedy, if one even comes, is not the same as justice. You know society better than I do. Do you think these men will be admitted to the drawing rooms of the aristocracy anymore? Do you think they will continue to be judges, ministers, successful businessmen?" He held up the paper, "This is justice. It also may do more to ensure that there is a genuine official response. Stealing the innocent children of poor immigrants to turn into the playthings of rich old men isn't something the government can afford to ignore. "

They both felt it even more imperative they visit Rowley House and talk to Anthony. Wolf sat down to write the duke a brief note requesting some time as early as possible. Within an hour of it being written and sent, they received a reply saying they could call at their leisure whenever they were ready. Tabitha went to change out of her day dress into something more appropriate for calling on a duchess, and they set off.

The duke's butler was expecting them and showed them into the drawing room. Rowley House was a magnificent Mayfair residence. The drawing room had a light, modern air, suggesting recent redecoration. The colours were pastels, with a delicate floral pattern repeated on the curtains and cushions. It was a pleasant, welcoming room that nevertheless displayed the wealth and taste of its owners in an understated manner.

Tabitha had been considering suggesting to Wolf that they redecorate parts of Chesterton House. She suspected the decor hadn't been updated since the early days of the dowager's marriage, if not earlier. Looking around her while they waited, Tabitha determined to ask the Duchess of Somerset for some decorating tips.

It only took a couple of minutes for the duke to appear. In the carriage on the way over, Tabitha and Wolf had agreed they would talk to the duke alone and then suggest he bring in his mother and grandmother.

Deciding there was no reason to beat around the bush, Wolf began, “Somerset, I was surprised to see the headlines in the newspaper today. I hope you realise that neither Lady Pembroke nor myself had any expectations you would reveal your father’s role in the whole sordid affair.”

Anthony smiled wistfully, “Pembroke, I appreciate that you and Tabitha were willing to enable me to hide my own family’s shameful role, but I could not let that stand. My father was not merely a participant in the horrors those poor girls suffered, he was the protagonist. He owned the house. He procured the girls. He invited those other men to abuse children and then had the audacity to blackmail them for something he was guilty of. The only way I could hope to begin to clear the stain on my family’s honour was by publicly acknowledging our role.”

“Anthony,” Tabitha said gently, “you are an honourable man. Anyone who knows you would never hold your father’s crimes against you.”

The duke laughed cynically. “Tabitha, you and I know that is not how society functions. I have no doubt whispers of his crimes will continue behind our backs for many years to come. But that was not what I aimed to prevent. People should be appalled. They should be appalled that I, his heir, an adult man, had no idea what my father was doing. I cannot blame them if they chose to spurn me for this.

"What I did aim to do by my actions was to clear the stain on my soul that my own father, a peer of the realm, a man privileged by birth to help rule this country, could have descended so low. Instead of helping to make life better for the people around him, he abused the most innocent and pure amongst them, their children.”

The duke paused, then added, “If I weren’t sure the inevitable censure it would burden my mother with, I would happily shout from the rooftops that he wasn’t my natural father. In truth, it is the one consolation I have at this point; his blood does not run through my veins.”

Tabitha and Wolf nodded in understanding. Tabitha wished

they didn't have more to heap onto the delicate shoulders of her friend. But they did, so she gathered herself and said, "Anthony, we have no wish to bring any further pain to you. Or your family," she added. "But, there is more we need to shine the bright light of day on."

The duke looked confused and asked, "What else can I help you with? I will forever be in your debt for making me aware of the foul stain my father brought on the Somerset name. You have just to speak, and I will do everything in my power to aid you."

"Thank you, Somerset. I hope once you've heard what we have to say, you feel the same way," Wolf answered.

He then proceeded to explain everything they knew to the duke. They didn't hold back. Wolf explained how he had become involved and everything they had discovered. He ended with their conclusions about who murdered the duke and why.

While Wolf talked, Anthony said nothing. As revelation after revelation unfurled, he became paler and paler. At one point, he slumped back in his chair in despair. He hadn't spoken at all while Wolf told the story. He hadn't protested. He'd seemed horrified when he heard about his aunt's abuse but didn't try to deny it. The revelation that his father's evil extended to young girls in his family wasn't unbelievable. When Wolf arrived at the theory of the duke's sister Hannah's likely imminent abuse, it looked as if every drop of blood had drained from the man's face. But again, he didn't protest.

By the time Wolf had finished his story, Anthony had his head in his hands. Tabitha could have believed he was quietly sobbing. But when he raised his head, his eyes were dry. However, he looked as if he had aged years in mere minutes, and his features were wracked with despair. "What do you want of me?" was all he asked.

Tabitha explained that they were unsure whether the actual murder had been committed by Anthony's mother, grandmother, or even the maid Annie. "I'm not sure it matters which of them it is," Tabitha admitted. "We have no doubt they planned it together."

"It would have been my grandmother," Anthony said with a certainty which surprised Tabitha and Wolf. "She would never allow a servant, or anyone, to commit a crime on her behalf. She is much too proud and honourable. If something she felt strongly needed to be done, she would have done it herself."

"We felt much the same way, " Tabitha said.

"I appreciate you are bringing this to me before going to the authorities," Anthony said in a resigned, sad voice. Tabitha was heartbroken she had brought so much pain to a dear friend. She knew he wouldn't hesitate to turn his grandmother in to the police, even if it meant the old woman would hang. He wouldn't invoke any special favours on her behalf, which made Tabitha even more convinced the solution she and Wolf had devised was the path to true justice.

CHAPTER 35

"I believe I need to speak to my grandmother," Anthony said, rising from his chair.

"We do not need to be here when you do that, " Tabitha offered.

They had suggested to Anthony how to rectify the situation and compensate Seamus, but not bring down Mickey D's wrath on Annie. He had found the plan acceptable. Wolf suspected the duke would have gone along with anything they might have suggested by that point.

Their imminent exit was interrupted by the entrance of the dowager duchess and the duchess.

"Ah, Mama and Grandmama, just the two people I wish to talk with, " the duke said.

Tabitha was about to say farewell when the dowager duchess waved her and Wolf back into their seats. "Lady Pembroke and Lord Pembroke, you need to be here while I say this; I believe you've been involved in a clandestine investigation regarding the theft of the Somerset Diamonds and my son's murder." Neither Tabitha nor Wolf knew what to say. The duke was about to confront the women anyway, but they still were surprised to have their investigation revealed.

"Don't try to deny it," the older woman continued. While her daughter-in-law had sat in a rather uncomfortable-looking armchair, the dowager continued to stand. "My maid Annie has heard rumours you were in Whitechapel asking questions of her relatives and others," the dowager duchess said rather pointedly. Even if she felt it beneath her to mention a criminal gang explicitly, she had no qualms about alluding to it.

"Of course, then there is the family scandal which has now graced the front page of a tawdry broadsheet. Rumours about you, Lord Pembroke, and your prior career have reached my ears. Your involvement in exposing my late son is clear."

"Grandmama," the duke protested, "do not hold Tabitha or Lord Pembroke responsible for the exposure of my father's great sins. I was the person who went to the journalist; any fault lies with me."

"Anthony, you dear sweet boy. You are many things but you didn't uncover those photos and that house alone. And you certainly would never have considered approaching a journalist. Someone suggested that to you, I have no doubt."

The duke ignored all the implicit insults in his grandmother's statement and instead returned her focus to the issue at hand, "What you believe me capable of is irrelevant. I am now the head of this family and chose to make my father's many crimes public."

The dowager harrumphed, "That is by the by at this point. I merely wish to make clear I know these two," she pointed an accusatory finger at Tabitha and Wolf, "have been intimately involved in uncovering our family's many scandals. And I believe they have now uncovered my particular crime. If there was any doubt of the matter, the look on your face, Anthony, tells me all I need to know."

"Grandmama, I understand why you killed Papa. If I had known what he'd done, what he would do to Hannah, I would have killed him myself."

"Would you have, Anthony dear? Would you? You have no idea the guilt I have carried for so long. How could I have been so blind? Perhaps I was wilfully blind and didn't want to acknowledge the awful truth that was clearly before me. And if I hadn't realised it then, the moment I walked in on Martin with his own daughter in much the same compromising position I had walked in on with Fannie, I knew. I knew in a heartbeat. In one horrifying moment, I replayed everything that had happened with my daughter, and every jigsaw piece fell into place. Martin had again laughed the moment off as familial affection, but the look on Hannah's face told a different story. I remembered that look on Fannie's face. The look I ignored when I failed my daughter. I gave birth to a monster and was blind in ignoring what he did to my darling Fannie. I couldn't let him do the same thing to Hannah."

Tabitha's heart clenched with sadness for the mother forced to say such things about her child. But she had to ask a question of the duchess, Cassandra, "Your Grace, did you not have suspicions about your husband?"

Two tears rolled down the duchess' face, "When Catherine came to me to tell me what she'd seen between Martin and my daughter, she believed I would deny it and need convincing. But I didn't. I believed every word," she continued, "Fannie and I were friends as children." And with these words, Tabitha and Wolf understood that Cassandra had also long known what her husband was, even if she hadn't wanted to admit to such knowledge.

"And yet you married him?" Wolf asked.

The duchess sighed deeply. "I was a silly young girl, raised to have no expectations but to marry well. Martin favoured me at my first ball and then asked my father for my hand. A Duke was so far above what my family had hoped for me. I was a quiet, shy, bookish girl of 18. There was no possibility of refusing such an honour. And what would I have said to my father that he would have believed? He would have discounted anything I might have to tell him as being girlish hysterics on Fannie's part or a reason to refuse a duke because I was in love with Maxwell."

The duchess paused, then continued, "I believe you now all know that Anthony was not Martin's natural son. I cannot tell you the relief I felt when I gave birth to a son. And then my husband's continued disinterest in marital relations meant there were no more children. And I gave thanks for that. But, then there was the one night when he," she paused, crying more heartily now, "when he forced himself on me, and Hannah was conceived. I knew from the moment she was born that the day would come when I might have to protect her from her own father. However, I tried to tell myself that Fannie was an anomaly and that no man was depraved enough to touch his own daughter. But I was a fool ever to believe that. When Mama came to me, I had no doubts about helping her to protect my daughter.

"I always wondered why he'd chosen me out of all the debutantes that season, a plain young woman from no great lineage or wealth. But I now realise why. He wanted a wife who he believed too much of a mouse ever to challenge him, no matter what he might do." Finally finished with her story, the duchess buried her face in her hands and sobbed.

Tabitha and Wolf were sure they knew the whole story now. Still, they wanted to hear it from the women themselves, "So, with your maid Annie's help, you set up a situation where it was inevitable that Annie's uncle's criminal gang would hear about the diamond necklace. You gave the butler the one night off, and Annie ensured word of that useful coincidence would also make its way back to her criminal family."

The two duchesses nodded along with Tabitha's narrative, and she continued, "You had ensured the robbery would take place on one particular night. You then drugged the duke's evening drink, laudanum, I'm assuming. You needed to be sure the robbery occurred before you killed him."

Tabitha paused and asked, "I'm assuming that if, for some reason, the necklace hadn't been stolen that night, you would have found another way to get rid of the duke?"

The dowager duchess answered, "Annie was sure her family would take the bait. But yes, if they hadn't, we would have regrouped and devised another plan. We had already sent Hannah to stay with my sister in the country for a few weeks. So, we'd bought ourselves some time."

As sympathetic as Tabitha felt towards the women before her, she couldn't help but ask, "Did you never think about the man you were framing for murder?"

"The man broke into our house and stole a priceless diamond

necklace. He's hardly an innocent," the dowager said with the haughtiness of someone who considered people not in her social class lesser beings whose function was to make her life easier.

Tabitha pointed out, "While it is true the man is a thief, he is not a murderer, and yet you set him up as one. If the police had tracked him down, he would have hung for a crime he didn't commit." The look on the dowager's face did not express remorse.

"Regardless, the truth has now come to light. I don't regret a thing. If those terrible stories in the newspaper have shown anything, it's that the world is better off without my son in it. My only regret is that I didn't kill him long ago.

"And now I have confessed, I have only one more thing to do." Saying this, the dowager duchess reached into a pocket in her skirt and brought out a small, ivory-handled gun.

"Grandmama, what are you doing with a gun?" Anthony cried.

"I will not subject you or the rest of the family to having our name dragged through the mud any more than it already has been. After that newspaper story, a very public trial will be the last nail in the coffin of our family's reputation and legacy. I have done what needed to be done. I can meet my maker with my head held high."

Everyone in the room seemed frozen, scared to make a sudden move but unsure what to do. "Catherine, Mama, you can't possibly mean to shoot yourself in the drawing room?" Cassandra, the Duchess of Somerset, cried.

"Of course not, my dear," the dowager laughed, momentarily bringing some relief to the room. "We've only recently decorated the drawing room, and you will never get blood out of all this silk. I will take my leave of you all and go to the library to take care of the deed. The drapes and curtains in there are awful and need changing anyway. My suicide will finally give you the push you need to redecorate."

If the dowager duchess hadn't been talking about taking her own life, Tabitha would have found the exchange amusing. As it was, she felt it was time for her and Wolf to intervene, "Your Grace, Lord Pembroke and I have no intention of going to the authorities and turning you in for the murder."

"You don't? Why on earth not?"

Tabitha turned her head slightly as she spoke and looked at Wolf, "Because it would not further the cause of justice. You are right; the world is a much better place without your son in it. He ruined many young lives, not merely his sister's. Left alive, he would have ruined many more, including his daughter's, I have no doubt. You are to be commended for having the courage to do what you did. I wish you hadn't implicated another man in the crime, but Lord Pembroke and I believe we have a solution. And a solution that will not ravage your family's reputation any further. And that will not require you to take your own life, " she added emphatically.

Tabitha and Wolf then explained the rest of their plan. Mickey D would never know Annie set his gang up. But he would be told the duke was murdered, coincidentally, by a family member and why. Anthony would provide handsomely for Seamus and his family to emigrate to America. The Rowley family would inform the police that, considering their recent high-profile scandal, they were no longer interested in trying to retrieve the Somerset Diamonds. Given how cold the trail had gone, without a peer of the realm breathing down Scotland Yard's neck, they'd probably be glad not to waste any more resources on the case. After a few months, Mickey D could safely fence the diamonds.

It didn't take much to persuade the dowager to give up her gun. As she did so, she made a point of saying, "Anthony, just because it will not have my blood and brain matter all over it don't think you can wriggle out of redecorating the library. The room's decor really is shocking."

EPILOGUE

A week later, Tabitha and Wolf had dinner together for the first time in days. The week had been a whirl of activity for both of them. Anthony, the Duke of Somerset, had bought a large manor house in Dulwich. The house had extensive grounds, including an apple orchard. All the girls had moved to the new house and were living under the watchful eye of Mrs Caruthers, Mother Lizzy. She had decided to come out of retirement permanently and was happily ensconced in the household. The house was large enough for more girls than they had rescued. Anthony and Tabitha had talked to Mother Lizzy about making room for other girls rescued from the streets.

Helping Anthony consumed Tabitha's days and many of her evenings. They both believed fervently that the girls should not be required to stay in the Holborn house, the scene of their horrors, a day more than necessary. The Dulwich house had been bought furnished, and Tabitha had worked diligently with Mrs Caruthers to assess what else might need to be purchased to enable a large group of young girls and the attendant teachers and servants to reside there comfortably.

With Tabitha's help, Anthony hired teachers. The girls were to receive an education. Not merely one good enough to enable them to go into service but to do more than be servants if they had the capacity and the desire. When told about the new house and about what it would mean for them, Tabitha had been quick to assure the girls, "But, if you don't wish to leave the house, if you don't wish to take up a career, there will always be a safe home for you in the Dulwich house, for as long as you need it. His lordship guarantees it.

Becky had never returned to Chesterton House and planned to move to Dulwich with the rest of her friends. Older than all the other girls, she was a firm favourite, particularly with the younger girls, and a lifesaver as far as Mother Lizzy was concerned.

Within the week, the decision was made that, while the Dulwich house still wanted for some necessary items, it was sufficiently furnished and now cleaned for its new occupants to take up residence. Mrs Caruthers had mostly undertaken the process of settling everyone comfortably, but Tabitha had been on hand to help ensure that everyone was comfortably situated.

Not for the first time, she marvelled at the girls' resilience. It had been less than a month since she and Wolf had accompanied Anthony to rescue the girls from the clutches of the madam who guarded them. Within such a short period, they seemed to have accepted their new situation and the safety and security Anthony had sworn to afford them. Now they happily bickered over which bedroom which girls would share, and the orchard rang with their giggles as they ran amongst the trees.

While Tabitha was busy, Wolf had been busy with his chores. His first task was to report back to Mickey D as planned. As Wolf had suspected, Mickey was happy enough to accept the version of Wolf's story and more than happy to accept that the diamonds were his to sell as he pleased. He confessed he believed emigrating to America would be the making of Seamus.

"One final thing Mickey," Wolf said, "This makes us even. I want your word on it."

While Mickey D could imagine many ways it might be to his advantage to keep Wolf on a short leash, he also acknowledged that the debt had been paid.

In all the commotion of the investigation, Wolf was tempted to forget Lady Ramford's party and the dowager countess' demand that he escort her. But, as if anticipating a possibly convenient memory lapse, the dowager sent Wolf a note reminding him of his obligation.

The evening had been as tedious as anticipated; all anyone could talk about was the Duke of Somerset's brothel scandal. Wolf was relieved to find that, while the dowager was thrilled to have more information on the scandal than anyone else, she somehow managed to not reveal his or Tabitha's role in uncovering it. As Tabitha had predicted, the dowager was most shrill and determined in her assertions of the victimhood of the rest of the duke's family and the extreme honour shown by his heir, the new duke. By the time the party was over, it was established that no taint of the scandal should be held against any of the surviving members of the evil duke's family.

Now the girls were settled, and Tabitha and Wolf were finally alone with time to talk. With the investigation concluded Tabitha was unsure how she felt about her life returning to normal. What was normal?

There was no doubt her life now held far more joy and purpose than it had two short months ago. She had Melly to love and cherish. Rat and the various members of her staff were getting on well with their lessons, and she was committed to ensuring that continued.

Tabitha had also assured Anthony she would continue to be involved with the school at the Dulwich house. He intended to create a trust to provide for the school and all its pupils. He wanted to make sure all the girls would be cared for, no matter that any heir of his might think otherwise. The trust would have a board of governors headed up by Tabitha.

Yes, there was joy and purpose to her life, finally. What else did she need? She looked over her wine glass at Wolf. At least in her mind, they had still not resolved the question of her permanent residence at Chesterton House. But more than the household accommodations she had forced on him with Melly and Rat, Tabitha realised their current situation couldn't last forever. Apart from anything else, Wolf would likely marry one day. The thought of such an event gave an unexpected tug at her heartstrings. She shook her head, exasperated at her own absurdity.

Seeing her shaking her head, Wolf asked, "What is it Tabitha? You're very quiet and solemn suddenly. Are there problems in Dulwich?"

Tabitha smiled, "No, everything is going to plan. I could not ask more of Anthony than he has proved himself ready to do to ensure a happier new life for those girls."

"Then what?"

"I was just considering what's next?" Seeing his confusion, she elaborated, "What's next for me, I mean. I know you asked me to help you settle into the household. But that won't take forever. This is your house now. You deserve the space and the freedom to explore what being the Earl of Pembroke means to you, without me hanging around reminding you and everyone else what it meant when Jonathan was alive. I believe I should start to think about setting up my own household."

As she said these words, Tabitha realised her eyes had grown wet. She felt absurd. She had nothing to be upset about. And yet, she felt an overwhelming sense of sadness she couldn't control. Wolf reached over and covered her hand with his large one, "Is that what you want to do, Tabitha?" he asked. "Do you want to leave me? I won't stop you if you do. But, if you are suggesting it merely out of concern for my feelings, let me put paid to that absurd idea immediately; I would have you stay and never leave." He paused, and Tabitha could have sworn he blushed slightly, "And not just to ensure the smooth running of the house. I don't want you to leave, Tabitha."

By this point, the tears in her eyes had begun falling silently in rivulets down her cheeks. She felt absurd; why was she crying? Was she sad? Happy? There was nothing to cry about. And yet, she couldn't seem to stop. Finally, getting control over herself, she realised her hand was still in Wolf's, "Even if it's not just me staying?" She asked.

Wolf laughed, squeezing her hand, "Melly, Rat, any other waifs and strays you choose to adopt, perhaps the odd puppy. Yes, please stay, all of you."

It was unclear where the moment might have led, but Tabitha and Wolf were saved having to find out by the entrance of Talbot, the butler. "Sorry to disturb you milord and milady, but the Dowager Countess of Pembroke is in the drawing room."

"Now?" Tabitha exclaimed, "These visits are getting earlier and earlier. What on earth would cause her to visit us while we're still at breakfast?"

Wolf chuckled, "There is only one way to find out. Lead the way."

The dowager was seated in the drawing room, her impatience visible by her tapping foot and sour expression, "How long did you expect me to wait for you to show yourselves?"

"Mama," Tabitha said as gently as she could manage, "we were eating breakfast. You surprised us with such an early call and we came immediately. Is something wrong?"

"Of course, something is wrong. You can't imagine I'd be up and about at such an ungodly hour if there wasn't. I won't beat around the bush; I know you two were involved in the investigation of the old Duke of Somerset's murder."

"We never denied the fact," Wolf pointed out.

"You made your involvement seem limited to his unpleasant extracurricular activities. But I never believed that was the extent of it. But that's neither here nor there. The point is, I need help and Jeremy, you seem to be the right man for the job."

Wolf answered carefully, "Lady Pembroke, whatever business I engaged in before ascending to the earldom is behind me. The affair with the Duke of Somerset and the Somerset Diamonds was a one-off, for a very particular reason. I have no interest in picking my old career back up."

"Jeremy! Manning, my butler, has been arrested for murder. The man has been with me since I left Chesterton House and is an invaluable member of my staff. I poached him away from Lady Ramford, you know. She's never forgiven me. It's inconceivable the man would murder anyone, he doesn't have it in him. And I need him. The house is at sixes and sevens without him, and this cannot continue. I have no interest in whether you plan to go back to your old career or not, but this will be a personal favour to me, and I will not accept no for an answer."

Wolf sighed deeply; no matter his desire to have a clean slate and put his thief-taking days behind him, fate had other plans for him. "Lady Pembroke, of course I'd be honoured to be of service to you."

AFTERWORD

Thank you for reading A Proud Woman. I hope you enjoyed it. If you'd like to see what's coming next for Tabitha & Wolf, here are some ways to stay in touch.

SarahFNoel.com
Facebook
@sarahfNoelAuthor - Twitter
Instagram
Sign-up for my newsletter for free stories and insider content

You can order the next in the series, A Singular Woman on Amazon.

And pre-order book 4, An Inexplicable Woman

Who is this mysterious woman from Wolf's past who can so easily summon him to her side?

When Lady Arlene Archibald tracks Wolf down and begs him for help, he plans to travel to Brighton alone to see her. What was he thinking? Instead, he finds himself with an unruly entourage of lords, ladies, servants, children, and even a dog. Can and will he help Arlene prove her friend's innocence? How will he manage Tabitha coming face-to-face with his first love? And how is he to dissuade the Dowager Countess of Pembroke from insinuating herself into the investigation?

Beneath its veneer of holiday, seaside fun, Brighton may be more sinister than it seems.

ABOUT THE AUTHOR

Sarah F. Noel

Originally from London, Sarah F. Noel now spends most of her time in Grenada in the Caribbean. Sarah loves reading historical mysteries with strong female characters; the Tabitha & Wolf Mystery Series is exactly the kind of book she would love to curl up with on a lazy Sunday.

BOOKS BY THIS AUTHOR

A Singular Woman

Wolf had hoped he could put his thief-taking life behind him when he unexpectedly inherited an earldom.

Wolf, the new Earl of Pembroke, against his better judgment, finds himself sucked back into another investigation. He knows better than to think he can keep Tabitha out of it. Tabitha was the wife of Wolf's deceased cousin, the previous earl, but now she's running his household and finding her way into his life and, to his surprise, his heart. He respects her intelligence and insights but can't help trying to protect her.

As the investigation suddenly becomes far more complicated and dangerous, how can Wolf save an innocent man and keep Tabitha safe?

An Independent Woman

Summoned to Edinburgh by the Dowager Countess of Pembroke, Tabitha and Wolf reluctantly board a train and head north to Scotland.

The dowager's granddaughter, Lily, refuses to participate in the preparations for her first season unless Tabitha and Wolf investigate the disappearance of her friend, Peter. Initially sceptical of the need to investigate, Tabitha and Wolf quickly realise that the idealistic Peter may have stumbled upon dark secrets. How far would someone go to cover their tracks?

Tabitha is drawn into Edinburgh's seedy underbelly as she and Wolf try to solve the case while attempting to keep the dowager in the dark about Peter's true identity.

Printed in Great Britain
by Amazon